ARMY RANGER WITH BENEFITS

the Men of
At-Ease Ranch

ARMY RANGER WITH BENEFITS

the Men of
At-Ease Ranch

DONNA MICHAELS

Entangled Publishing, LLC
2614 South Timberline Road
Suite 105, PMB 159
Fort Collins, CO 80525
Visit our website at www.entangledpublishing.com.

Lovestruck is an imprint of Entangled Publishing, LLC.

Edited by Heather Howland
Cover design by Heather Howland
Cover art from iStock

Manufactured in the United States of America

First Edition March 2018

To Mel and Sandy for their unceasing support! And to the readers who asked for Vince's and Leo's books. I hope you enjoy! Thank you from the bottom of my heart.

Chapter One

Georgia—the last thing on Vince Acardi's mind.

At least it was that morning.

Great song. Nice state. But he had a not-so-great reason for heading to Columbus on his second flight of the day from hell.

The day had started off fine. The sun was shining. The kitchen was quiet, except for the sound of eggs cooking on the stove and bacon sizzling in the oven that filled the room with a delectable, smoky aroma. He'd been halfway through preparing breakfast for the twenty-plus residents of At-Ease—the veteran transition ranch he co-owned with three of his former Ranger buddies—when he received the call responsible for slicing ten years off his life.

And burning his bacon.

When Vince had still been an active duty Army Ranger, he and his younger brother—also a Ranger—had listed each other as points of contact, opting to spare their parents the heart-stopping call, should there be one.

There was today.

And damn if Vince's heart hadn't stopped beating for a full ten seconds as the official on the other end of the phone informed him Captain Dominic Acardi had been admitted to the base hospital at Fort Benning that morning, with non-life-threatening injuries.

That last part had eased the invisible band squeezing Vince's chest, allowing air to finally travel to his starved lungs.

Thank goodness for his friends. They'd rallied around him.

Stone Mitchum, one of his Ranger buddies, had set a hand on his shoulder. "Go. Take care of your brother. Don't worry about things here."

"Thanks. I'll be back before the wedding."

It was three Saturdays away. Surely his brother would be fine way before then.

Jovy, Stone's fiancée, gave Vince a hug. "If your brother needs you longer, you stay there and don't worry about us."

"No way am I missing the wedding." He'd winked. "I've got the food ordered. Even if I have to just fly in for the ceremony and fly back out to take care of Dom, I'll be here."

She'd smiled. "Then you'd better get packed and get going. Your flight leaves in less than two hours."

Leo, his friend and the reason behind Foxtrot—their construction company—and At-Ease, pushed away from the wall where he'd been leaning. "I'll be in the truck."

The rest of the day had gone downhill from there.

Traffic slowed to a crawl near the airport. When he finally arrived, he'd boarded the plane, not a minute to spare, only to find himself wedged between two worst-case scenarios: a mother with a crying child, and a hefty dude who snored the whole three and half hours until they touched down in Atlanta. From there, Vince boarded a connecting flight on a plane not much bigger than Cord's horse trailer and truck.

At least now he was seated next to a sweet senior citizen.

Thank God the baby and dude from the other flight were nowhere in sight.

"Do you dig older women?"

Make that a sassy senior citizen.

"I'm not asking for me, silly." She snickered and slapped his arm, apparently reading shock in his expression. "For my daughter. She's single again and in need of a good man. A solid one." A boney finger poked his bicep. "Like you."

Willing the plane to fly faster, Vince gave her a noncommittal shrug, more than happy to offer up his right nut if the pilot could hit Mach one. "I haven't dated much lately, ma'am," he replied with his best neutral tone.

"Ah." She nodded, a knowing twinkle lighting her eyes. "You're holding out for *the one*."

The one.

He'd been there once. Had his shot at a once-in-a-lifetime soul mate. It would never happen again. That was the reason it was called *once*-in-a-lifetime, not *several*-in-a-lifetime. He was absolutely not holding out for another "the one."

"Something like that," he said.

"Well, you'll know when you've found her." The lady grinned. "It'll feel like you were hit with a ton of bricks. Or a rocket. Or a good sock in the teeth…if you have your own teeth. Mine were gone ages ago." She opened her mouth and tapped her dentures with her finger as if she thought he'd like to see them.

He didn't. And now he was willing to give up his left nut to get to Columbus faster, too.

"But you get my meaning," she continued with a wink. "The moment you meet her, you'll be momentarily stunned… almost painfully so, but it'll be worth it. Trust me."

What he trusted were the good manners his mother had ingrained in him to nod politely to the well-meaning woman, when he really wanted to turn away, close his eyes, and worry about his dumbass brother in peace.

Thankfully, the pilot announced their descent, saving Vince from further conversation...and sacrificing his manhood.

. . .

Today was the day.

Emma Roberts could feel it.

Anticipation hummed through her body and fluttered her pulse. Something special was going to happen, and she hoped with all her heart it meant Stephan would ask her out.

Dr. Stephan Greenwald was the newest and youngest doctor to join the practice where she worked as a medical transcriber and coder in a wing of doctors' offices attached to the hospital.

He was also her high school crush.

"Maybe today's the day Stephan finally asks you out." Her mother's hopeful voice echoed Emma's thoughts as she cradled the phone to her ear at work. "After all, it's been well over a decade since you started to pine over him."

A reminder she didn't need.

From the moment Emma had set eyes on the tall, blue-eyed, light-haired senior on her first day of freshman year, she was smitten. Her extremely shy teenage-self was content to crush on him from afar, but when they were paired as lab partners for a science project, she nearly died. Forced to actually talk to the guy—after her tongue remembered how to function—she discovered he was every bit as nice as she'd imagined, and that he had a girlfriend in a neighboring school district.

It didn't stop her from daydreaming about him, though, even after he graduated and moved up north for college and eventually med school. As time moved on, so had Emma. She even dated and entered several relationships, but she thought of him often.

"I just think it's fate," her mother continued. "The soldiers you've insisted on dating have all broken your heart, and now Stephan shows up. He's the one who got away."

He wasn't the one who got away. Not exactly. He was more like the one she wished she'd had a shot at. But her mother was right. When he showed up six months ago as the new doctor, it felt as if fate was giving her that shot.

Until she found out he was in a relationship. Not with the high school girlfriend, but some Boston chick who didn't like it down south. The Yankee lasted two months, then left Stephan to head back north.

Perhaps that was fate stepping in again.

"Maybe," she said, not wanting to give her mother false hope, or add to her anxiety. Her mother, thoughtful as she'd always been, had moved to Florida to care for Emma's sick aunt. She didn't want to increase her stress. "I have a feeling something's going to happen soon."

"I hope so, hun." A soft sigh filled her ear. "He needs to open his eyes and realize the best thing to ever happen to him is right in front of him. You know he'd be lucky to have you, Em. Any man would."

Her mother had always been her cheering section.

Emma smiled. "Thanks, Mom. I need more fans like you."

"I'm your biggest," her mom cheerfully replied. "That's why I'm also glad you've given yourself a deadline with Stephan. I like the guy, don't get me wrong, but you've wasted enough time pining over him."

She held back a sigh. "I know." Once Stephan was available again, Emma had silently given him four months to ask her out. Four months since his breakup seemed like plenty of time. Especially given the lingering looks and smiles they exchanged.

And yet, she was nearly down to the wire.

"Then you also know I know when to shut up." Her mother chuckled. "I'll let you get back to work, dear. Good luck with your doctor."

At this point, Emma would take all the luck and well wishes she could get.

After hanging up, she slipped the phone back into her pocket. Interacting with Stephan during his first week, she'd been happy to discover he hadn't changed at all—well... except for filling out his tall frame. The man was even more gorgeous, if that were possible.

He wasn't pretentious like some of the doctors, either, nor was he a snob. Stephan was down-to-earth, often stopping by her section to chat with her and her best friend, Macy, the other transcriber, and even sat with them sometimes in the hospital cafeteria, instead of joining his peers in their private lunchroom.

But the best thing about him was his nonmilitary status.

Her mom hadn't been wrong about her dating history.

Not that she had anything against the military or those who served. She'd just promised herself she was done dating military men. Three times Emma had swum in those waters, and all three times she'd nearly drowned.

Her first ex thought it was fine to sleep in her bed and the beds of other women during deployment.

That got him dishonorably discharged from her life. Stat.

Her second ended the day he finished training and was assigned a new duty station. He left her with an "it's been fun" kiss on the cheek and moved on. Without her.

But the third one...that was the worst.

After training, he was assigned to the base and asked her to move in. For nearly a year, Emma had thought she'd found the one. Faithful and attentive, Adam had always showed her how much he cared through little notes and special outings. He was a Ranger, so he deployed without notice. That was hard, but she'd kept her head up because they had a future together. Or so she thought. In the end, she hadn't been an important enough part of his life. When his duty station changed, he left her behind, too.

She got it—the men and women who served had a lot on their plates, both emotionally and physically. But God, she was so tired of being "good enough for now," but not "good enough for forever."

It was time for a change, and that included sticking with men in the private sector.

Even though the practice was located in the hospital at Fort Benning, Stephan had never served. He was hired through the CHRA—Civilian Human Resources Agency.

That made him even more perfect.

Watching as he walked down the hall and into his office catty-corner from her desk, Emma admired his exceptional "private sector." Having just returned from an early lunch, the man removed his lab coat from a hook on the wall and slipped it on, covering her view.

No matter. He was just as sexy in his doctor gear.

"Girl, you should take a picture. It lasts longer," Macy muttered from behind her. "I understand admiring his sexiness. Lord knows, I do it myself. I just do it more discreetly."

Emma snorted as she turned to face her coworker. "Yeah. Right. By taking a photo of him."

"Hey. I told you I was taking your picture. It was dumb luck Dr. Hotness happened to walk by."

"Walk by?" Emma smirked. "He was leaning against the counter here, talking to me at the time." She pointed to the counter that surrounded their rounded cubical located in the middle of the practice. "And if I recall the picture correctly, you barely got my ear in it."

Macy's brows rose, along with her shoulders. "Because you moved. Not my fault I got a frame full of hottie."

Ducking their heads, they chuckled softly. With parallel halls of patient rooms flanking their sides, they'd learned to keep their conversations hushed.

"All kidding aside." Her friend nodded toward Stephan's office. "When is your hotness deadline?"

That self-imposed deadline, again.

She was beginning to wish she hadn't told anyone.

"Two and a half weeks." Emma sighed.

She really thought the guy would've asked her out by now. He wasn't in a relationship. Nor was he gay. The few times she'd run into him in town, he'd had a different beautiful woman on his arm, and given their body language, the ladies weren't just for show. And after overhearing a conversation with his buddies, she knew asking him out wasn't an option. He preferred to do the asking.

So Emma never took the initiative. She just flirted and waited.

And waited.

"Okay. So two and a half weeks," Macy repeated, glancing at the calendar that separated their workspaces. "That puts you right at…the hospital fundraiser gala brunch."

Emma nodded. "I chose that as my stopping point right from the start. Four months is plenty of time for him to make a move, and the gala gives him an excuse."

"Agreed." Macy glanced around, then moved closer. "But I think it's time you helped the good doctor along."

"Helped?" She frowned. "How? I've put out signals and flirted, but I refuse to throw myself at him. He doesn't like that."

Her friend waved a hand in the air. "Girl, that's not what I meant."

"Good."

"You're going to throw yourself at *another* man."

"What?" She reeled back. "Are you crazy?"

"Nope, but I *am* right." Macy folded her arms across her chest and smiled smugly. "How do you think I landed Dupree?"

Her husband? Emma shrugged. "I thought he was your brother's friend."

"He was, and wouldn't give me the time of day until I suddenly stopped mooning over his skinny ass and started showing up at the same places as him...with another man." A big smile curved her lips. "Sometimes a guy just needs to be reminded what's in front of him. That's all I'm sayin'."

Emma was going to regret this. "Reminded...how?"

"It's a well-known fact that a guy wants what he can't have. And up until now, Stephan knows he can *have* you, thanks to those signals you mentioned earlier."

"So you're saying I need to let him know he can't have me?" She'd never thought about that before.

"No, girl." Macy shook her head and frowned. "You got to *show* the man that."

Stephan walked out of his office right then and sent her one of his sexy smiles before continuing down the hall to reception. Halfway there, he stopped, turned around, and walked straight to her.

"Emma, I've been meaning to ask you something."

Her heart dropped to her knees. Good Lord.

Was this it? Was he finally going to ask her out? Right there in the middle of the office? In front of Macy?

She smiled up at him, hoping it came across as friendly and not like an eager teenager with a crush. "Yes?"

"Can you take these to radiology?" He set a folder on the counter in front of her face. "I missed the courier."

With her smile still in place, she nodded. "Sure. I'd be

happy to." Because she was an idiot. And a chump.

"Thanks. You're the best," he said, treating her to another one of his brilliant smiles. The kind that lit his eyes and fluttered the hearts of every female within a twenty-foot radius.

"Yep. You definitely need to find yourself a man," Macy muttered under her breath as Stephan disappeared into one of the patient rooms. "That dummy had the perfect opportunity, and he blew it. He needs a nudge."

"He'd never ask me out here." For some reason, she felt compelled to defend him. "Not at the office." Emma grabbed the file and headed for the door.

What had she been thinking?

She hadn't. That was the problem.

Macy's outrageous suggestion mixed her up. Confused her. With her mind playing devil's advocate, she marched from the wing of doctors' offices into the hospital section of the building.

She wasn't the type of person to play games. To use a man to get another. *Although, the suggestion did hold merit,* she thought, weaving through the busy corridor. It wasn't just men who wanted what they couldn't have. Women were just as bad. Sometimes worse. It was human nature. Therefore, it was feasible that if Stephan saw her with another guy, endorphins, testosterone—or some other kind of hormone— could kick in and wake his cute ass up.

She pulled the door open to radiology and walked inside. Slow day. Only a handful of people sat in the waiting room, and no one stood at the window. Since it was slow, she didn't bother to go in the back. "Hi, Sally." She handed the file to the receptionist. "This is from Dr. Greenwald."

The woman took the file and smiled. "Has he asked you out yet?"

Darn. Did everyone know about her crush?

"No." Emma sighed.

Pity darkened Sally's gaze. "Well, hang in there."

Nodding, Emma turned around and marched for the door. She was going to do better than "hang." She was going to do something about it. No more pitiful stares. No more waiting for Stephan to ask her out. It was time to up the ante. Time to play her final card. To utilize her last resort.

Macy's advice.

Now all she needed was a man willing to pretend to date her for a week or two, to show Stephan other men found her desirable.

Shoulders back, chin held high, she opened the door into the corridor, and it jolted in her hand with a sickening thud.

Followed by a muffled curse from the other side.

Emma's heart rocked in her chest. She just smacked a stranger with the door.

"Oh my God. I'm so sorry." She stepped aside to shut the stupid thing, and tried to assess the damage.

A tall man with broad shoulders that tapered into a lean torso pushed a clump of dark hair out of his amber eyes and blinked. Relief coursed through her to find no blood or bruising on his face.

His handsome face.

Her pulse hiccupped.

"It's okay," he said in a sexy low timbre she felt to her toes.

Hysterical laughter bubbled up her throat. Just her luck. She whacked a gorgeous guy. The only thing that could've been worse would've been to find Stephan on the other side of the door.

Exhaustion lined her victim's eyes and mouth. "No harm done, ma'am."

Ma'am?

Disappointment crashed through her body and cancelled

the tingling in her chest. He was military. Of course he was. She was on a freaking Army base.

With a curt nod, he brushed past her, rubbing his shoulder as he strode down the hall. After he disappeared around a corner, she shook her head and walked back to the office, determined to put the embarrassing moment out of her mind.

At least she wouldn't have to worry about running into him again.

Chapter Two

Vince rotated his aching shoulder, scowling at no one in particular. Why the hell did the hospital have doors that opened into the corridor?

Icing on the cake from his day from hell.

The woman sure was pretty, though...

Focus. Dom was one floor up, and the reason Vince was in Georgia. Not to find a date.

Arriving at the elevator lobby, he eyed the people milling about and decided to use the stairs. He needed to get to Dom soon. His thickheaded brother would try to leave to get back to his men, no matter what kind of injuries he suffered. And since Vince had no idea what those injuries were, other than non-life-threatening, he increased his pace.

An image of the cute brunette flashed through his mind again as he took the steps two at a time. Color had risen into her cheeks, deepening the blue of her horrified gaze. It would take a hell of a lot more than a door to do any actual damage to him. Something she'd never know, since the chances of running into the beauty again were slim to none.

Forcing her out of his mind, he concentrated on his brother.

A brother whose grumbling Vince heard echoing down the hall the instant he stepped onto the floor.

"I don't need any damn pain medication. Just give me my gear and shove me on a plane."

Relief eased the tightness from Vince's shoulders. His brother would be fine.

"You won't do your men any good with cracked ribs, a dislocated hip, or back spasms." A calm, tolerant, feminine voice drifted out as Vince neared the room. "You need therapy if you want to be cleared to join them on the next mission."

"Next mission?" his brother's voice boomed. "What the hell, Doc? I can't just sit around. I'm not made that way. I'm fine. Just clear me so I can get the hell out of here and do my job."

"Sorry, Captain Acardi," the doctor said, her tone still calm and patient. "You're asking me to *not* do my job, and *I'm* not made that way."

Hovering just outside the room, Vince smiled. Two points to the doctor for using his brother's words against him.

"If you want me to clear you, then you'll come here four times a week for therapy."

"Four?" Dom asked. "Why not seven?"

A soft chuckle drifted into the hall. "I appreciate your sudden enthusiasm, but I want you to heal, not overtax the muscles and cause more damage."

As much as Vince was enjoying his brother's losing verbal battle, he decided it was time to make his presence known.

With the smile still on his lips, he braced for the impact of his brother's injured appearance and entered the room. "My apologies, Doctor. Dom was born with an oversize PITA gene he never did learn how to control."

The doctor lifted a perfectly arched brow as she met his

gaze. "And you are?"

"Vince Acardi." He extended his hand. "The PITA's older brother."

"Dr. Palmer," she replied, shaking his hand.

Average height, auburn hair pulled back in some sort of a bun, green eyes full of intelligence. Pretty in the kind of way his brother had a weakness for. Dom always did have a soft spot for redheads, but his charms were clearly not working on this woman.

Which probably explained Dom's grimace. That…and pain from his injuries.

Jesus, he was mess. Taped ribs. Cut on his cheek. Bruises on his forehead that matched the bruising on his arms and chest. Eyes sunken in a face with skin that appeared too tight.

"Don't worry," he said, releasing her hand. "I'll make sure the PITA is at therapy four times a week, and that he takes his medication like a good soldier." Vince suppressed a grin when his brother flipped him off behind the doctor's back.

With both hands.

"Good." She nodded, then turned to Dom. "I know you want to rejoin your men, Captain, but you can't. You're not capable now. At best, you're subpar."

Holy shit.

Vince barely refrained from sucking in a breath as he watched his brother's mouth slam shut. No one, outside of family, ever dared to call Dominic Acardi feeble.

This was great.

"But I promise you this," she went on as if his brother's knuckles weren't cracking in his clenched fists. "If you follow my instructions for the next two to three weeks—and those of the physical therapist I assign—then you'll be ready to command the next mission."

His brother groaned. "Two weeks?"

"Or three."

Vince's heart dropped to his knees. Damn. He'd hoped to be back at the ranch in a couple of days. Leaving his kitchen to someone else for two weeks was inviting disaster. Jovy and Stone's wedding menu aside, he had his hands full with everyday meals.

There were veterans with food allergies, diabetes, certain likes and dislikes, and several with social issues who opted to eat in their bunk instead of joining everyone else at the table in the main house.

Before leaving that morning, he'd briefed Beth about the food allergies, but the rest of the preferences were stored in his head. He made a mental note to relay them to Leo when he checked in later.

Dr. Palmer looked his brother over one more time. "Now that I know you have someone here to take you home, I'll get your discharge started." She turned to Vince and held out her hand. "Nice to meet you, Mr. Acardi. Good luck," she added with a slight quirk to her lips before exiting the room.

His brother blew out a breath. "What the hell just happened?"

Releasing the stranglehold on his glee, Vince laughed all the way to the foot of the bed. "You were just put in your place by your very pretty doctor. But I agree with her a thousand percent."

Muttering an oath, Dom flipped him off again.

He chuckled. "I'm guessing you haven't had the chance to glance in a mirror. Trust me, bro. You look like hell."

His brother smirked. "Explains why I feel like hell."

"Want to tell me what happened that spurred the call that sucked ten years off my life?" He held Dom's weary stare, knowing it wasn't likely he'd get an answer, or the whole one, but he thought he'd try.

Frustration flashed through his brother's eyes. "I was positioned on the roof of a building that collapsed."

Shit.

Vince held his emotions in check. "You were damn lucky."

Dom lifted a shoulder, but the anxiety pressing down on his brow told Vince what his brother kept inside.

"You weren't the only one on that roof."

His brother swallowed and shook his head. "I was with an Iraqi informant. I've no idea what happened to him."

That explained the haunted look.

"Leo still has ties there," he said. "I'll call him later and see if he can find anything out for you."

Dom slowly exhaled, and relief brightened his expression. "Thanks." He tossed the covers back and grimaced. "How's he doing?"

"Great," Vince replied, grateful a pair of scrubs covered his brother's bottom half. "He's off the bottle. Taking on more responsibility at Foxtrot. Even joined a bowling league."

"Good to hear." A smile tugged his brother's tight lips.

Vince agreed. It was a far cry from the guy who'd mixed medication with booze in an attempt to silence memories of one of their final missions.

"Do you have an extra shirt?" Face drawn and pale, his brother gripped the bed rail and slowly rose to his feet. "Not much left of my uniform."

And not something Vince wanted to see. "Yeah, in my rental car. Don't be in such a hurry. We still have to wait for the nurse to come in with the papers." He pointed to the bed. "Sit your ass back down before you fall down. I'll go find the top half of your scrubs."

Dom answered with a glare before shuffling to a chair in the corner, then proceeded to curse through his clenched teeth as he lowered himself onto the cushion.

Vince cocked his head. "You know, pain meds will take the edge off."

"Like I told the doc. I don't need them," the idiot replied, sweat beading across his forehead and upper lip.

He sighed.

It was going to be a long two to three weeks.

• • •

Day one-hundred-and-five down the drain.

Emma sighed as she turned onto her street after work. She really thought something special was going to happen today. Like Stephan asking her out. She'd felt it. But, other than whacking that cute soldier with the door, nothing out of the ordinary had occurred.

An image of the guy with thick, dark lashes rimming warm brown eyes flashed through her mind. Darn shame he was military. Although, even if he wasn't, it wouldn't matter. She was no quitter, and she'd put a lot of time and effort into getting Stephan to ask her out. Not to mention years of pining over him. It wasn't over yet, though. A lot could happen in seventeen days.

The instant Emma pulled into her driveway, all thoughts of Stephan and the deadline disappeared from her mind. Right now, she had a more immediate problem.

Prickles of concern spread across her shoulders. An unfamiliar car sat in her neighbor's driveway.

It wasn't his. The Army Ranger was still on a mission with his unit.

Most of the time, those guys left and returned without notice, but Dom wasn't back. She knew this because fifteen minutes ago she passed his truck on her way off the base. His "parked" truck. Which meant he hadn't returned.

So who in the world was in her neighbor's house?

Intent on finding out, Emma got out of her car with Dom's house key in hand—the key entrusted to her for keeping an eye on the place whenever he was gone—and sneaked into his yard.

The day she'd moved into the house next door, he'd shown up in her driveway and pitched in. The fact he never once made a move on her was refreshing. They became fast friends.

Unease raced down her spine. For over a year now, she'd never had an issue with his place. Emma glanced in the windows on her way to the back of the house. Relief and alarm vied for top billing when she saw nothing.

Keeping her panic in check, she sneaked past the pool and hot tub and onto the back porch, surprised to find the door intact. And locked. No sign of forced entry. With adrenaline kicking up her pulse, she used the key to slip quietly into the kitchen.

Then stopped dead.

A tall man, with his back to her, stood rummaging through Dom's cabinets.

Everything inside Emma tensed up tight.

Holy crap...

Intruder!

Who else had she expected to find when a stranger's car sat in the freaking driveway? The cleaning lady?

Oh yeah, that's right. *She* was the freaking cleaning lady.

With her heart beating out of her chest, Emma reached for her phone, only to remember it was in her purse...on the front seat of her car.

Darn it. Why hadn't she dialed 911 instead of playing cop?

Too late to retrace her steps, she said a silent prayer and launched herself at the man's back. In a series of moves too quick for her mind to register, she was flipped through the air and landed on her back with a thud.

As she worked to catch her breath, Emma stared up at a pair of familiar, thickly lashed brown eyes, crinkled in a frown.

Chapter Three

"You!" Emma blinked up at the man she'd hit with the door earlier that day. "What are you doing here?"

His frown remained as he reached for her. "Who are you?"

Alarm replaced Emma's momentary stupor. She slapped his hand away and scooted backward on her butt. "I could ask you the same thing. Are you following me?"

Idjit.

Of course he wasn't. She'd only just arrived. Technically, she'd followed him.

Plus, there was the small fact that this wasn't even her house.

"Following you?" He gave her a weird look. "Lady, I don't even know who you are."

Scrambling to her feet, she eyed the knives sticking out of the block on the counter to his right. "Ditto. Let's call the police and let them sort it out."

Why were the good-looking ones either taken, conceited, gay, or crazy?

"Emma?" A gruff voice called from the doorway to the living room behind her.

Twisting around, she found her neighbor leaning against the doorframe. "Dom? When did you get... Oh my God!" She sucked in a breath. "What did he do to you?"

Deep red, purplish bruises covered his face, neck, and arms. She couldn't tell where one ended and another started. They were everywhere. Even his fingers.

Overcome with a fierce protectiveness, she placed her body between the two men, held up her fists, and glowered at the intruder. "You lay another hand on him and I'll...hit you so hard you won't be able to tell me who you are because... you won't remember your name."

Lame.

Yeah, but she was running on adrenaline and had no control of her mouth. She did, however, have control of her fists, and refused to let anything else happen to her friend. Dom was a lean, muscled, fighting machine. It didn't compute in her brain for him to receive such a beating without putting so much as one mark on the other guy.

The intruder balked. "Wait a minute. You think *I* did that to him?"

Before she could reply, spurts of laughter rumbled behind her, intermixed with bouts of coughing and an occasional muffled oath.

"Never happen." Dom choked on a laugh as he moved around her. "Damn, that hurts." Doubled over, he waved a hand at her and the other guy. "Emma, meet my brother, Vince. Vince, meet my neighbor, Emma."

Brother?

Lowering her fists—just an inch, because she still didn't understand what was going on—she tried to recall what Dom had told her about his brother.

Former Army Ranger who now worked on a ranch.

"From Texas?"

"Yes." His guarded expression eased as he thrust out his hand.

Still in defense mode, she jerked back.

"Hey." He frowned and held his hands up. "It's okay. I just wanted to say it was nice to finally meet my brother's neighbor. He told me you watch his place when he's gone."

She glanced from his hands to the concern in his warm brown eyes. "Sorry. I-I'm still processing." Heat rushed into her cheeks as she slowly offered her hand. "Not sure what's taking my brain so long."

Or why she shook like a chihuahua in a blizzard.

What the heck?

"It's okay. It's normal." He gently shook her hand and motioned toward the high-backed stools that bordered one side of the center island. "You'll be fine. It's just the adrenaline wearing off."

Right. Because she was an idiot who'd just tried to take on an intruder.

She eyed her injured neighbor as he slowly shuffled across the kitchen to ease his battered frame onto one of the chairs on her right. Her mind finally registered the fact he wore a pair of gray sweats and an unzipped hoodie over a bared torso that looked like one big bruise, with a bandage wrapped around the middle like a mummy. Probably too painful to slip on a shirt, she reasoned, and her heart squeezed. "Shouldn't you be lying down?"

"Don't bother," Vince said. "I've tried all afternoon to get him to lie down and take his pain medicine. He refused both. It's like beating a dead donkey."

"You mean horse," Dom corrected.

Emma smiled, catching his brother's meaning. "No, I don't think he does."

"Hey." Dom's brows knit together, and he would've

pulled off the offended expression if not for the amusement flickering in his eyes. "I thought you were my knight in purple kittens."

She glanced down at her uniform and snickered. Work required everyone to wear scrubs, even the nonmedical staff. Most days, she wore solid ones. Today, though, had felt like a printed set kind of day. They made her feel happy, and since she woke up feeling it was going to be a special day, she'd reached for the kitten ones.

"I appreciate you watching over the place while I'm gone." A large, badly bruised hand covered hers on the counter, while his gaze darkened to navy and bore deep. "But don't ever try to stop an intruder on your own again, Emma. I'd rather they robbed me blind than for you to get hurt. You hear me?"

"Yes." She brushed her thumb lightly across his hand, careful not to hurt him. "Why are you home? What happened? Is the assignment over?"

Dom stiffened and released her. "No. The guys are still on the mission."

With her earlier stupor all but gone, she finally got a clue. "You were hurt, and they sent you back here."

His top lip curled. "I should be with my men."

"Best thing you can do for your men is recover," Vince said. "You fell through a *roof.*"

"Jesus, Dom." She sucked in a breath. "You're lucky to be alive."

Her neighbor's scowl deepened, but he remained silent.

She knew that look. Saw it plenty of times on several men. It was the I-can't-talk-about-the-mission expression, warning her not to bother asking him questions. Any attempt to get him to speak would be exactly as his brother had stated, and she wasn't into beating a dead donkey.

In fact, she suddenly felt drained of energy.

"Here." Vince slid a mug in front of her. "Drink this. You should stop shaking soon."

"Thanks." She cupped the mug and watched him head to the stove. The resemblance was more obvious now. Same dark hair as Dom's, but Vince wore it a little longer, and his eyes were a warm brown, where his brother's were a stark blue.

Mmm...chamomile.

Her favorite tea. How had he known?

Wait a minute.

Frowning, she turned to Dom. "Since when do you have tea in the house?"

On more than one occasion, she'd slipped some into his cupboard, only to retrieve the unopened box out of the trash a day later.

"Since I made a supply run," his brother replied over his shoulder while stirring something on the stove that smelled so incredible her stomach rumbled.

Dom shifted on his seat. "Civilian life has turned you soft, bro."

Vince chuckled, and the low sound rippled through Emma. "Don't waste your breath trying to pick a fight with me." He smirked at Dom. "You know it won't work, *princess.*"

She choked on her tea. "Princess?"

Her neighbor was tall and broad and oozed so much testosterone females swooned two states away. There was nothing feminine about the guy.

"Forgive my brother. He thinks he's funny," Dom grumbled.

Vince turned to face them both and grinned. "I don't *think.* I *know.*"

Emma laughed, warmed by the lighthearted banter, and when the men insisted she stay for dinner, she agreed, only leaving long enough to retrieve her purse from her car. Not cooking was always her favorite dinner option, especially when someone else was much better in the kitchen.

Vince was the real deal. She had no idea chicken, tomatoes, and cheese could taste so good in a soup. A *soup*. She also discovered "princess" was a childhood nickname given to her neighbor when he was a baby.

Vince pointed to his brother with a spoon. "His lashes were so long, and his features were so perfect, women were always mistaking him for a girl. It just sort of stuck."

Glancing at several days' worth of stubble covering Dom's clenched jaw, and the muscles bulging beneath his unzipped hoodie, she shook her head. "Yeah, not seeing anything 'princessey' about him now."

Same with his brother.

Equally blessed with long lashes and faultless features, Vince was just as tall and broad, and Emma knew firsthand his body was full of lean muscle from when she'd jumped on his back.

An act that normally would've embarrassed her, if not for the stark concern she'd harbored for his brother at the time.

Yeah. The Acardi brothers were far from "princessey."

"Damn straight." Dom glanced at her. "Enough about me. How do you know my brother? You acted like you recognized him when you were on the floor."

Shoot. Even injured and in agony, the man hadn't missed a trick.

Vince cleared his throat. "We ran into each other at the hospital today."

Understatement of the freaking year.

She snickered, and could tell by the way his lips twitched that he was holding back a grin. "Your brother's being polite," she told Dom. "I nearly took him out with a door. I keep forgetting the ones from radiology open *into* the corridor."

"It wasn't that bad. I hit it with my shoulder. No big deal,"

Vince reassured her. "Besides, I wasn't exactly watching where I was going, since I was in a hurry to get to a certain stubborn SOB before he tried to check himself out of the hospital."

Dom shrugged. "You need better friends, bro."

"Friends my ass. You know it was you. Besides, you can choose your friends." Vince scoffed, and a second later, he echoed his brother's chuckle.

Envy squeezed Emma's heart. The comradery between the two awakened her longing for a sibling that stemmed back to childhood. According to her widowed mother, "it hadn't been in the cards" while her father had been alive. And since her mother never remarried or even looked at another man, it'd been just the two of them. Not that she'd had a bad childhood. Emma had just always wanted the relationship with a sibling like the ones her friends had.

"So, how are things with your doctor?" Dom asked, turning his attention to her and pulling her back to the present.

She stifled a sigh. "The same, although, for a moment there, I thought he was actually going to do it today."

Vince frowned. "Do what?"

"Ask me out." Odd. She never blushed, but for some reason, the Texan's unblinking scrutiny sent a rush of heat into her cheeks.

Dom stood and shifted his feet. "How much time is left?"

She was *really* starting to regret ever mentioning the darn deadline.

"Seventeen days," she replied.

"There's a time limit on him asking you out?" Vince's gaze bounced between her and his brother.

"Four months ago, Emma set a deadline for a doctor she works with to ask her out," Dom answered before she could, pausing every three or four words to breathe in.

The idiot was in pain, and it was getting worse. It wasn't the first time Emma marveled at the stupidity of men and their pride. Although, to be fair, she knew several women who fell under that category, too.

She, of course, wasn't one of them.

"Remind me again, why aren't you in bed?" In fact, she was beginning to wonder why they even allowed him to leave the hospital. He kept alternating between sitting and standing, as if neither brought any relief.

In a typical defensive move, he straightened his shoulders and cocked his head. "Because I'm hungry."

She glanced at his untouched soup. "I can tell."

"Getting to it," Dom grumbled.

Vince's chuckle echoed across the island. "She's got your number."

And the Texan got her attention with his pleased expression and contagious grin. His cheerfulness was going to drive Dom nuts. That made her smile widen.

"Don't think I didn't notice, Emma." The obstinate man tipped his head again. "You're trying to change the subject."

Keyword was "trying."

"Let's get back to your doctor deadline," he said.

"Yeah, I need to get this straight." Vince set his spoon down and scratched his jaw. "You've been waiting four months for this doctor to ask you out? Does he have a pulse?"

"Yes." She laughed, aware of the heat infusing her face again. "And before you ask, no, he's not gay or attached. And it hasn't exactly been a full four months. More like three." After his breakup, she'd kept her attraction to herself, not wanting to be his rebound. But once he started dating again, she set her *hospital gala brunch* deadline. "My coworker thinks if I pretend to date another guy—you know, casually to show I'm desirable to other men—Stephan will come around."

Dom lifted an eyebrow. "Forbidden fruit *is* always more tempting…"

Vince shook his head. "That's because we're idiots."

Emma blew out a breath, relieved to find neither censure nor judgement in their gazes.

A smile twitched Dom's lips. "Speak for yourself, Vinny."

Vince grinned outright. "You would need a smack upside the head with a sledgehammer—or tank—to get a clue if someone like Emma was trying to get your attention."

"True." Her neighbor shrugged. Then winced.

Enough was enough.

Having watched the man suffer all through dinner, Emma set her spoon down and frowned at him. "You left the hospital. Fine. You don't want to lie down. Fine. But why aren't you taking your pain medication?"

"Don't need it."

Irritation prickled her neck. Men and their foolhardy notions about showing weakness.

"Yes, you do," she said. "You just don't want to look like a…a…*princess*."

Vince's snicker ricocheted across the room, but his brother didn't bat an eye.

"That's not it." Sitting down, Dom shook his head and winced. Again. "I've seen too many good men go from injured to addicted." Determination filled his gaze. "That's not happening to me."

She understood his reluctance and his concern. Over a decade ago, her grandfather fell off a roof and broke his back, and after his recovery, he had a hard time weaning off the morphine.

"I wouldn't let that happen," Vince said.

Emma believed him. Just because he appeared all teasing and smiles didn't mean the guy was a pushover. Or stupid. There was an underlying strength, a stubbornness, and intelligence behind those amber eyes.

Probably had made him a great Army Ranger when he was active duty.

Emma slipped off her stool and headed to the medicine bottles she spotted on the counter by the fridge. No morphine, but there were muscle relaxants, and they could be highly addictive, too.

"Your concern is understandable, Dom," she said, turning to face him. "But you barely sit for two minutes before you have to stand. Then you sit again, because you can't stand." Enough was definitely enough. "There's a difference between concerned and stupid. Taking medication for the first few days is not going to make you an addict." She set the pills in front of him.

Approval flickered through Vince's eyes as their gazes met. "That's what I've been telling him." He slid a glass of water next to the pills.

Her stubborn neighbor stood with a grimace. "I said no."

Emma jammed her hands on her hips and lifted her chin, prepared to do whatever it took to square off with her hardheaded friend. "For goodness sakes, Dom. Just take the medicine, because if you don't, you leave me no choice but to call a certain female who we both know would jump at the chance to pamper you."

Apprehension flickered through his gaze a second before his eye twitched. "You wouldn't."

"Yes. I would."

Vince's lips quirked. "Now, this sounds like something I need to see. Call whoever she is and get her over here."

She laughed. The Texan really was quite cute. Too cute for her own good.

Alarm bells rang in Emma's head. Her brain had no right—or permission—to think thoughts like that. Shaking them away, she refocused on her neighbor.

His gaze narrowed. "You're bluffing."

"Oh really?" Emma lifted a brow while fishing the phone from her purse hanging on the back of her chair. "I happen to have Chelsea's number. A few weeks ago, she texted me to put in a good word for her. We both know she's just chomping at the bit for a chance to be with you."

The blonde was one of many groupies that fawned over him at the local bar and grille, except Chelsea was a bit more over-the-top than the others. Lordy, if that woman ever got wind that Dom was back—and injured—she'd be on his doorstep with chicken soup in one hand and her suitcase in the other. He wouldn't be able to sneeze without her handing him a tissue, glass of water, a cold compress for his forehead, and a marriage license application.

His jaw clenched. "Are you blackmailing me?"

If blackmailing the stubborn man got him to take the medication to give his body some relief and a chance to heal, then so be it. Just to make sure he took her seriously, Emma began to scroll through her contacts. "It's your own fault. If you won't take the medication now, you'll take it for her so she'll go away."

"Fine." He grabbed the pills. "I'll take the damn things. But on one condition."

Unease trickled down her spine. "What?"

"You fake date my brother."

Chapter Four

Vince stiffened. "Me?"

He empathized with the bewilderment clouding the woman's gaze. That hadn't been the condition he expected, either. Hell, he didn't even know why she needed help. This doctor of hers sounded like an idiot. No red-blooded man in their right mind would pass up a chance to ask her out on a date.

"Yeah, you," Dom replied. "It's a win-win. You help Emma out so I don't have to worry about some dickwad taking advantage of her, and in turn, I get a break from your mother-henning."

Of course. He should've known his brother would bend things to suit his own agenda. Typical Dom fashion.

"First off, I don't mother hen. That's Stone." Vince scoffed, recalling how his friend had hovered around Leo earlier that year, afraid he'd do something crazy while intoxicated again. Luckily, those days were behind them. "But if you'd like some mother-henning, I could always veto your request not to call Mom and let her know you were injured."

Vince hadn't been keen on keeping it from their parents in the first place. The only reason he'd agreed was to minimize his brother's stress level.

Dom turned his back to Emma and flipped him off.

Vince ignored it. "Besides, I'm only here for a couple weeks."

"And he should spend that time with you," Emma said.

"No. He shouldn't. And it's the perfect amount of time." Dom glanced at Emma. "That's what's left on your deadline, right?"

Another blush filled her face, and the color deepened the blue of her mesmerizing eyes as she nodded.

Damn, the woman was pretty.

And transparent.

No doubt, the poor thing was mortified her neighbor was trying to convince his brother to pretend to date her.

Truth was, Vince would be happy to date her for real. Emma was witty and beautiful and fiercely protective of her friends, considering how she'd jumped on his back, then placed herself between him and his brother to keep Dom safe.

A pang of long-buried emotions ricocheted through his chest. More than a decade had passed since a woman had cared about him with such conviction. It had taken a long time to get to a good place in his head. Lately, since his buddies in Texas had starting falling for their women left and right, he was warming up to the idea of dating again.

Dating. Nothing more.

Just not with this woman.

No. Emma was his brother's neighbor. The one Dom relied on when he deployed, and the one he suspected kept his unruly brother in line. The last thing he wanted was to jeopardize the relationship if things went south before he left.

Or, heaven forbid, one of them got attached.

"The hospital fundraiser brunch is three Saturdays from

now," she said. "If Stephan doesn't ask me out by then, I'll take what's left of my self-respect and move on."

Good for her. Seemed like she was better off without the guy anyway. Although, it was possible the doctor was interested but had a rule about dating a coworker. Vince could understand the reluctance to act if that were the case.

Dom grinned. "So, then my brother is the ideal candidate."

Jerk.

Taking pity on the woman for being a pawn in the guy's strong-arm tactics, Vince tried to give her an out. "Maybe Emma already has someone lined up."

His brother turned back to Emma. "Do you?"

She shook her head.

Damn it.

"There. You see?" Dom's gaze met his. "Perfect."

The urge to wipe the smug smile off the idiot's lips was strong, and he would have if it weren't for the pain still pinching his face.

"Of course," his brother continued, "if you two would rather, I could always toss these pills in the trash where they belong, and we could forget all about any of this."

As much as he hated being manipulated, Vince hated to see his brother suffer. He shook his head. "No. Take the pills. I'd be happy to help Emma out while I'm here. If that's what she wants."

A pair of cobalt-blue eyes met his gaze, and the mixture of relief and pissed off woman made him smile. Yeah, she wasn't entirely thrilled with his brother's maneuvers, either.

"Yes, thanks, Vince," she replied. "I appreciate it." Her gaze shifted to his brother. "What I *don't* appreciate is being manipulated, but since I just pulled the same stunt on you with Chelsea, and in essence I'm kind of getting ready to do that to Stephan, I won't ream you a new one."

Dom answered by swallowing the pills, then made a show of opening his mouth to prove he wasn't hiding them.

"You're a goof." Smirking, Emma stuffed her phone back in her purse, then stepped between the chairs to place her hand on said goof's shoulder. "You know I love you like a brother. And God, Dom, you look bad. Really bad." Her voice broke, and her eyes filled with tears. "I hate knowing you're in pain."

In an instant, the teasing and smugness disappeared from Dom's face, and a much stronger expression appeared.

Panic.

Muttering a curse, Dom leaned closer and winced when he slid his arms around her. "It's okay, Emma. I took the pills, and will take them for a few days; just don't cry."

Well, damn. Vince bit back a smile. Too bad she hadn't deployed her waterworks sooner. Poor woman wouldn't have been coerced into dating him.

Fake dating, his mind corrected. *Casually.*

Drawing back, Emma sniffed. "Sorry. I don't know what's wrong with me. I don't usually cry."

"I know. It's freaking me out," his brother said, sinking back down onto his chair. "Vince always dealt with tears better than me."

He laughed. "True. You're more like Brick."

The parallels between his younger brother and Stone's were always a source of amusement. Both men hated tears, and were magnets to the opposite sex. Although, their reactions differed.

Dom reached for the basket of Italian bread. "So how *is* Romeo?"

Vince folded his arms across his chest and grinned. "Engaged."

Dom's gaze snapped to his. "No fu—uh, no way."

"I know." He still found it hard to believe at times.

"Wow. A one-eighty." His brother rubbed his jaw. "Lady-killer to monogamist."

"Lady-killer?" Emma arched a brow, then grinned at Dom. "So he's like you."

Vince laughed. "With one exception. Unlike my brother, Brick used to reciprocate the advances."

Dom was no saint. But, unlike Brick, he was in command. Vince knew his brother took his leadership role seriously. Nothing came between him and his men. Rangers first. Always. He'd never allow a woman to get close enough to jeopardize his priorities.

His brother grunted. "That's why it doesn't compute."

"Oh, trust me, bro. It gets better."

"She a nun? Stripper? Witch?" Dom fired off. "She has to be special."

He nodded, not bothering to hold back a grin. "Beth is special. Very special. She's Cord's kid sister."

"Fuck me," his brother muttered, then glanced at Emma. "Sorry."

She laughed. "No worries. I gather Brick served with Cord and broke some brotherhood code."

"Something like that." Dom's attention returned to him. "Cord let him live?"

"Well, apparently, there was a brawl at a motel that everyone missed." What Vince would've given to have been a fly on the wall that day. "They had to pay for the damages."

Dom chuckled—or tried to, at least. "Sounds like you missed a good fight."

"Yeah," Vince said. "But they got over their issues and the ranch is cool again."

"That's good." Emma's gaze met his while she nodded her head toward his brother. "It means there's hope for Neanderthals."

Vince threw his head back and laughed. Emma had wit

and brains, and held her own with his brother. He liked her. "You really do see past Dom's handsome hero facade."

Most women swooned.

"Clearly," she replied, the corners of her mouth twitching while playful amusement lit her eyes.

Apparently still shocked by the news about Brick's engagement, his brother didn't seem to realize they were dissing him. "I never thought I'd see the day." The idiot shook his head. "Cord's gone soft."

"Love will do that." Vince shrugged.

Dom's gazed snapped back to his. "Love? What are you talking about?"

"Cord moved in with Haley."

The instant that news sunk in, his brother's jaw dropped. "Drew's widow?"

He nodded.

"Just what the hell's going on in Texas? You better be careful, bro. Society is assimilating your unit."

True. And it was great, but something his active-duty-minded brother wouldn't conceive.

Dom cocked his head. "Only three of you left."

"Two," he corrected. "Stone's getting married in two and a half weeks."

"No shit? Wait...two...?" Disgust erased the disbelief in his brother's eyes. "Damn it, Vince. You should be at the ranch helping them get ready, not here nursing me."

He held up his hand. "There's time and plenty of people there to help with preliminary stuff." Even though he was the peacemaker of the two brothers, Vince could be just as stubborn. A fact his brother knew all too well. "Don't even think of trying to use that to get me to leave. It won't work. I'm not going until you can at least get off the...couch by yourself."

He'd wanted to say shitter, but refrained because of Emma. No reason to be crude, although, sometimes that was the only way to get through to his thickheaded sibling.

She sat, regarding him with an expression that mirrored his brother's worried frown. "I can help with Dom, if you want to leave sooner."

Sweet of her to offer, but not even his Ranger buddy's wedding would tear him from his injured brother's side. If Dom was still too incapacitated to take care of himself two and a half weeks from now, then Vince was staying.

Before he could reply, his brother set his spoon down and straightened his shoulders. "No need." What little color Dom had in his face slowly ebbed away. "I'll rest, take meds, do therapy, and whatever else the doctor orders. So, Vince, you continue to plan to cook for Stone's wedding, and Emma, you continue to plan to attend that fundraiser brunch with your doctor, because I'm going to make the fastest damn recovery in the history of Fort Benning."

"Yes, sir." Emma saluted, pulling a laugh from Dom that quickly turned into a coughing swear.

The idiot grasped the counter to stay upright.

Vince rushed around the island to shove a shoulder under his brother's arm and grip his hip. "Come on, that pill is kicking in. Let's get you to your guest room before you fall down."

"Guest room?" Emma moved the chairs out of the way.

He nodded. "Stairs are off-limits right now."

Truth be told, his brother couldn't handle them. Hell, Dom was barely managing to shuffle across the kitchen with Vince absorbing the full brunt of the weight. Son of a bitch was heavy. The action brought back memories of active duty.

Some good.

Some bad.

Pushing them aside, Vince concentrated on getting his brother through the living room to the hallway.

"Something told me to change the sheets yesterday," Emma called over her shoulder as she rushed ahead. "Just wish I'd listened."

He wanted to tell her not to worry. His brother wouldn't give a shit about clean sheets, and the groan rumbling through Dom's body confirmed it. Considering the hellholes military missions sent them into, a musty sheet was a luxury.

By the time Vince got his brother to the room, the bed was changed, and the poor guy was too exhausted to do little more than grunt in pain as he settled onto the mattress.

Emma fussed with the pillows, then disappeared only to show up a minute later with another armful, which started the fussing again. Vince had to give the woman credit. She wasn't a quitter. She set a goal and didn't give up until it was accomplished. No matter the obstacle.

In this case, his brother's mutterings and grunts. Emma ignored them and remained on course with her task until she was satisfied Dom was as comfortable as he could be, under the circumstances.

Vince stood back and kept out of the way, and damn, he enjoyed the show. The fact his brother could only lie there, completely at Emma's mercy while she took charge, was priceless. But his favorite part was the way the thin material of her scrubs conformed to her sweet curves as she crawled all over his brother's bed to accomplish her mission.

Yeah. He really liked that part.

Which wasn't wise, especially since they were about to go on a fake date and there was nothing fake about the hard-on pressing against his zipper.

What had he gotten himself into?

That thought remained uppermost in his mind long after his brother fell asleep and he'd walked Emma home. But it was unwanted and time to focus on something else, like checking in with the guys back at the ranch.

Retreating into the kitchen, he pulled out his phone and dialed his buddy.

Leo picked up on the first ring. "Hey. How's your brother?"

"Battered to shit. Cracked ribs. Back spasms," he replied. "So, hopefully, two to three weeks of physical therapy will give him back enough mobility that I can get back in time for Stone's wedding."

"Is he spitting nails?"

Over the years, his Ranger team and his brother's team had met and worked different orders on the same op. Leo knew Dom well enough to recognize limitations didn't sit well with the obstinate guy.

He leaned his back against the counter and smirked. "More like spikes."

Leo chuckled. "Thought I felt a disturbance in the force."

"Yeah. That was him refusing his pain meds," he said. "In order to get the bastard to take the pills, I had to agree to pretend to casually date his neighbor while I'm here."

"What? Why?" his friend asked. "Is there something wrong with her?"

He shook his head, even though Leo couldn't see him. "No. Emma is very attractive."

A fact Vince was *still* trying not to think about. Much.

"Then why does she need a fake boyfriend and not a real one?"

"She needs to go on a few fake dates to *get* a real one," he replied, then went on to explain the situation. "So, after we show up at a few of the same places as this Stephan asshole, and he sees someone else finds her desirable, I'm sure he'll make a move and I'll be off the hook."

Which was good, his mind insisted.

"Sounds like you have your hands full."

The image of a sweet, scrub-covered ass flashed through Vince's mind. He straightened from the counter and shook the vision from his head. His hands were not going anywhere near Emma's delectables.

"Speaking of hands being full, how are things there?" he asked, changing the subject. "Is my kitchen still standing?"

Leo laughed. "Yes, it's just as you left it. Don't worry about a thing. Beth and Jovy will handle the cooking just fine. I forwarded your text of food allergies, preferences, and who prefers to eat in solitude. It's now printed out, color coded, and pinned to a board in the kitchen."

He smiled and shook his head, knowing full well Stone's fiancée was responsible. "But they have Jovy's wedding plans to take care of, too." He hated to dump this on them, too.

"Hello? Have you met Jovy? She's the queen of multi-tasking and organization." His buddy chuckled. "And Beth plans events for a living, so quit worrying. We're good here. Worry about your brother and your fake girlfriend."

He laughed but didn't rise to the bait. Instead, he thought it was time to ask the favor Dom needed. Vince just hoped it didn't bring up too many negative memories for his friend. "You still have contacts in Iraq, right?"

The phone was silent a beat. "Yeah. Why?"

He explained what had happened to his brother, and his concern for the missing informant, then glanced at the microwave clock. "It can wait until tomorrow. I know it's early across the pond."

"Actually, Farid is probably already up," Leo said. "I'll call him now, then get back to you to let you know what he says."

"Okay. Thanks." Vince hung up and set his phone on the counter.

That went fairly easy. Hopefully, the same could be said for his dealings with Dom and Emma over the next few weeks.

Too bad he had a sinking suspicion that helping the pretty woman could prove tougher than helping his stubborn brother.

Chapter Five

The next day, Emma entered the cafeteria with Macy, anxiety quivering her stomach. It was nearly time to start the ruse. Her last shot at Stephan.

"I'm not going to stay long," her friend said, sitting down with a smile on her face to rival a Cheshire cat. "Just long enough to meet your man. I can't believe you found someone so fast. Damn, girl, my cousin Latisha has nothing on you. You're a quick worker."

She sat facing Macy and the cafeteria entrance in order to keep an eye out for Vince. Earlier that morning, she'd filled her friend in on Dom's brother and their tentative plan. "I just got lucky."

"Well, this location was genius." Eagerness lit the woman's gaze as she glanced around the room. "There's quite a bit of staff here. Word is bound to get out. Whose idea was it?"

She brushed an imaginary crumb off the table, finding the Formica cool and reassuring to the touch. "Vince's."

Last night, he had insisted on walking her home.

Unnecessary, but sweet. And during the one-and-a-half-minute walk to her house, they made plans to meet for lunch during Dom's physical therapy.

"I can't wait to meet Vince," Macy said loud enough for everyone at the nearby tables to hear.

Emma tried not to cringe. Maybe this wasn't the best place to meet until they discussed a game plan and rules—the very purpose of this lunch. Well, that and getting the rumor mill started.

It wasn't like she had a ton of time. Emma just hoped they didn't appear too awkward, considering they knew next to nothing about each other.

"I bet he's hot. He is, isn't he?" Grinning from ear to ear, the woman practically vibrated in her seat.

Dammit. Macy was still using her outdoor voice.

Behind her happy expression, at least, Emma hoped it appeared happy, she sent her friend a warning glare. "Yes," she replied in a much quieter tone. "He's tall, dark, and handsome."

All true. Emma was determined to keep as much truth in the ruse as possible.

"That's wonderful," her friend said in a much quieter tone. "I hope for your sake he's good in bed."

She sucked in a breath. "Macy."

"What?" The woman shrugged. "It's hard to find a guy who is handsome and good in bed. I got lucky with my Dupree. That's how I knew he was a keeper."

"I'm not going to find out. It's not like that."

"Oh, I get it." Macy winked. "He's actually not handsome."

Emma shook her head and leaned closer. "No. He is very attractive. But this is fake, remember? F.A.K.E.?"

How many times did she have to drill it into her friend's thick head? It was Macy's idea in the first place.

"I know. But if he was…and you two did…no one would blame you," her friend insisted. "It's all right to get into character…and for the character to get into you."

Emma gasped. "Macy!"

Her crazy friend blinked. "I'm just saying, if he's hot and you're in the role…go for it. Ride the Lone Ranger."

She smiled. "He's not that kind of Ranger."

"What kind is he?"

"The late kind." Vince stood by the table, appearing out of nowhere.

Emma's heart leaped. "Hey…hi." Heat flooded her face as she scrambled to her feet, wondering if he overheard any of that conversation.

"Sorry," he said. "It took longer than expected to get Dom out of the car and downstairs."

An image of her stubborn neighbor flashed through her mind. She smiled. "Let me guess, he refused to use a wheelchair."

"Correct." A mischievous gleam entered Vince's eyes. "Care to guess what he told me to do with it?"

She laughed. "No need. I'm sure I know." No doubt it included several colorful words and Vince's well-formed backside. Not that she noticed that. Yeah. Okay. Yesterday, she totally did.

The clearing of a throat drew her attention to her friend, now standing with a huge grin on her face, her curious gaze raking Vince down, then up. Worried about what might come out of the woman's mouth, Emma made a quick introduction.

Smiling, he shook her friend's hand. "Nice to meet you, Macy."

Appreciation lit Macy's face. "Likewise. You two lovebirds enjoy your lunch. I need to pick my guy up at the repair shop. His car is on the fritz again."

Emma had no idea if any of that was true, but she went

with it. "All right. See you back at the office." The heat returned to her face when Macy gave her a fist pump of approval behind Vince's back. Making sure he didn't turn suddenly and see her crazy friend, Emma grabbed his arm and pulled him in the opposite direction to the food. "So, shall we get in line?"

A few minutes later, Emma sat down with him at a table off by itself in a quiet corner. She didn't want anyone to overhear their conversation, plus it lent to the appearance of wanting to be alone.

"How long is Dom's appointment?" she asked, wanting to keep their talk light while they ate.

"An hour," he replied. "So this works out great."

She nodded. "And we're already getting curious glances." A few people she knew were smiling at her, and several of them fanned themselves.

Even though it helped with the facade, she wished her foolish body would stop blushing. It made no sense. This wasn't real, and yet, heat still swarmed her cheeks whenever she received a thumbs-up.

"Then I'm guessing this will help." He reached across the table to cover her hand with his.

Her stupid blush wasn't the only thing to increase. Her heartbeat surged, too. Blaming it on the unexpected contact, she refused to believe it had anything to do with his light, warm touch, or the delicious scrape of calluses across her skin.

Nope. Couldn't be that.

"Yes," she finally replied. Her voice sounded a little breathless to her ears, so she covered her confusion with a smile. "Have you done this before?"

"No." He laughed and released her hand.

She found the act of breathing a little easier, which was odd, since it was Stephan who usually affected her pulse. For this to happen with Vince, too, caught her completely off guard.

Had to be a fluke.

She eyed the man sitting across from her, smile dimpling his face, gaze warm and open, and her breath caught again.

Shoot. What was wrong with her?

Nothing, her mind reasoned. Vince was a lean, handsome, sexy man, and it was only natural her body would take notice.

Whoa. Hold on. Since when had her body gotten involved? It was just her pulse. Her body was not taking part in this pretense. There would be no notice-taking allowed.

"I figured to make it look real, we need to act as if it is," he said. "So, we need to say and do things any normal man and woman would do if they were interested in each other."

Made sense.

She nodded. "And we'll need to know a few basic things about each other as well."

"A few basic things. Let's see…" He tapped his finger on his stubble-ridden chin that she took no notice to at all, since it wasn't allowed. "I'm from New Jersey. My parents still live there. I'm the oldest of two sons. A Libra. Like to take long walks on the beach at night under the moonlight. Don't smoke. Will have an occasional beer with the guys. Would do anything for my family and friends. I'm at peace in the kitchen, and I make a mean cannoli." He grinned. "Your turn."

His friendly nature immediately put her at ease.

She smiled. "Okay. I'm from right here in Columbus. The only child of a widow. My mom moved to Florida to be with her sister who recently started chemo. I'm a Pisces. Love to lay out under the stars. Don't smoke. Will also have an occasional beer with the guys, but prefer a wine cooler. Would do just about anything for chocolate. Make a mean peach pie. And I'm at peace reading on my porch swing."

He grabbed a napkin, pulled out a pen, and started writing things down.

"What are you doing?" she asked.

"Making a note about the stars. Oh, and that chocolate thing, too."

She laughed and smacked his arm. "You're a nut."

He smiled. "Guilty."

The guy was such a contrast to his brother's more serious demeanor. It was a surprise, and admittedly refreshing.

"So, I take it your outlook on life is 'glass half full'?"

His smile widened. "More like three-quarters full."

"Never would've guessed."

"How about you?" he asked, digging into his lunch.

"Me?" She'd never given it much thought. But no one had ever accused her of being pessimistic. "Half full."

"Well, we'll have to work on getting that up to three-quarters," he teased. "There may be some chocolate involved."

Narrowing her eyes, she pointed her fork at him. "Oh, I see what you're doing there."

"What's that?" His innocent gaze didn't fool her for a second.

And darn it, it was cute.

"You're speaking my language," she replied.

He immediately picked up the pen and wrote on his napkin again.

Smiling, she shook her head. "Yep, you definitely got all the sense of humor in your family."

"Dom has a sense of humor. It's just covered in layers of sarcasm," he said, his gaze turning serious. "I have to admit, I'm just a little curious as to why you and my brother never hooked up."

"Me and Dom?" She raised a brow. The guy was gorgeous, but there weren't any sparks. "Never crossed my mind. For one, he's military, and my track record there sucks. And for another, he's too…"

"Intense," Vince supplied with a grin.

"Yeah. That." She nodded. "It's going to take a strong woman to handle your brother."

Admiration lit his eyes. "You're strong, and you handled him just fine last night. I quite enjoyed watching him concede to you."

Now that was funny. She laughed. "Dom knows I won't put up with any of his bull. He also thinks of me as family. His whole unit does. They treat me like a kid sister. My chances of getting a date plummet to negative two thousand when they're around."

"Warn everyone off, do they?" His lips twitched, while understanding warmed his gaze.

She sighed. "Yeah, despite my protests."

"I'm guessing they approve of your doctor, otherwise Dom wouldn't suggest I help you."

"True." She reached across the table to touch Vince's hand. "And I really appreciate your help."

Awareness immediately shot up her arm and fluttered her pulse. Again. Funny, the few times she'd come in contact with Stephan had never mainlined a zing to her chest. Then again, she'd never touched him outright.

Vince's gaze narrowed, and his body stilled as if he felt it, too. Apparently, it wasn't just all the humor this Acardi brother possessed. No. The handsome Jersey boy turned Texan held all the sparks, too.

Not good.

She drew her hand back and cleared her throat. "So, what's our game plan?"

Other questions—personal ones—resounded in her head, but she refused to ask them. He was not her real boyfriend. Heck, he wasn't even a candidate. He was an out-of-towner.

A visitor. A military man. The guy was a pawn, a tool to help her finally land on Stephan's radar.

"Depends."

Her heart skipped a beat. "On what?"

"On what your doctor likes to do."

"His name is Stephan," she corrected, tired of everyone referring to the guy as "her doctor" when it wasn't true. Yet. "And...I don't know what he likes to do. I only see him at work, although, I've bumped into him once or twice at Antonio's."

The first time she'd seen him at the Italian restaurant, he'd been with his former girlfriend back when he'd just arrived, and the second time he was with a buddy sitting at the bar surrounded by a bevy of beauties.

"Ah...Antonio's." Vince grinned. "It's still open?"

She nodded. "I take it you've been there?"

"Once or twice," he replied. "Do you remember what day of the week he was there?"

"No. Why?"

Vince shrugged. "Just wondered if he had a pattern we could use to show up there."

"Oh." She shook her head. "Sorry. I don't remember the exact day."

"It's all right. How about hobbies? Sports? Art? Charities? Anything he attends regularly."

Again, she shook her head. "I honestly don't know. I mean, I'm sure he has them, I just don't know what they are." Which, come to think of it, was odd. Why didn't she know any of that? "He discussed college football with one of the other doctors once, but I don't remember what team."

A frown creased Vince's brow.

"I'm sorry." She sighed. "For someone interested in the guy, you'd think I'd know more about him. It's just that he doesn't really talk about those things at work, and I don't socialize with him outside of it."

His frown remained. "Can I ask you a question?"

Uh-oh… "S-sure."

"Why are you interested in him? Specifically. Why him?"

It was a simple, easy question. So why was she suddenly at a loss for words? That wouldn't do. She lifted her chin and gave it some thought. "He's smart. Compassionate. Funny. Good-looking…a-a-and he makes my heart flutter." That last part sent heat rushing into her face again. It was too weird discussing another man with a man who fell under the exact same description.

Vince held her gaze for a moment, then nodded. "Okay. Good enough. Then there's only one thing to do."

There went her heart rocking in her chest again. "What's that?"

"I need to see him."

She stilled. "See him? What do you mean?"

"He's a doctor, isn't he?" Vince lifted a shoulder. "Get me an appointment to see him."

Emma raised both brows and blinked. "I…are you sure?"

"Yes. Of course," he said. "It's a no-brainer."

And above and beyond.

"I don't know what to say." No one had ever done anything like that for her before. To willingly see a proctologist just to get information for her was more than she'd ever ask of him. "You really don't need t—"

"Ah." He waved a hand at her. "No big deal. This way I can drill the doc while he's examining me."

Emma's big mistake was sipping her soda. She choked as carbonation shot down the wrong tube. He was too much. She coughed into her napkin. "You and your sense of humor."

"What?" He half frowned, half grinned.

He was messing with her again. Using the word "drill" when he talked about a proctologist exam. The man was too funny.

"I'm not sure what I did to put that smile on your face, but I like it. You should always smile," he said, pulling his buzzing phone from his pocket.

Because she didn't know how to respond to the compliment, or even if she should, Emma decided to ignore it. She jabbed a thumb toward his phone, instead. "Is that the master beckoning?"

His lips twitched as he answered the text. "Yeah. The Earl of Happiness is done with therapy early and demands my presence."

"I have to get back to work anyway." She rose with him, and together they emptied their trays, then set them on a stack near the trash can.

That's when one of her friends approached. "Hi, Emma."

Quick on the uptake, Vince stepped close and slipped an arm around her waist.

"Oh, hi, Kelly." She made a hasty introduction, and repeated it several times to various friends before she and Vince finally made it out the door and to the elevator.

He removed his hand from her waist, only to grab her hand and bring her knuckles to his lips.

She swallowed past her suddenly dried throat. "W-what's that for? No one's here."

His warm, firm lips continued to brush her knuckles and steal her breath. "True, but there are several women watching us down the hall."

"Ah." Now she heard the snickers and sighs, and did some sighing of her own once they entered the vacant elevator and the doors closed. Gently tugging her hand free, she moved a few feet away and found the act of breathing much easier. "Well, that should get the gossip mill going. Thanks."

He leaned against the far wall, arms folded across his chest. Sexy grin dimpling his face. "My pleasure."

Hers, too.

No. She lifted her chin and exhaled slowly. She could handle it. Her stupid deprived body was just thirsty for the attention. No big deal.

It would just have to wait for Stephan.

Then her mom would be happy. She would be happy. Everyone would be freaking happy. Because the alternative wasn't an option. She wouldn't even consider it.

The elevator stopped on her floor.

"Don't forget to make that appointment for me," Vince said, pushing away from the wall to step to her side. "We don't have a big timeline."

She nodded. "I'll stop by tonight to let you know how I made out."

Normally, it was tough to get one on short notice, but she was friends with all the girls in the office. Hopefully there would be a cancellation and they could pencil him in that week.

"Why don't you come over for dinner?" His grin was easy and light, nothing suggestive at all about it.

But still, she shook her head. "Sorry. I'm already doing something with Macy," she lied and stepped off the elevator.

He was too nice. Too handsome. Too kind.

No. Overexposure to the sweet man was dangerous with a capital *D*. He confused her. Muddled her brain. Her survival sense kicked in. He was prior military, which was a big negatory. She needed to stay the course and keep her distance whenever possible.

Chapter Six

The sun was slicing through the blinds in the guest room as Vince got Dom out of bed the next morning. After only a few minutes, he tuned out his brother's bellyaching about not being able to dress himself and thought instead about Emma.

The woman confused him.

Late last night, she'd stopped by just long enough for a glass of iced tea and to tell him about a last-minute cancellation that'd allowed her to get him an appointment first thing this morning. Her gaze had lingered on him, and what appeared to be regret flashed through her eyes.

What the hell was all that about?

And then there was yesterday's lunch. He was still trying to figure out what had happened during that time. They were holding a nice conversation, having a little fun, because, damn, the woman was easy to talk to, and then she touched his arm, and *bam*...a strange current had surged through his body.

He'd only ever felt a connection like that once before. Decades ago. A lifetime ago.

With his soul mate.

Each other's firsts, they'd been inseparable all through high school. Everything was planned. She wanted to see the world beyond New Jersey, and was supportive when he'd joined the Army in the spring of their senior year. After basic, scheduled for that summer, he'd planned to propose.

He never got the chance.

Connie was everything good in the world—she *was* his world—until a car accident took her from him.

Ever since, Vince had closed that part of himself off and never had a deep connection with another woman. Never allowed himself to get that close.

To feel a similar zapping with Emma threw him off balance. His first instinct was to run. Get as far away from the woman as possible. But he was a Ranger. He didn't run. Hell, maybe it wasn't even real. It could've just been his stupid mind playing tricks on him because he'd gotten on so well with her.

He nodded. That had to be it.

"Good. Then let's go," his brother said, bringing his mind back to the present.

"Go where?"

Dom frowned. "What the hell do you mean, go where? To Kelley's for a drink. You just nodded you'd take me."

"What? No way." He shook his head. "First of all, you're not going to a bar at eight in the morning. And definitely not while taking medication. Second, I never agreed. And third," he said, waving at the floor, "where the hell is your other sock?"

"On the bed where you left it," Dom replied, narrowing his gaze. "I've got a better question. Where the hell are your thoughts?"

Mumbling, he grabbed the sock and carefully put it on his brother's foot.

"Did your check in with Leo not go so well last night?"

Dom asked. "Is everything okay at the ranch? Because if it's not—"

"Everything's fine," Vince said, cutting him off. "You're not getting rid of me that easily. You'll have to go through a lot more PT—and not skip out on your sessions early—before I'm satisfied enough with your progress to even consider leaving."

Dom grumbled as Vince finished helping him get dressed. "Has Leo gotten through to anyone about my friend?"

"Yes," he replied. "He called me late last night to tell me he finally got word to his contact."

His brother blew out a breath. "So now we wait."

"Yeah. He'll call the minute he hears anything." He watched Dom grip the dresser and slowly pull himself to his feet.

Knowing better than to try and help, Vince stood back, ready to assist if necessary. The macho idiot preferred to do it himself, claiming it gave his muscles a workout, but Vince knew it was just Dom being pigheaded. With pain erasing the color from his brother's face, it was obvious the muscle relaxant remained in the bottle that morning.

"So much for keeping your word to Emma." He shook his head.

Dom frowned. "What are you talking about?"

"You take your muscle relaxant, and I pretend to casually date Emma for a few weeks," he reminded. "Since it's as obvious as the pain on your face that you didn't take any today, does that mean I don't have to date Emma?"

A muffled oath mixed with a grunt as Dom lumbered near to stare him straight in the eye. "I won't take that poison more than once a day and prefer to take it *after* PT. So, no, asshole, you still have to play Emma's boy toy." His smug expression turned pensive, and he cocked his head. "Why? I thought you two got on well together."

"We do." *Too well*, he thought, motioning for his brother to move out of the room, but the idiot didn't budge. "I just wanted an answer about the medication."

Mostly true. Vince did want to know that, but also wasn't opposed to having a reason to back out; although, in truth, he wouldn't. Not after giving Emma his word. He'd never leave her in the lurch.

Dom set a hand on his brother's shoulder. "Sorry. Deal still stands. Just promise me you won't hurt her. Emma's a gem."

He frowned. "Of course I'm not going to hurt her. I think you know me better than that."

Expelling a breath, Dom released him and shook his head. "Look, I know you don't go around hurting women. It's just that Emma is like a kid sister to me, and I don't want to see her upset."

"She'll be fine."

"And I'm not blind," Dom said. "I know she's beautiful, so just promise me you won't get carried away and sleep with her."

He reeled back. "Jesus, Dom. I'm not really dating her, so there will be no need for me to be anywhere near her bedroom." He rubbed his suddenly throbbing temple. "Besides, for me to be able to hurt her, she'd have to have feelings for me, and we both know all her feelings are tied up with Stephan."

Dom nodded. "Fair enough. And despite what you think, I don't want to see you get hurt, either."

His brows shot up. First his brother throws him under the bus, then in the next breath, he was worried about him. Vince held back a snort. Typical Dom. Never predictable. "Again, it's *fake*. We're just friends. And it's only a little more than two weeks."

Dom hesitated. "So, what are your plans to help her

today?"

"I had her get me an appointment with the guy," he said. "This way I can extract information from her doctor without stalking."

Dom's eyes widened. "You're going to see her doctor?"

"Yeah."

"For an exam?"

"Yeah." He frowned, unsure what the big deal was. "Why?"

Dom released him and stepped back to lean against the doorframe. "No reason." His lips twitched as he scratched the bridge of his nose with his thumb. "Smart thinking."

"Thanks," he said. "I thought so, too. This way, I can play the new-in-the-area card and ask him to recommend places he frequents."

"That's a good way to get to know him."

He nodded.

"Intimately," his brother added, still fighting a stupid grin.

Vince wrinkled his nose. "What the hell's your problem? I wouldn't go that far."

"But *he* might." Dom snickered.

Irritation prickled Vince's spine. "Why do I bother?" Fighting the urge to shoulder-check the idiot, he pushed past and muttered, "Asshole," on his way out the door.

For some reason that increased his brother's amusement. Bastard's laughter followed him down the hall, along with a hissed breath and several curses.

Good. He hoped the exertion hurt like hell.

Dom was acting odd that morning. Then it hit him. What if his brother *had* taken his medication—despite his claim he only took it after PT—then forgot? Vince's heart dropped to his knees. That would definitely explain the strange behavior.

"You going to be okay while I'm gone?" he asked.

Dom scowled. "Yes. I'm not helpless. I'll survive the hour while Stephan gets to know you."

"Don't you mean while I get to know him?" he asked.

"Ah, yeah, right. That, too." His brother nodded with a grin, and was still smiling when Vince left for his appointment.

All the while he drove, and even while filling out paperwork, Vince kept thinking about his brother. Damn. If Dom really had taken his pain pills and forgotten about it, then Vince was going to have to take over administering the medication.

Christ. He ran a hand through his hair. That wouldn't go over well with his control-freak brother. But he couldn't have the guy doubling up on doses.

"Vince?" Standing in front of an open door, a sour-faced nurse called his name while glancing around the waiting room.

Showtime.

He pushed thoughts of his brother aside and approached the woman with a grin. "Good morning, ma'am."

Her eyes widened, and an answering smile erased the grouchy from her face. "Morning."

As he followed her down a hall, he passed a section in the middle where Emma and her friend Macy sat behind a rounded counter. He winked at them on his way to an examining room where, once inside, he sat while the nurse took his vitals. Her shoulders were less rigid, and her features were much softer by the time she left.

A twinge of guilt flickered through him for wasting her and the doctor's time. An actual patient could've used his slot. But, his mind reasoned, although he wasn't having issues, Vince hadn't seen a doctor in a while, so technically, it wasn't a waste.

The door opened a few minutes later, and his thoughts zeroed in on his task—extracting information to help Emma secure a date with the Brad Pitt clone walking into the room.

"Hello, Mr. Acardi." The man held out his hand and cracked a smile full of perfect white teeth in his perfect face. "I'm Dr. Greenwald."

Vince was already on his feet, shaking the man's hand before the last name registered in his brain. "Greenwald?" He cocked his head. "I went through basic with a Brian Greenwald. Any relation?"

The doctor's smile widened. "He's my older brother."

"I'll be damned." Vince snickered, releasing the man's hand. "What's he up to? I lost track after I joined the Rangers."

Leaning back against the exam table, the doctor folded his arms across his chest and shook his head. "Lucky bastard's stationed at Fort Shafter in Honolulu."

Vince whistled. "Sweet draw."

"Yeah. I plan to take our parents there this Christmas." He motioned for Vince to take a seat alongside the small corner desk, then sat in the chair in front of it. "So, you're a Ranger?"

He nodded. "I left the military two years ago, though."

"Really?" Doc Greewald glanced at Vince's stats the nurse had keyed into the computer. "What do you do now?"

"I'm part owner of a Texas ranch and construction company where veterans live and work." No need to get into specifics. He was there to ask the questions.

"Texas? What are you doing in Georgia?"

He exhaled. "My brother. He's stationed here and was recently injured on a mission. Dislocated a hip."

The doc winced. "Ouch."

"Yeah. I'll be in town until he's done with physical therapy or can drive himself there. Right now, though, he can barely get out of bed on his own." With personal stuff out of the way, Vince was ready to start grilling. "It's been a while since I lived here, so tell me, Doc—what do you do for fun? I'm already going stir-crazy."

The guy laughed. "First off, call me Stephan. And I doubt the area's changed much, but me personally, I like to hike at Flat Rock Park on the weekends, and often join the Tuesday night bike ride."

"At the river walk?"

"Yeah," Stephan replied. "And when I can, I head to Kelley's. Great food. Live bands. Dancing. It's always a good time. Tonight, I'm bowling with a few friends over at The Peach Bowl. They have open lanes after the leagues."

Perfect.

Vince knew the place well. In fact, he knew all the places. Showing up at The Peach Bowl with Emma tonight would get the ball rolling, pun intended.

"So, Vince, you don't seem to be in any pain." The guy switched back to doctor mode. "Are you having issues, or is this just a routine exam?"

Pushing back another stab of guilt, he shrugged. "Just routine."

"All right." The doc rose to his feet. "Let's get started. Drop your pants."

Drop my...

Vince frowned. What the hell for?

He watched the guy walk to the counter and pull two gloves from a box. Alarm trickled down his spine.

What kind of doctors did Emma work for?

He'd assumed it was a general practitioners' office, but one glance at the diagram of lower anatomy on the far wall explained the whole thing.

Literally.

Dr. Stephan Greenwald was a goddamn proctologist.

A great many things became clear. Emma's astonishment over his offer to let Stephan examine him, for one thing. The woman had looked at him as if he were crazy, and right now, he was having crazy thoughts—like leaving before Stephan snapped on that last damn glove.

As Vince eyed the door, an image of his brother's smirking face came to mind, along with the bastard's laughter.

That son of a bitch.

Dom's strange behavior had nothing at all to do with double dosing medicine, and everything to do with being an asshole.

Jerk *knew* and said nothing. Bastard also knew Vince would go through with it once he found out, because to tell the doc it was a mistake would ruin his credibility as someone interested in Emma. No man worth his salt would date a woman without knowing what she did for a living, or who she worked for. And even though he didn't really know the woman, he'd given his word to help.

So Vince couldn't leave, and was about to pay a big price for assuming. But he wasn't the only one who was going to pay.

Hell no.

Reaching for the button on his jeans, he began to formulate a plan. His brother seemed to have forgotten one very important thing.

Vince didn't get mad, he got even.

Chapter Seven

Emma still couldn't believe Vince was going through with the exam just to help her out. *Her.* A nobody. She was practically a total stranger. That was so far above and beyond anything she'd ever expected, he practically lived on Mars.

He deserved a thank you. When she got home from work, she was making him the biggest, best peach pie of her life.

"Girlfriend, you have got to tell me your secret," Macy said, staring down the hall at the closed exam room door Vince was in. "What did you do to get that gorgeous man to agree to let your doctor fist his goods?"

"Macy!" Emma sucked in a breath as she glanced around to see if anyone had heard. Thankfully, reception was too far away, and none of the nurses were in the hall or at their station. "Shh…and you know the doctors don't do that."

"No, they just probe where the sun doesn't shine."

Emma shook her head. Better to just shut up, then her friend would move on to another subject.

"Wait." Macy tipped her chin. "Maybe that's how Vince swings. I mean, maybe that's why he suggested it."

"Maybe we should change the subject," Emma said, glancing around again.

Her friend exhaled and waved a hand. "All right. Fine. You can tell me what you're going to do to make it up to the guy."

"Make him a pie."

"The poor man deserves a hell of a lot more than pie for putting his ass on the line. Literally." Macy smirked. "But, since your peach pie is to die for, I'd say it's cool. Even if he fell into the other category."

Emma narrowed her gaze and cocked her head. "What other category?"

"The one where the guy didn't know what kind of doctor you worked for," Macy replied.

Didn't know?

"Nah." Emma shook her head. "He knew."

"So you *did* tell him." Macy raised a brow. "That's good. Could you imagine if he didn't know?" Her friend slapped a hand to her chest and shook with glee.

Macy was right. It was a good thing Emma told him. Only, she couldn't quite recall doing that. But, she must have…at some point. Probably.

Her heart sank.

What if she hadn't?

The exam room door opened, putting an end to her dire thoughts and sending her pulse into orbit.

She needed to…what? Play it cool with Stephan, but smile at Vince? Ignore them both? Or maybe hide in the bathroom and hyperventilate.

She exhaled slowly. No. If she wanted to hook up with Stephan, she needed to stay put and see this through.

Since Vince was supposed to be someone she was interested in, it would probably appear odd if she didn't at least smile at the guy.

She watched as the two men walked out. They were shaking hands and laughing like old friends.

Okay, so maybe she was in the clear. Vince had to know what kind of exam—

"Maybe he *did* like it," Macy mumbled, the smile evident in her tone as she broke through Emma's thoughts.

Ignoring her friend, she waited, heart pounding out of her chest as Stephan walked Vince down the hall toward the billing desk, then returned alone.

Setting the folder in the basket on the counter, he smiled down at them. "That patient went to basic with my brother."

Which explained the comradery.

"Don't that beat all?" Macy said. "Emma knows him, too."

Son of a beeswax.

Her heart lurched, and even though she wanted to smack her friend, she refrained.

Barely.

"You know him?" Stephan frowned, interest and—dare she label the other emotion in his eyes as...apprehension? "How?"

Blurting out Vince was interested in her and vice versa seemed a little weird, so she decided to ease into it. "He's my neighbor's brother."

Macy kicked her shin.

She swallowed a curse and was about to add the interested in each other part when her phone vibrated in her pocket.

"It's a small world." Stephan straightened from the counter. "I'd better get back to work. See you ladies later."

Nodding, she pulled out her phone to find a text from Vince asking if she could take a quick break and meet him in the corridor outside the practice.

Shoot. Trying not to panic, she watched Stephan disappear into another exam room. What if Macy was right and he hadn't known this was a proctology practice? Her stomach knotted. Was he breaking up with her before they even started to pretend date?

That'd be just her luck.

She stood, ready to face the music, whatever it may be. "I'll be back in a few minutes," she told Macy before heading to Vince.

By the time she reached the corridor, anxiety beat an erratic tune in her chest. She studied his features for signs of anger, but only found a friendly expression.

Probably acting since people were mulling about. She noted a few females smiling at him as they passed. But he didn't notice. He straightened from the wall when he spotted her.

"Hey." Smiling, he grabbed her hand to draw her closer.

Emma hid her surprise behind her own smile and fought to get her racing pulse under control.

"Thanks for meeting me," he said, still holding her hand. "I needed to talk to you."

Here it comes. He was breaking up with her.

"Oh?" she said through a suddenly dry throat.

He leaned his shoulder against the wall and nodded. "I wanted to let you know we're going bowling tonight with Stephan."

She blinked. He wasn't backing out?

Her apprehension disappeared and then the rest of his words sunk in. "He invited us to bowl?"

"Not exactly." Vince chuckled. "Once we both realized I went to basic with his brother, we got to talking, and when I asked him what he did around here for fun, he mentioned he was bowling tonight. A perfect opportunity to surprise him."

He wasn't the only one surprised. Why did it have to be bowling? Emma hadn't bowled a day in her life. Any chance of impressing the guy just hit the gutter.

Still, Vince just went above and beyond for her, and seemed so happy to put her in close proximity to Stephan outside of work, she couldn't burst his bubble.

"Yeah, it'll be great." She smiled and squeezed his hand. "For a minute there, I thought you were calling me out here to back out."

A frown creased his brow. "Why would I do that?"

Good one, Emma, now you have to talk about the exam. Idiot.

She cleared her throat and stared at his neck. A sexy, lickable birthmark sat at the base. Damn. And if that wasn't enough, little sprigs of hair were visible where his shirt buttoned. But that didn't mean anything, she told herself. She swung either way on the chest-hair debate.

Stephan's was smooth. Emma knew thanks to a charity softball game their practice participated in two months ago. He'd removed his shirt in the dugout to don the team's T-shirt. He had a lean, well-defined frame.

Vince, on the other hand, was an Acardi, and like his brother, Dom, he had too much testosterone not to have hair on his chest. And since she refused to think of her fake boyfriend in a sexy light, Emma pictured that hair wrapping around to cover his back and shoulders, too.

That dimmed the sexy light. A little.

"Emma?" he said. "Look at me."

She forced her gaze to meet his. "Yeah?"

His eyes weren't strictly brown. There were little flecks of gold surrounding the pupils, which…wasn't mesmerizing at all. Nope. Not at all.

"When I give my word, I keep it," he said, those gold flecks deepening several shades as his gaze turned earnest. "I won't back out. I promise."

No man had ever really had Emma's back before. Dom and his buddies were trustworthy, of course, but she knew better than to count on them, because they deployed on a moment's notice and weren't always around.

So for this man, a man she barely knew, to stand here with honesty in his gaze and a promise to help on his lips, it said a lot for his character...and threw her for a loop.

A huge one.

Overcome with the strongest urge to hug the man, she squeezed his hand instead. Emma wasn't a hugger. It was an act she never took or gave lightly. It required investment and trust. Even though she was starting to trust Vince, she knew he wasn't sticking around. He lived in Texas. Had a job and a life in Texas. Plus, he was military. They're wired a certain way, a way which, for some reason, never seemed to include her. No. She had no plans to drop her guard to let him in deep enough to reach the "hug zone."

Fake hugs for performance sake, sure. But not real ones. She was saving those for someone who "stuck."

A nonmilitary guy with no intention of leaving town.

A guy like Stephan.

"Okay," she said, then cleared her throat because her voice sounded hoarse.

He smiled, and his gaze brightened. "Good. Now, tell me why you thought I'd leave you in the lurch."

Dropping her gaze back to his neck, she shrugged. "It dawned on me when you were in the exam room that I...uh... never told you what kind of specialists I work for." Finding the courage, she lifted her gaze to his again. "Did you know?"

"No."

Her stomach lurched. "Oh my God, Vince. I'm so sorry." Without thinking, she set her forehead to his chest, unsure whether to cry, or curse, or laugh. "I don't know why I thought you knew. I'm so sorry."

"It's okay." Grasping her upper arms, he gently pulled her back and dipped down to meet her gaze. "I don't blame you. My brother, on the other hand…him I blame."

She widened her eyes. "Dom *knew* you were coming here and didn't say anything?"

"Not about the practice. But he did say things, all right." A scowl rippled across Vince's face. "He told me it was a good idea, and a great way to get to know Stephan. Intimately."

I'm gonna kill him.

Sucking in a sharp breath, she slapped a hand over her mouth, torn between laughing and cursing. And she rarely cursed.

Vince released her to lean back against the wall and shove a hand through his hair. "Bastard was grinning all morning long." His scowl deepened. "I thought maybe it was the pain meds making him loopy. Now, I know different."

Emma removed her hand from her mouth. "Sorry. It's my fault. I didn't think about it. I assumed—"

"Hey." He grinned. "Don't worry about it. I don't get mad, I get even. That's the other reason I asked you to meet me out here."

"Oh?" She raised a brow.

"Seems to me my brother is going to need a sitter while we go bowling tonight." His grin turned devious. "Do you still have Chelsea's number?"

She laughed, loving where his mind dwelled. "Yes, I do."

It was time to show it went both ways.

"I've got you covered, Vince." Emma winked at him and scrolled through her contacts. "Leave this to me."

Chapter Eight

Ten minutes to seven, Emma knocked on the door and breezed into the kitchen, looking cuter than she should, wearing jeans and a rust-colored top with slits in the arms that showed off her tanned shoulders. With more than his interest pricked, Vince regained perspective by turning his attention to what she carried.

The biggest damn double-crusted pie he'd ever seen.

"Sweet." Dom eyed the dessert from his chair at the corner of the island. "Is that peach?"

She walked to him and held the pie under his nose. "Yes, it is."

Dom inhaled, closed his eyes, and moaned. "My mouth is watering just thinking about it." His eyes snapped open. "Vince, prepare to enjoy someone else's great cooking for a change. Emma's an excellent baker. The rec center holds a bake sale every year, and her stand always sells out." His brother paused to frown. "That's coming up soon, isn't it?"

"Yes." She nodded. "Next Saturday. And don't worry. Your brother is definitely going to enjoy this pie." She drew back and walked straight to Vince, and with a flourish, handed him the pie. "I made this for you."

Unexpected warmth spread through his chest. No one, other than relatives, had ever baked for him before.

Dom gazed longingly at the pie. "Just him?"

"Yes, unless he wants to share." She turned a hard stare on his brother. "He stuck more than his neck out for me today, thanks to you."

Amusement twitched the asshole's lips, but longing continued to rule his gaze as he watched Emma grab the pie and a knife and cut a large piece of what looked to be peach perfection. "It was just a little joke. We do it to each other all the time. Tell her, Vince."

True. Growing up, they pulled pranks almost daily. The bigger they got, the bigger the prank. But at the moment, he felt no need to enlighten Emma. The show was too enjoyable.

Nodding his thanks, he took the big plate of pie she handed him, and could've sworn his brother wiped drool from his mouth. Not one to miss an opportunity, Vince made a show of lifting a forkful close to his nose and inhaling.

"Emma, if this tastes as incredible as it smells, then my brother is right. I'm in for a treat." Holding it there a few seconds, he waited until he heard his brother grumble before finally shoving the forkful in his mouth.

An instant, in-your-face introduction to the sweet, succulent fruit pleased his palate. Damn, Dom wasn't kidding. He savored the flavors until he finally swallowed. "This is terrific." The combination of fresh peaches, cinnamon, and nutmeg was killer. He took another bite. Then another. And yet another, enjoying the drool-worthy treasure, vaguely aware of his brother's bellyaching.

"Aw, come on, Vince. You can spare a slice."

"Why should he?" Emma jammed her hands on her hips and stared his brother down.

A sweet little Georgia peach taking on the Jersey dragon. It was possibly more delicious than the pie.

Dom shifted in his chair. "Because he already got me back."

She raised a brow, but remained silent.

"I fell off the couch when he came home, and he left me on the floor. Took me ten damn minutes to get to my feet."

Damn straight. "Tell her why you fell on the floor."

Emma narrowed her eyes at his brother. "Why?"

Dom's gaze dropped to the counter and he shrugged. "Because pain radiated across my back and hip."

"Yeah." Vince scoffed. "From laughing too hard after I flipped you off when you asked how the probing went."

Bastard had laughed so hard he'd winced, and eventually rolled off the couch and onto the floor.

"What?" Dom stared at him with an innocent expression. "I was talking about your interrogation of Stephan."

Vince snorted. "You were, my ass."

"Yeah," Dom deadpanned. "That, too."

At the time, he'd thought about helping his brother up, until the idiot continued to snicker.

Like now.

No, wait...that was... "Emma?"

"Sorry." Her face was flushed, and her eyes were bright as she slammed a hand over her mouth. "I'm going to hell, I know," she said through her fingers. "But that was kind of funny."

He blew out a breath. "It'd be funnier if it'd happened to someone else."

A second later, her laughter mixed with Dom's and drew a grin from him, because she was right.

Dammit.

It *was* funny.

He waved his fork at them, lips twitching. "Now you're

both on my shit list."

"Understood." His brother nodded. "But can I have some pie?"

Taking pity on the guy, he cut him a piece and pushed it close. "Yeah, we have time." No reason to withhold a slice of heaven when, any minute, retribution was due to ring the doorbell.

"Emma?" He pointed to her creation.

She shook her head and settled onto a stool. "No thanks. I taste-tested through the process."

An act Vince understood all too well. He cooked the same way. Always guaranteed a delicious outcome.

Halfway through his pie, Dom stopped to frown at him. "Wait...what do you mean you have time? Are you going somewhere?"

"Yeah." Vince carried his fork and plate to the sink, then grabbed plastic wrap and covered what was left of his thank-you gift. "Emma and I have our first date tonight."

His brother's gaze bounced between him and Emma. "Great. Where?"

"At the bowling alley," Emma replied. "Stephan will be there."

Dom cocked his head. "I knew you were going to play the new-in-the-area-and-looking-for-fun card, bro, but I never thought he'd actually tell you where he was going to be tonight. How the hell did you manage to find that out? What did you have to do? Two fing—"

"Don't finish that sentence," Vince cut in. "Or I'll be forced to book the sitter for more than one night."

His brother's brows crashed together. "Sitter? What sitter?"

"The one due any minute now."

"Ah, to hell with that," Dom grumbled, waving his hand in the air. "I don't need watching. Cancel whoever it is."

Headlights flashed through the kitchen window as a car pulled into the driveway.

Vince grinned at his brother. "Too late." This was going to be good. "It's true what they say about payback."

His brother's spine stiffened. "What the hell did you do?"

"*We*," Emma corrected, jabbing a finger at Vince, then herself. "Payback's a *beeotch*, and this one happens to wear flip-flops." Smiling, she headed to answer the knock on the back door.

All the color drained from his brother's face. "Oh, hell-fucking-no." Dom rose to his feet, no doubt ready to take flight.

Vince clamped a hand on his brother's tense shoulder and pressed him back in his seat. "Now don't be rude."

Before his brother could react, Emma opened the door and grinned. "Chelsea, thanks so much for coming on such short notice."

"You're a dead man walking," his brother muttered, shaking him off. Then cursed under his breath, no doubt in pain from the sudden movement.

"No, I'm a smart man getting even," he said, then turned his attention to the woman entering the house.

"It's my pleasure," Chelsea told Emma. "Thanks for calling."

To say he was surprised was an understatement. The way his brother had acted, Vince assumed the woman was an ogre. Instead, an attractive woman, with hair the color of honey, wearing cute glasses, a bright-yellow sundress, and matching flip-flops rushed forward.

"Dom, oh my goodness, look at you." She set her large yellow purse on the counter, then turned to his brother and cupped his face. "What happened? You should be in bed. You look awful."

Vince snickered. "We tried telling him that." He thrust

his hand out. "I'm his brother Vince, by the way."

"Nice to meet you, Vince," she said. "I'm Chelsea, and he's in good hands now. You two go have fun. Don't worry about a thing."

"Thanks, Chelsea. I appreciate that." He smiled. "My brother can't do the stairs yet, so we have him set up in the guest room down the hall."

Dom's jaw was clamped so tight his lips nearly disappeared. Vince held back a grin. He wasn't through just yet.

"And help yourself to some of my peach pie," Emma said, walking close to slip her arm through his. "If he gives you any trouble, call me."

Good one.

Vince led a smiling Emma to the door where he turned around to face the other couple. "Oh, and he hasn't had his shower yet. He'll need help, but if it's too much, don't worry, I'll take care of it when I get home."

He wanted to make his brother uncomfortable, not poor Chelsea.

"Oh." She blinked, then moved behind his brother to pat his shoulder. "No worries. I'm sure we can manage."

Dom's hands were curled into fists on his lap, and his left eye twitched as he glared across the kitchen at Vince. Exactly the look he was going for. It embodied how he'd felt that morning during his exam.

Mouth curving into a grin, Vince saluted his brother before ushering a snickering Emma out the door.

Once they were in his car and on their way, she turned to him and laughed. "Oh my God, did you see Dom's face? It was priceless."

"I know." He grinned. "Thanks for getting her to come over."

"Are you kidding?" Emma chuckled. "She told me not to

worry about a thing. Even offered to stay the night if I wanted to take you back to my place."

Vince's heart dropped to his gut. "What?"

Emma laughed. "I know. She's eager to spend time with your brother."

That wasn't the reason for his reaction. No. That would be the part about Emma taking him back to her place.

His favorite body part woke up and *hell yeah*-ed the suggestion. But, since this wasn't a real date, that body part wasn't invited tonight.

He turned onto another road, and after a few minutes of silence, glanced at his quiet passenger. She was staring at him.

"What?"

Emma shrugged. "It's just that I half expected to walk in tonight and find you and Dom with busted lips or something."

The woman had no idea how close Vince had been to doing just that when he'd returned from his appointment. It was only thoughts of tonight's planned torment for Dom that had kept his fists to himself.

"Thought had crossed my mind, believe me. So did dosing his meal with laxative so he'd have to ask Chelsea for help cleaning up."

"Oh my God." Emma covered her mouth and laughed. "You didn't, though, right? Not that I'd blame you."

He smiled, liking the flush in her cheeks and the gleam happiness brought to her eyes. She needed to be happy more often. No man could resist the sparkle in those baby blues.

Including him.

Alarm bells went off in his head. He gave himself a mental shake.

The best thing to do was keep her in this happy mood tonight—so *Stephan* would take notice and take action. Because the longer Vince was around this woman, the more he was going to like her. Which was bad. He was there to help. Not hinder.

Or hurt.

"No, I didn't put anything in his food," he finally replied, glancing sideways at her.

She brushed a strand of hair off her face and cocked her head. "You know, there's a chance my pie could send him to the bathroom, too."

He raised a brow. "Did you do something to it?"

"What? No." She laughed. "I'd never do that to you or him. I just meant that maybe the fruit and his medication won't agree with each other."

"Ah. I see." He pondered this as he turned into the bowling alley parking lot and parked near the entrance. Pocketing the keys, he turned to smirk at her. "Now you're just trying to make me feel better. Easing my need for revenge because of my uncomfortable ordeal this morning."

Her eyes twinkled under her raised brows. "Is it working?"

The woman had a whole lot of things working that had no business working.

He shifted in his seat. "Yeah. It is." So was the fact she appeared to genuinely want him to be happy.

In a few short days, he'd gotten to know her well enough to realize she had the power to capture more than his attention. She was beautiful, smart, had a great sense of humor, and baked one hell of a peach pie. The woman was dangerous to his well-being. Because of this, he needed to hook her up with Stephan. And fast.

Tonight, Vince would do what he could to make the doc notice Emma.

Chapter Nine

Emma wasn't sure why Vince's gaze suddenly turned serious, but before she could question him, he blinked, and a friendly expression returned to his handsome face. Which was a relief, since she needed to bring up what they should do on their "date."

"Are you ready?" he asked.

"Almost." She nodded, then glanced down at the skinny jeans she brushed with her hand. "I...we should probably discuss what...well, how we should act."

Shoot. She better not stumble over her tongue all night. It was no way to impress Stephan or his friends. And she knew all about the influence of friends.

It was Macy's suggestion that put Emma in her current predicament. So, yeah, she knew how much influence a friend had, and counted on Stephan's friends tonight. If she made a good impression, perhaps they'd encourage him to pursue her...despite her date.

She sighed.

Vince touched her arm. "What's wrong?"

"Well, I was just wondering…what if Stephan doesn't ask me out because of you?"

"I gave that some thought." His gaze was confident and sure as he turned in his seat to face her. "How about this? We'll make it clear that we're keeping things casual. Hanging out and having a good time, but not attached."

That kind of made sense.

"Yeah." She rubbed her chin. "Okay. That could work."

He smiled. "Okay then. Tell me what you want me to do tonight. How close are we supposed to be? Have we been dating? Kissed? Slept together yet?"

Slept together?

Butterflies—on freaking fire—swarmed through her belly at the thought of having sex with the man.

But he wasn't the man she wanted to date, so she immediately banished the thought. Her heart was set on Stephan. Not an ex-soldier leaving Georgia in a few weeks. Been there, done that, no thanks. There was no reason to entertain thoughts of any kind other than friendship where Vince was concerned.

Bringing her mind back to the conversation, she decided to take a logical approach and keep things as truthful as possible. "No. We haven't." She couldn't bring herself to say "slept together" while staring into his warm brown gaze. "I think this should be our first date. So we haven't done anything, yet."

Yet being the optimal word. She wasn't stupid. At some point, they were going to have to kiss in front of Stephan. She really hoped she wouldn't like it. In fact, Emma was counting on that. Otherwise, things were going to get complicated.

He nodded. "Makes the most sense, too. He knows I'm here to help my brother, so once he realizes Dom's your neighb—"

"He already knows," she spoke up, remembering her

conversation with Stephan right after the exam. "He told Macy and I about you going to basic with his brother, then Macy—and her big mouth—told him I knew you, too."

A smile twitched his lips. "That woman's a firecracker. I'm surprised she didn't tell him I was your boyfriend."

"Yeah." Emma rubbed the shin her friend had kicked. "Darn woman knows we're just supposed to be casual."

He sat back in his seat. "Okay, since this is our first date, then hand holding it is." He glanced at her and winked. "Are you ready?"

No. Yes. Lord give her strength.

She nodded again and reached for the door.

"Don't even think it," he said. "I get the doors for women I date. And don't try to give me any crap about our date being fake, because it needs to appear as real as possible."

Releasing the handle, she turned to him and saluted. "Yes, sir, General, sir."

His chuckle filled the space between them. "You can drop the rank, smart-ass. But," he said in a tone that matched the mischievous gleam entering his eyes. "I'm not opposed to the 'sir.'"

She snorted. "That'll be the day."

"Can't blame a guy for trying." He smirked as he got out of the car.

Admittedly, Emma felt a little odd waiting while he walked around to open her door. None of the guys she dated did that. They opened doors to restaurants and places they frequented, but never made her wait in the car until they could get her door.

It was new. And kind of nice.

Warmth spread through her chest, and when he held his hand out to help her from the car, a rush of heat filled her cheeks. Lordy, the man was attentive. And because it made her wonder if he was attentive in other relationship aspects, she shut off those dangerous thoughts and took his hand.

After helping her from the car, he continued to hold on to her. Emma tried her best to ignore the tingling spreading up her arm as he ushered her inside and through a crowd to a counter where he rented a lane and shoes.

"They're part of a team, right?" She motioned toward people in colorful shirts.

"Yes." He reached for her free hand again and guided her around the crowd. "Probably in a summer league."

She nodded like she knew, but the man was too astute.

He stopped and smiled down at her. "You've never bowled before, have you?"

"That obvious?" She wrinkled her nose. "Sorry, probably should've warned you. But I did think to bring socks."

She'd had the foresight to shove a pair in her purse before taking the pie to Dom's.

Bringing their entwined hands up to his mouth, he brushed his lips across her knuckles. "Good thinking. And I apologize. I should've thought to ask you sooner if you'd ever bowled," he said, those warm lips of his grazing her skin with each word.

Her mind was oddly fuzzy.

"I could've run through the basics with you," he continued, lowering their hands. "But there's really not much to it. I'll help you the first few times. You'll catch on quick. Everyone has their own style. You'll discover yours by the end of the night."

Style?

She was about to ask him to elaborate when a familiar laugh sounded in the distance.

Glancing around Vince's broad frame, she spotted Stephan sitting in a row of chairs with two other doctors she recognized. "I see Stephan," she told Vince, relief flushing away half of her nerves. Better yet, she knew his friends and their wives who occupied the other seats. "He's on lane twenty."

"Luck is with you." He smiled. "We got lane twenty-six. It's an end lane, and close enough to him that he can see us, but not hear us."

She relaxed even more. "We won't have to be on guard the whole night."

Maybe she'd actually have some fun.

"Vince? Is that you?" Stephan asked from behind her date.

Mind suddenly blank, Emma stood frozen, unsure whether to step around Vince and say hi, or pretend she hadn't recognized his voice.

She hoped to God she didn't look like the idiot she felt.

"Ready?" Vince mouthed to her, then took the decision from her by turning so they both faced Stephan. "Hey, how's it going?" Vince tugged her close and slipped his arm around her waist. "I believe you know Emma."

At the contact, her heart pounded hard in her chest. Or was it because of the way Stephan looked at her?

Shock, and something unreadable widened his blue eyes. "Yeah...Emma...hi. I didn't know you bowled."

As much as she would've loved to boast about stats and leagues to impress the guy, she knew the moment she rolled— more likely dropped—a ball everyone would clue into her novice status.

Better to keep it real.

"I don't," she said. "It's my first time."

Warmth entered his blue gaze. "Well, we all have to start somewhere. I'm sure you'll do fine."

"Yeah. She'll do great," Vince said, pulling her in closer. "Thanks for mentioning this today, and the other activities. If Emma's game, I think maybe we'll check them out. She graciously agreed to come here with me tonight to keep me company."

Oh, nice one, she thought, hiding a grin as she nodded. This way it wouldn't look as if they were stalking the guy. Which, yeah, she supposed they were. Plus, he made sure Stephan knew they weren't exactly on a date tonight, either.

Stephan's amicable expression didn't alter, except for a quick blink. "Good. I think you'll enjoy them, too."

"I'm sure we will," she finally said.

"Starting right now." Vince grinned down at her. "Let's go find you a ball." Then he glanced back at Stephan. "Thanks, again, for the tip."

"Sure thing." He nodded. "Have a good time."

"You, too," Vince said, before tightening his hold on her waist and leading her away.

Emma was torn between leaving Stephan standing there, and following Vince's lead. Was she missing an opportunity? Maybe he was jolted enough to ask her out already. Although, he'd never ask her while she was with a guy, so it was probably best to get on with her casual not-quite-date.

Vince released her waist and grabbed her hand again. "You're doing great," he whispered as they walked to their lane.

"Super." She snickered. "Because I have no idea what I'm doing."

Understatement of the year.

She sat on a plastic seat in their assigned lane to don her shoes, while he fiddled with the control panel. A few seconds later, their names appeared on the screen above for all to see.

Great. Not much chance of keeping her lack of prowess a secret. But she was glad Vince knew what he was doing.

"So, what next?" she asked while he swapped shoes.

"Simple." He smiled. "Now we go find our balls."

Emma couldn't help it. She laughed. "Lordy, I've got to be the easiest woman in Columbus if I'm fondling balls with you in the middle of our first date."

Setting a hand at the small of her back, he chuckled while they walked to the racks of balls. "You want to find one that's not too heavy or too light, and your fingers fit in the holes just right."

"So, basically, I need to fondle balls until I find one that feels good in my hand."

He threw his head back and laughed. "Exactly."

For the next five minutes, they joked and fondled balls together, until they each found the right one. Of course, Vince insisted on carrying their selections back to the lane. Emma did her best not to notice how the muscles in his arms rippled from the act.

When they got back, he set their balls on the contraption he called a ball return that separated their lane from the one next to them, which, thankfully, was empty. Glancing past him, she spotted Stephan a few lanes down. He stood, ball in hand, nearly touching his chin, with his gaze transfixed on the pins.

Was he saying a prayer? Offering up his firstborn? Calculating the distance?

She had no idea.

He stood that way for nearly half a minute before taking three steps and releasing the ball with a flip to his wrist. It landed with a thud and looked like it was going in the gutter, then made a sharp left turn and sliced through the pins, knocking them all down.

Turning around, Stephan glanced at her and smiled, his chest puffed out with pride. Her heart skipped a beat. Was he looking at her differently? Maybe it was her imagination. Or wishful thinking. Either way, she smiled back and gave him a thumbs-up.

"I take it that was the doctor's strike I heard?" Vince asked.

She frowned and refocused on her "date." "You can hear a strike?"

"Yeah." He nodded. "It has a distinctive sound. Here, let me show you."

"Okay." She moved off the lane and watched by the score table.

He grabbed his ball, stood in a similar pose as Stephan, took three steps, then released it. She noticed a few things. The thud wasn't as loud. The ball didn't curve, it went straight, hitting the pins off center, knocking eight down. But most of her attention rested on him. Damn, the man had amazing shoulders.

And a really great butt.

She cleared her suddenly dry throat. "That did sound different."

He nodded and threw a second ball, but she vaguely noticed the remaining pins falling. Her attention gravitated to the play of muscles rippling beneath the polo shirt stretched tightly across his back.

Warmth spread through her body in an unexpected rush.

This was bad. All wrong. He was just helping her. She didn't want to be attracted to the man.

Emma exhaled. She needed to get a grip and focus on their plan...not his butt. Although, gripping his butt was a good plan.

No. She shook her head. Vince wasn't the endgame. Stephan was.

Straightening her spine, she forced her gaze to remain on the ball he gripped a third time.

"Normally, you'd go next, but I want to show you the difference in sound. This time, I'm going for a strike." He glanced over his shoulder at her and winked before turning around.

Just like when Stephan had smiled at her, her heart

skipped a beat.

Shoot.

She was in trouble.

So were the pins. This time his ball hit with a louder thud and powered down the lane. She swore the pins either fainted or jumped off to avoid the decimation of Vince. The ones taking their chances exploded in a flurry of white until nothing remained.

"Did you hear the difference?" he asked, walking back to her.

"Yes." She saw it, too.

Both men achieved the same results through different methods. Methods that epitomized the man.

Stephan took the round-about approach, while Vince took the straight and narrow, hitting them head-on.

She refused to analyze which one gave her more tingles.

Instead, she walked to the ball return. "All I'm going to know is the sound of a gutter ball."

"That's okay," he said. "It's normal when you're first learning. Don't let it discourage you. Take the next few turns in a row to get a feel for the ball."

She nodded, then assumed the same stance as the guys, holding the ball up near her chin and inhaling. *I can do this.* Emma blew out the breath, took three steps, swung the ball back…and dropped it.

Crap.

The pink menace rolled backward toward the chairs.

Heat rushed into Emma's face. Great. She hoped Stephan and his buddies hadn't seen that. No way was she going to look.

Stopping the ball with his foot, Vince picked it up and handed it back to her. "Also normal when you're first learning. Don't sweat it."

Grateful for his understanding attitude, she smiled.

"Thanks. The bugger slipped out of my hands." She was such an idiot. "Let's try this again."

He stood back and nodded.

Going through the same motions, she increased her grip on the ball, and this time, released it in the right direction. It landed with a thud louder than Vince's, but rolled much slower, managing to knock down one pin.

She turned around and shrugged. "At least it wasn't a gutter."

"Exactly." Vince smiled. "That really wasn't bad. Can I give you a few pointers?"

Surprise and some unknown emotion rushed through Emma. It was refreshing that he'd asked first, instead of telling her how she should do it. In her experience, limited as it was, military guys were men of action. They acted first, sought permission—or apologized—later.

"Yes, please do." She waited for the ball to return, then grabbed it and walked to the middle of the lane again.

"First off, it's good to use the dots and arrows on the lane." He pointed to marks on the floor she hadn't really noticed. "I stand just left of the middle so my arm is lined up between the center arrow and the one next to it. This is good for throwing a straight ball. You can also throw a straight ball from the side, you just have to aim at a different arrow on the lane."

"I'd like to use the middle," she told him. There was more room for the ball to stay on the lane.

"Okay, then put your toe here." He tapped a dot with his foot.

She moved to the spot. "Now what?"

"It's good to remember that when you release the ball, wherever your arm ends up is exactly the direction the ball is going to roll," he said. "So you want keep your elbow close to your side and try not to drop your shoulder when you release.

So, let's practice the swing without releasing the ball."

Vince got right behind her. She could feel his heat, his strength, as he cupped her hand while she rehearsed her swing a few times. If she were made of stronger stuff, she probably would've made a better student. But, damn...it was hard to concentrate with his body brushing hers with each movement.

"Ready to try it on your own?" he asked, warm breath hitting her neck and ear.

Goose bumps danced down her arm and she nearly dropped the ball. Not cool.

She nodded, and when he moved away, she drew in a deep breath and rejoiced at the return of brain function. Goodness, that was crazy. Her body still tingled where they'd touched.

Refocusing on her task, she stood on her dot, and noticed Stephan watching from the corner of her eye. Great. More pressure.

Praying she didn't drop the pink eyesore behind her again, Emma stepped forward, and using all of Vince's tips, released the ball—straight down the center, where it remained, hitting the middle pin and knocking seven down.

"Holy crap." Grinning, she turned around and clapped, accomplishment warming her blood. "I did it." She rushed down the lane and launched herself at a smiling Vince. "It stayed on the lane."

"You did great." Wrapping his arms around her, he lifted her off the floor and swung her around.

"Thanks to you," she said, squeezing him tight.

Emma knew what she did was insignificant, but, God, she felt good.

So did being in Vince's arms.

He was hard and hot, and she felt unusually feminine and soft. It was strange and wonderful. And he must've felt it, too, because he stilled, then slowly lowered her feet to the floor.

But didn't release her.

The friction of her body sliding down his lean frame sent a rush of awareness straight to all her good parts. They'd been dormant for so long. Too long. He drew back to gaze into her eyes. Breath caught in her throat. Those amber flecks of his were like warm honey, and she clutched his shoulders as she melted against him.

He lifted a hand to lightly trace her lip. "Emma..." he said in a low tone that sent a ripple through her belly. "I'm going to kiss you now."

Her heart jumped in her chest. "Okay," she whispered just before his mouth brushed hers.

Warm and soft, Vince's lips caressed hers until her mind fogged over and toes curled in her rented shoes. Both were temporary, but fit so right. Then those amazing lips grew bolder, firmer, kissing her with a purpose she didn't understand...and didn't care.

It was unexpected and amazing, but all too soon, it ended when he suddenly broke the kiss and set his forehead to hers.

"That was..." She exhaled, at a loss for words.

"Perfect," he supplied.

She smiled. Yes, it was perfect.

Warmth enveloped her like a soft blanket.

"Stephan saw the whole thing." Vince drew back to kiss her nose. "That should get him thinking."

Stephan?

Disappointment rushed through her veins like ice water.

He did that for Stephan?

Of course he did, her mind chided. That's why they were there. He was acting, trying to get Stephan's attention.

But, for a minute...she thought...

Wrong.

She was an idiot. Her fake date was on track. *She* was

the one who'd gotten caught up in the moment. Lost in a kiss that wasn't real. A kiss she'd always dreamed of sharing with Stephan.

How could her body have such strong reactions to a man who was just acting?

But she couldn't fault Vince for that. Or take offense.

"Perfect," she echoed, and stepped out of his arms.

At least now she knew what she was up against in her quest to win Stephan's heart.

Her body.

For some reason, it wanted the wrong man.

Chapter Ten

A half hour after he walked Emma to her door, and Chelsea to her car, Vince sat in the hot tub with his brother and cracked open a beer.

He needed it.

Things hadn't gone at all as he'd expected tonight. His innocent acquiescence to help his brother's neighbor land her childhood crush took a right turn into the danger zone the instant their lips had met.

There hadn't been anything innocent about it.

Sure, he expected to enjoy the kiss. What red-blooded man wouldn't? Emma was a beautiful woman. And he liked her. But, damn, he hadn't expected the intense connection or strong sparks.

What the hell was up with that?

"For someone who just exacted revenge, you don't look too smug." Dom regarded him from across the hot tub. "You obviously don't have any idea what hell you put me through tonight."

Too consumed with his own troubles to enjoy his brother's

discomfort, Vince shrugged.

"Something happen tonight?"

Vince snorted and drank his beer. "Don't know what you're talking about."

"Bullshit." His brother cocked his arrogant head. "Your thoughts are obviously elsewhere. I hope they aren't on Emma."

"And if they are? You're the one who volunteered me—no, *blackmailed* me—into dating her."

"*Fake* dating, bro," Dom corrected. "And I didn't have to twist your arm too hard. I see the way you smile at her."

He waved a hand. "I smile at everyone like that."

"Not with your teeth." Dom laughed. "Hell, you expose your gums like one of those slick dudes on those fancy magazine covers. It's embarrassing."

Vince laughed, too. "You're full of shit."

"True, but you're delusional if you think you're not attracted to her." His brother shook his head, coming way too close to the truth. "So what happened?"

Damn man and his intuitive powers.

Sinking farther into the water, Vince rested his head against the concrete and closed his eyes. "What makes you think something happened?"

"Normally, you talk my damn ear off and constantly smile."

Also true.

Dammit.

And the man wasn't going to drop it. He was like a rabid dog with his teeth sunk into a pound of flesh.

With his eyes still closed, he lifted a shoulder. "We kissed in front of Stephan."

Although, truth be told, Vince hadn't even realized it at the time. All he knew was he needed to taste the smiling woman pressing her soft curves into him. Hell, he'd wanted to kiss her since she whacked him with the door that very first day.

"And?"

Vince opened his eyes and frowned over his beer. "What do you mean, 'and?'"

"Well, of course you're going to kiss in front of the guy." Dom rolled his eyes. "No better way to make the guy jealous and take notice."

He nodded.

"So what's the problem?" His brother's gaze narrowed. "He didn't care?"

"No. I mean, yes. I guess." He blew out a breath. "I was too busy getting knocked on my ass."

Light entered the blue eyes scrutinizing him. "Ah. She made you feel it, did she?"

And a hell of a lot more than he'd expected, but couldn't let her know. She wanted Stephan. Which was why he'd mentioned the man the instant he caught his breath. Although, why she'd responded with such an odd look puzzled him. It appeared almost…pained.

Which made no sense. Must've interpreted it wrong. Hell, with all the craziness going through his mind at the time, that had to be it.

"Nothing wrong with that, bro," Dom said. "Don't beat yourself up about it. Emma's hot. And you're breathing. Of course, you're going to feel it."

If only it were that simple.

"It was more than that," he said with a shake of his head. "It was like…I don't know…like I was back in high school."

There. He said it. He voiced the discontent whispering in his head all damn night.

His brother sat up and muttered a curse. "What are we talking here? Connie potential?"

Maybe.

"I don't know." He sucked down the rest of his beer and set the empty bottle on the paver. "That's why I'm freaked out. I can't go through that again." He refused to open himself up like that, especially to a woman who wanted another man.

Dom shoved a hand through his hair. "Sorry, Vince. I didn't mean to put you in this position. Maybe I can get the doc to okay more therapy. This way I might be able to shave a few days off your stay."

Vince stilled while alarm shot through his chest. "No. Don't mess with it. Look how far you've progressed with just two therapy sessions. You never would've been able to get in this hot tub three days ago."

"Exactly my point. Imagine my progress if we upped the sessions."

"No. Too much strain could set you back. Just leave it as it is. I'll be fine," he insisted. No way would he forgive himself if his brother jeopardized progress because of him. No way. If that's the case, he'd quell any and all feelings for the woman. Blood before lust. "Now that I know the danger, I can safeguard against it. I've resisted temptation before. Hell, I've done it for nearly a decade and a half."

Granted, those women never sent shockwaves of awareness through him with just one touch, but his brother needn't know.

Dom closed his eyes and leaned his head back. "Who knows? Maybe you've done enough tonight to get the doc to finally ask her out tomorrow."

"True," he said, refusing to label the sinking feeling in his gut, or the tightening in his chest as anything but relief.

It was also the reason he decided to make a fresh batch of cannoli in the morning and deliver it to Emma at work. That didn't exactly scream casual, but in that moment, Vince didn't care.

Hell, maybe he'd get lucky and Stephan would be around

to witness the act. It might even add fuel to the fire. Because when Vince had spotted the guy watching them after that amazing kiss, there was no mistaking the clenched fists, or the envy darkening the man's eyes.

Yeah, he definitely needed to visit her at work.

For Stephan's sake.

It had absolutely nothing to do with the long dormant need knotting his gut.

. . .

"So, how long have you been seeing each other?" Stephan asked Emma the next morning.

Wow. Her butt had barely hit her chair when he'd approached her cubicle. Heck, she hadn't even had the chance to fill Macy in on her date.

The unexpected action and question momentarily stole her voice. She glanced at her friend. The smiling woman sat back and regarded her with a lazy grin, clearly comfortable to watch the show.

"Vince?" She cleared her throat and shrugged, hoping to appear cool. "Oh, we aren't actually seeing each other. He's my neighbor's brother. It's more of a casual thing."

The fact she'd had a great time, that it'd felt more like a real date than a fake one, was all Vince's fault. He made her feel at ease. Like she could do no wrong, and he was happy to just hang out. The guy had learned more about her in two days than Stephan had learned in six months.

How was that possible?

Because he had to, her mind reasoned.

But he didn't have to take the time to teach her to bowl. To actually walk her through it. Most men would've just told her to do what they did.

Not Vince. He was perhaps the most patient man she'd

ever met. Which didn't compute because the military men she'd dated had never been good with patience.

Or maybe she'd dated the wrong men.

"So you've known him a while," Stephan said, more than interest filling his gaze.

She nodded. "A long time." Dom had mentioned his brother early on. "But I didn't meet him until four days ago."

Stephan's brows rose. "Boy, he didn't waste much time asking you out."

"Some men are like that," Macy chimed in. "They see what they want and go for it. They don't need to wait...say six months...or a decade to act."

With heat rushing into Emma's cheeks, she returned the foot-to-the-shin maneuver and ignored Macy's yelp.

Stephan glanced from her to Macy, then back. "Well, he seems like a nice guy."

"Yeah." Her friend nodded, a devilish grin on her face. "A nice guy packing mouthwatering cannoli."

Emma sucked in a breath. *She did not just say that.*

"Good morning, everyone," Vince said from behind.

Squeaking, Emma jumped and turned to face him. "Hey...I didn't see you."

"I know." His gaze softened. "Didn't mean to scare you. I just wanted to drop this off." He set a dish of mouthwatering cannoli on the counter between him and Stephan. Emma pressed a hand to her fluttering stomach to keep the relief inside—and to keep herself from smacking her not-so-funny friend in the arm. "I couldn't stop thinking about you, so I made these this morning to give me a reason to see you while Dom's at PT."

Real or not, his words put a smile on her face. "Thank you." She stood. "I had a great time last night."

So much so, he'd dominated her dreams.

Not Stephan.

Emma tried not to read too much into that. Just like she wouldn't read too much into the way her heart skipped a beat when his gaze dropped to her lips.

"Yes, thanks, Vince," Stephan said, breaking the spell. "I'm assuming we can have some, too." He held up a cannoli.

Vince nodded and grinned. "Yes, of course. Help yourself."

"That's all I needed to hear. Make room." Macy jumped to her feet and reached for one.

Smiling, he grabbed one and handed it to Emma. "Let me know what you think."

"Okay." Holding his gaze, she took a bite and promptly echoed Macy's moan as the confection melted in her mouth.

Stephan stilled and swallowed audibly, while Vince's gaze darkened to a deep whiskey color that warmed her from within.

"This is the best thing I've ever tasted," she told him before taking another bite.

Satisfaction eased his mouth into a grin. "I'm kind of partial to your peach pie."

"Emma baked you her pie?" Stephan raised both brows and blinked when Vince nodded. "You're a lucky guy."

A few of the nurses drew near, eyeing the goodies.

"May we have some?" one of them asked.

"Help yourself." He stepped aside and grinned at her. "There's another batch at Dom's. He threatened to skip PT if I tried to leave the house with both trays."

"I don't blame him," Macy said, reaching for her third treat. "These are the bomb."

"Amen," one of the nurses said between bites.

Chuckling, he turned to face her. "I better let you get back to work."

She nodded, trying to stop the blush threatening to invade her cheeks. "Thanks for the cannoli."

"My pleasure." He sent her one of his sexy grins before leaving the office.

"Mmm...mmm." Macy sighed. "That man looks just as good walking away."

"Amen," the same nurse said again.

Emma smiled, and was still smiling two hours later when break time rolled around. She saved her file and stretched back in her chair.

Her friend grinned. "I can't believe Stephan came right up to you this morning and flat-out asked you about Vince. Finally, you have movement! You and Vince need to keep it up. It's working."

Yeah, but in both directions.

How was it possible to be attracted to two men at the same time? Stuff like that only happened in the movies or in a book. Not in real life. Especially not in hers.

Good thing Vince wasn't attracted to her.

Chapter Eleven

Several hours later, Emma entered her neighbor's backyard with a strawberry-rhubarb pie. She couldn't show up at a barbecue without bringing one. Vince had texted the invite to her after lunch, stating they needed to strategize their weekend and suggested doing so by the pool.

"Hi, Emma," Dom greeted her with a wave, standing near a patio table already loaded with food. The man wore board shorts and an actual smile.

Her heart lifted. She hadn't seen it in a while. She missed the grin.

It appeared less strained with pain, and for that she was grateful, but she wished he was fully clothed. His beautiful, muscled body was covered in bruises that were turning that ugly yellow-brown. In truth, it was hard to look at him and not cry.

She inhaled slowly and cleared her hot throat. "How are you feeling?"

"Better now." He grinned, reminding her of his brother. "You brought pie."

She laughed. "I see how it is. It's not me you're happy to see. It's my pie."

"*I'm* happy to see you," Vince said, stepping onto the back porch.

His words and presence sent her heartbeat racing, and she nearly dropped the pie.

Darn it.

He, too, wore board shorts, but thankfully, he still had a T-shirt on. The last thing she needed to see was his naked torso.

It's probably covered in hair, all covered in hair, she told herself as she headed to the table to set down her pie.

"Thanks," she told him, remembering to be polite. "I brought dessert."

"You didn't have to," he said, stopping next to her. "But something tells me I'll be glad you did." She lifted the pie for him to sniff. "Mmm…strawberry-rhubarb. I haven't had any in years."

Dom stepped close and cupped both their shoulders. "Then you're in for a treat. Peach isn't her only specialty. All of her pies rock."

Between his praise and Vince's admiring gaze, she wasn't sure how to react.

"Whatever you're cooking smells amazing," she blurted. "Do you need any help?"

Vince shook his head. "No. I got it covered. You two sit down. The burgers are almost ready." He headed to the grill.

"Grab yourself a drink and take a load off." Dom motioned to a cooler near the porch. "And while you're there, can you grab me another beer?"

She laughed. "A ploy to get what you want."

He set a hand over his heart. "You wound me."

Grabbing their drinks, she snorted. "Takes more than that to get through your thick skin." She glanced at the griller a few feet away. "Vince, you want a drink?"

"Yeah. A beer. You can set it on the table." He turned to her and smiled. "Thanks."

The fluttering in her stomach was strictly due to hunger. End of story.

She placed the drinks on the table and sat down. It felt good to get off her feet.

Vince carried over a plate of sizzling burgers that smelled so amazing her stomach didn't flutter—it growled. Loudly.

She grinned despite the heat in her cheeks. "Think you woke up a beast."

"Wouldn't be the first time." Dom snickered, reaching for a patty. "My brother inherited our nonna's cooking prowess. She could make cardboard taste delicious."

Vince's phone rang, cutting off his laugh. He fished it out of his pocket and answered, "Hey, Leo." After listening a few seconds, he smiled. "Hang on, I'm going to put you on speaker. I'm with Dom and Emma." He set the phone on the table and tapped it. "Can you hear me?"

"Yes," a low, rather sexy voice responded. "Hello, Dom and Emma."

Vince grabbed a patty. "I just finished grilling, so we sat down to eat."

"Burgers?" Leo asked, voice wistful.

"Yeah," Dom said, his mouth full. "They're delicious. Too bad you're not here."

"Bastard. Enjoy it for me."

"I am."

They laughed. Emma took a bite of her own burger and nearly moaned. Dom wasn't kidding about Vince's cooking.

"I'm calling to let you know my buddy may have found your friend," Leo continued, and Dom went still. "He's going there on Sunday to check in person."

Relief eased the stiffness from her neighbor's shoulders.

"Thanks."

"Yeah, Leo. Thanks," Vince said. "That's good news."

"Hopefully, it's him and he's okay," Leo said. "So, how are the burgers?"

"Amazing," Emma said between bites. Seriously amazing. Maybe he'd be open to feeding her every day in exchange for pie?

A groan emanated from the phone. "Vince, I've missed your cooking, man. Everyone has."

He sat up. "Why? Is my kitchen okay?"

"Yes. Relax," Leo said. "Everything's covered, it's just that the girls don't cook like you. Although, Jovy's pierogi were delicious, and Beth makes a mean pork barbecue."

Vince frowned, a flash of envy darkening his gaze. "Jovy made pierogi?"

Her heart squeezed. Memories of making them with her grandfather flashed through Emma's mind. Some of her favorite times.

"Yeah, she did," Leo replied. "Homemade."

Vince shook his head. "She's been holding out."

Dom leaned forward. "That's okay. We have Emma's homemade pie."

"Yeah." Vince's warm, amber gaze met hers. "Strawberry-rhubarb today."

Another groan emanated from the phone. "My grandmother makes pie, too, but I haven't had one in years."

"I'd be happy to make one for you if you're ever in town," she offered.

His warm chuckle echoed through the line. "Thanks. I just might take you up on that, seeing as Mother Hen here and the whole damn gang voted for me to drop in and check on Vince and Dom."

Vince raised a brow. "Stone wants you to come here? When?"

"There's a little lull between jobs right now, so how does Sunday sound?" Leo asked. "I'm hoping I'll have more concrete news for Dom by then, too."

"You're always welcome here," her neighbor said, reaching for his beer. "You all are."

"Appreciate that. I'll see you Sunday."

Emma leaned toward the phone again. "I'll have your pie ready."

"I appreciate that, too. Thank you," Leo said. "See you all on Sunday. Enjoy your burgers."

A second later, the phone was silent.

By the time the meal ended, not only was Emma no longer hungry, she would no longer look at a grill the same again. She loved the grill. The grill was her friend, but nothing she'd tasted from her backyard, or anyone else's, had ever made her moan. Until today.

"I can't believe I ate that whole burger," she said. "The combo of mesquite and Italian flavors was flat-out amazing. I think you just ruined me, Vince."

He laughed, a measure of pride lighting his eyes. "Well, thank you. I'm glad you enjoyed it, because I'm pretty sure I'm going to eat all of your pie." He nodded to his nearly finished second helping of dessert.

"Think again." Dom loaded his plate with his third slice. "There's still two more pieces left and they're mine."

Vince raised a brow. "Don't bet on it, bro."

Smiling, she sipped her wine cooler, more relaxed than she'd been in a long time. The sun was setting, the air was warm but not oppressive, and a soft breeze blew the hair off her face as the solar lights slowly kicked on. A great transition into evening, and it was nice to sit and enjoy it with the brothers, especially at the end of a workweek.

"Where are you two pretending to date this weekend?" Dom asked, scraping the last of the pie from his plate with a fork. "And don't even think of siccing Chelsea on me again. I can manage a few damn hours by myself."

She hid a smile. "You telling me you didn't have a good time with your groupie?"

Dom gave her the stink eye and grumbled into his beer.

Vince chuckled. "I got the same answer from him last night."

"So, where are you two heading tomorrow?" her neighbor asked again, completely ignoring all talk of Chelsea.

Emma let it drop and shrugged. "I'm not sure. I think Stephan told Vince he likes to jog or hike or something on the weekend."

"Yeah." He nodded. "At Flat Rock Park. But he never said what day or time, so we may not even bump into him. Have you ever jogged or hiked before?"

Laughter rippled up her throat. "No. Like bowling, I've never hiked or jogged, either, although I have been known to sprint from mice."

He smiled. "I'll be sure to keep your path rodent free."

They had just settled on a time to meet in the morning when her phone rang. Rubbing a hand on her pant leg, she sent her hosts and apologetic look, and answered. "Hi, Mom."

"Hi, sweetheart."

Her mother's tone was relaxed, so Emma let herself relax, too. Must just be a social call. Not bad news about her aunt.

"How was your week?" her mother asked. "Any movement with Stephan?"

Emma got up and walked out of earshot. "Good, and not really. But he does seem a little more interested in my personal life. Maybe that's something?"

"I would say so. Could it be because he saw you kiss your neighbor's brother at the bowling alley?"

Heat rushed back into her face, shock halting her pacing. "H-how'd you know about that?"

"I'm a mother. I have my ways." Her mother's chuckle filled her ear. "What does Vince look like? Is he handsome like his brother?"

Emma turned and let her gaze trail over the man, and her heart literally halted for two full beats. He'd lost his shirt. It was gone. Leaving him in nothing but his board shorts.

Lord have mercy, the man was tan and broad and lean, and had just the right amount of hair on his chest and abs without concealing his incredible muscle tone. His back and shoulders, however, were free of hair. That sucked. She needed that ape scenario. Needed something negative about the guy, because most of the off-putting things she'd tried to imagine about him had been proven wrong.

On his left bicep, she noted he had a tattoo. There. Some people would list that as something negative—too bad she wasn't one of them. His tattoo of an eagle clutching a Ranger banner in one talon and a flag in the other, was sexy as all get out.

Darn it. The man was hot as hell, and her whole body responded with a rush of tingling heat.

"Emma? Are you there?" her mom asked.

Crap. She'd forgotten she was on the phone with her mom. Dragging her gaze from the lean hunk of temptation, she cleared her throat. "Uh...yeah."

"Do you find him attractive?"

Only with every freakin' fiber of her being.

Thing was, she didn't want to find him attractive. "It's complicated," she told her mom.

Thank goodness the man didn't seem interested in her beyond helping out. If he had been, she was apt to make a huge mistake and fall into bed with him. That would muck everything up.

"You've been wanting a chance with Stephan for so long, honey," her mother reminded her. "Don't blow it now. Not when you're so close. Otherwise, you'll always wonder what could have been. Promise me you'll keep that in mind."

"I promise," she said, and meant it.

Her mom was only reiterating the thoughts in Emma's head.

"I'll call you in a few days to see how you're doing. Good luck with Stephan," her mother said before hanging up.

What she needed was good luck resisting Vince. There was no use in denying it. Emma was attracted him. Big time.

Bracing for the impact of awareness, she hung up and strode back to the table. Every hair on her body stood up in an attempt to get close to the man. "Sorry about that."

Vince shook his head. "Never apologize for talking to your mom."

"You coming in the pool?" Dom rose to his feet and slowly made his way to the steps at the shallow end. His brother, on the other hand, moved past her and dove into the deep end.

She watched Vince swim under water to the middle of the pool where he surfaced and slicked the hair off his face. Water trickled down the muscles of his lean body, dripping off the sprigs of hair clinging to his well-defined chest and six-pack abs. Heaven help her, she was never more envious of anything in her entire life as she was of that water.

"Come on, Emma." Dom slowly submerged. "The water's warm."

Doubtful. Vince was in the water. It had to be hot.

"No," she said, already making her way to the gate. "I have a few things I need to do tonight since I'll be busy tomorrow. Thanks for dinner. It was amazing as usual, Vince. I'll see you in the morning."

Before she could change her mind, Emma strode home and didn't stop until she was safely inside. Distance was the best defense against the temptation of the wet, hard-bodied guy she was only supposed to be *casually* interested in.

A grill wasn't the only thing she was never going to look at the same again.

With luck, Stephan would ask her out soon, and then Emma wouldn't have to go on any more fake dates with her neighbor's hot brother.

Chapter Twelve

Heaven?

Hell?

Vince lingered somewhere in between as he hiked behind Emma the next day. The view of one of his favorite parks was lost on him, thanks to her captivating curves. He used to frequent the place while stationed nearby, enjoying the peaceful solitude of the trails and the muffled thud of his sneakers pounding the ground, keeping pace with his accelerated heartbeat.

Not today.

No. Today his heart beat to a different master. Emma. The beautiful woman ruled his pulse.

Dressed in shorts and a tank top designed to drive him mad, his fake date proved there wasn't anything fake about her gorgeous body. Awareness hit him in an unexpected wave. And when they rounded corners, he was hard-pressed not to notice the gorgeous ripple of her bouncing breasts.

More than his tongue swelled.

But calling a halt to their hike because of blue balls was

not an option, so he soldiered on.

And suffered so good.

Held prisoner to her long, supple, shapely legs, his gaze never strayed on the straight paths, but his imagination—the disobedient bastard—soared with sinful thoughts best left in his head.

He wanted to kiss and lick every mouthwatering inch of the beauty, starting at her ankles and working his way up to the promised land. This attraction was getting stronger and out of control. It reminded him of raging hormones back in his teens.

What the hell?

His body acted as if he hadn't had sex in years when, in fact, he'd enjoyed several hours with a pretty waitress in Dallas just last week.

The uncontrollable need made no sense.

It was making him a jerk, too.

Emma was taken. She was Stephan's soon-to-be girlfriend. Or at least that was what Vince told himself to try to keep his desire in check. But it was hard.

And so was he.

Dammit.

The things he wanted to do—

No. He halted those thoughts. This was wrong and damn stupid. Deploying restraint drilled into him through years of training, some not far from where they now hiked, he ripped his gaze from her sweet ass to stare over her shoulder at the trail ahead. There were other concerns prevalent in his mind. Like the ranch.

He knew his friends were more than capable of taking up the slack his absence created, but it didn't stop his concern over some of the veterans dealing with socialization issues. Time and perseverance helped him build a rapport with a few of them and he hated to jeopardize their progress by disrupting their routine.

According to Leo, everyone was doing fine. He hoped it was true and not just his buddy blowing smoke up his ass to keep him from worrying. But experience had taught him not to stress about situations he had no control over, and right now, At-Ease was one of those.

Unlike his brother.

The stubborn fool had insisted on coming with them to the park today. Dom wanted to stay active because he didn't have physical therapy until Monday. They left him back near the parking lot to walk around the level path. That was over an hour ago. Vince hoped the idiot wasn't doing anything stupid.

"You know what?" Emma stopped suddenly and twisted to face him.

Swallowing a curse, he grabbed her hips to avoid plowing her over. "Sorry. Are you okay?" Once they both had their footing, he released her and stepped back.

She nodded. "Yeah. And I'm sorry, too. I shouldn't have stopped so quickly. It's just that I realized something."

He frowned. "What?"

"Do you hear that barking?" She placed a hand behind her ear as if to listen.

He noted the sound of dogs in the distance. "Yeah."

"I don't mean the dogs. I'm talking about my feet." She grimaced. "These puppies are done. Besides, this place is too big. We've already tried two different trails. The chances of running into Stephan are slim. My feet vote we stop. Just the thought of hiking back to your brother makes them want to cry."

He smiled. "No need to be cruel to your puppies."

"Thanks." Nodding, she moved past him to head back the way they came. "Stupid flat feet," she mumbled, walking with a slight limp.

Memories flashed through his mind of missions and training from long ago, where he'd trekked with blisters or a bum foot. It always made the distance seem twice as long. He hated the thought of Emma going through something similar.

Not while he was around.

"I have an idea."

Without waiting for her to respond, he scooped her up into his arms and smiled at her startled oath.

Gripping his shirt, she blinked. "W-what are you doing?"

"Giving your puppies a rest."

This time her eyes widened. "But...you can't carry me all the way. It's so far."

He chuckled, heading back. "I've trekked dozens of times in full gear that weighed more than you."

"At least let me get on your back. You know...like piggyback," she said, looking way too cute and feeling way too good in his arms.

He nodded, and in two quick maneuvers, flipped her around.

"Holy crap." She gasped as she clutched his neck from behind. "You're crazy." She laughed, loosening her hold while she wrapped her legs around his hips.

She sounded happy. He liked that. A lot.

She felt good wrapped around him. He liked that a lot, too.

Hooking his arms under her knees, he hoisted her up a little more on his back. "How's that? Better?"

"Yes. Thanks." Her voice was a little breathless.

He could relate. The woman interfered with his damn breathing. Between the heat from her body and the way her soft curves pressed against him, he fought to keep his eyes from crossing as awareness skittered down his spine.

Sweet torture.

"I can't believe you're carrying me," she said a few

minutes later. "I feel bad."

He glanced sideways at her. "No need. Just because I'm not active duty like Dom doesn't mean I've gone soft."

She chuckled. "Yeah, soft isn't a word I'd use to describe you."

Since that sentence could lead them into trouble, Vince decided to ignore it. "I haul and lift a lot working at Foxtrot."

"Like what?"

"Tools, boards, bags of cement, cinder blocks, you name it," he replied.

"Foxtrot is the construction company created in conjunction with the ranch, right?" she asked. "Both to help veterans?"

Since it was a safe subject, he was more than happy to answer her questions. "Yes, me and my buddies—Stone, Brick, and Cord—created the ranch for veterans who have trouble transitioning back into civilian life."

"How the heck big is the ranch house?" she asked. "It has to be huge to house everyone. Or do they sleep in tents or trailers or something?"

"They sleep in the male and female barracks we built, but come up to the main house for chow."

"Which you cook," she said with a smile evident in her tone.

He nodded. "Yes, but several of the vets help with food prep. They look forward to it, too." It was good for them to have something to do. To feel useful.

"Is that why you also have the construction company?" she asked. "To give them jobs?"

"That's part of it, but it also helps generate income to keep things going."

Taking a deep breath, he braced himself for the question he knew was coming.

"What made you all start this?"

And there it was. He exhaled slowly, then answered, "Our other buddy, Leo. He was hurt on the same mission our Ranger brother Drew was killed. Leo witnessed it. Couldn't help. It messed him up pretty bad. We all retired soon after. He was still on pain meds because of his injury, and drinking to silence it all in his head, spiraling worse than we realized until one time, he did both too close together—maybe on purpose, maybe not...we don't know, he doesn't even know—but he ended up in the hospital and nearly died. That's when we realized we had to do something. Had to help other veterans trying to cope."

"Wow." Her voice was soft, and he could tell it was full of emotion.

"It's hard enough dealing with flashbacks. We all deal with them," he said. "But I can't imagine having a photographic memory like Leo. It's no wonder he sought solace in a bottle and pills. He wanted a break."

She cleared her throat. "Well, it's a good thing you all were there to help him through," she said quietly. "And now you're helping more veterans, too."

"It's an honor." He was only too happy to help. "We saw a need and felt compelled to do something."

"Which is so great. Most people wouldn't do anything, and yet, you all did." Her hold on him tightened.

She was so easy to be around. Not judgmental or opinionated. She was someone he would be happy to have as a friend.

Coming to the end of the trail, he pushed the past from his mind and concentrated on the now, like his scowling brother meandering several yards away.

"You really did carry me all the way back," she said, that smile evident in her tone again. "You have to be the sweetest man I have ever met."

Sweet?

"Not sure I want to be sweet." He frowned, coming to a halt. "Hot. Irresistible. Unforgettable, maybe." He flipped her around until she was in his arms again. "Now those I can live with."

She laughed. "You're all of those, too."

"Well, all right then." He returned her smile, not in any hurry to release her.

Still grinning, she raised a brow. "You can put me down now."

"I know."

She laughed again. "Are you planning to carry me all the way to the car?"

"Maybe." Now that it came down to it, he didn't want to let her go.

Dom lumbered close, both brows raised. "Is this a new way to hike? Or is Emma hurt?"

"Not hurt, but her puppies are barking," he replied with a grin.

"What puppies?" His brother glanced around. "I didn't hear any barking."

Emma laughed. "He's talking about my stupid feet. Your brother was kind enough to give me a lift."

"Was he now?" Dom lifted an eyebrow. "Something tells me it wasn't such a hardship."

Vince sent the idiot a warning look, but didn't get a chance to follow it up with words.

"I know." She glanced at Dom and nodded. "He didn't strain at all. It was as if I weighed less than a feather. I wish." Her gaze returned to his. "But you can put me down now."

Despite his brother's deadpan expression, Vince knew disapproval lurked just below the surface. Nodding, he set a smiling Emma on her feet and stepped back. He wanted to remind Dom that he and Emma were just putting on a show...only, they hadn't acted today. Not once.

"Oh my God. I don't believe it. There's Stephan." Emma smiled and stepped close to cup his face. "I'm going to kiss you. Hope that's okay."

Without waiting for a reply, she pulled his face toward hers and kissed him.

Chapter Thirteen

Vince wasn't sure who was more surprised, him or his brother. Considering it was his job to respond—a job his brother volunteered him to do—he wrapped his arms around the woman and kissed her back.

There went that zapping again.

That crazy energy zinged through his body. Just like it had when they'd kissed at the bowling alley.

Mindful of their surroundings and the people and families milling about, he reined in his need to explore Emma's sweet taste, and let her control the embrace.

It did nothing to lessen his enjoyment.

She brushed her lips over his, once, twice, nipping and drinking as if she enjoyed it every bit as much as he did. Soft and slow, she continued the sweet torture, until Dom cleared his throat.

"You can stop now," his brother said. "Stephan's gone."

They broke apart, blinking. But he kept his hand on her hip in case the guy decided to double back. At least that's what he told himself.

"Thanks." Emma inhaled, then exhaled slowly, as if she, too, had gotten caught up in the moment. "Do you think he saw us?"

Apparently, not the same moment.

Hit with a cold wave of reality, Vince released her and glanced around while the awareness throbbing through his veins died a sudden death. A stark reminder not to get caught up in playing his role.

"Yeah," Dom replied. "He stopped dead in his tracks before disappearing up one of the trails. I think you threw him for a loop."

Vince could relate. He was still reeling, both from the effects of her kiss, and his momentary lapse in reality.

She smiled. "Good."

Yeah. Great.

"So, what are you two going to do now?" Dom asked. "Stick around?"

Vince shook his head. "Nah. That would seem too contrived."

And he needed to move. Walk around. Take a cold shower. Do something to expel his sudden pent-up energy.

She nodded. "I agree. What do you think we should do tomorrow?"

Since there was a big difference between *should* and *want*, he went with his gut. "Nothing. A day or two without bumping into him will work in our favor."

Besides, he needed the damn break to get his head out of his ass and fix his perspective. He was starting to like the woman too much.

She nodded again. "Yeah, there's such a thing as coincidence and then there's manufactured. Besides, I usually hang out with Macy on Sunday," she said, brushing her palms over her hips. "And I have the feeling I'm going to need a spa day tomorrow, or at the very least, a damn good massage."

"Yeah." Dom chuckled. "I'm betting your calves are going to be tighter than a—"

"Don't finish that," Vince cut his brother off, well used to Dom's more than colorful antidotes.

"What?" The idiot grinned. "All I was going to say was wound clock."

Emma laughed.

Vince snorted. "Right."

His brother's innocent gaze didn't fool him for a second.

"I was." Dom narrowed his eyes and shook his head. "You need to get your mind out of the gutter, bro."

Wasn't that the truth.

• • •

The next afternoon, Emma was sitting on her porch with Macy, enjoying an ice-cold glass of sweet tea after several hours of long overdue pampering at the spa.

She sighed. "My legs feel like rubber. And who knew Frieda did nails, too?" Holding out her hand, she gazed at the slices of watermelon painted on her tips. "They're works of art."

"I think she was partial to you," Macy said.

She turned to her friend. "Me? Why do you say that?"

"Well, I did hear you tell her you wanted to have her baby." Her friend snickered, swiveling her ice in the glass. "Hell, it sounded like you were making one, the way you were moaning."

Setting her tea on the table that separated them, she snorted. "You're full of shit. But the woman did work some magic. My calves are nowhere near as tight as they were this morning."

Emma could barely walk, and when she did, it had been at a much slower pace than poor Dom.

"Girl…" Macy 's eyes widened as she sucked in a breath. "You've been holding out on me."

"*Now* what are you talking about?"

"Vince." Macy set her glass near Emma's and pointed behind her.

She'd deliberately chosen the chair that placed her back to her neighbor's house. It was bad enough she could hear the brothers swimming. She didn't need to see them through the open gate. Friday night had been hard enough.

Emma suppressed a groan at her word choice.

"Good Lord that man is fine." Her friend sighed. "Why didn't you tell me he was solid muscle like his brother? As a matter of fact, why are you sitting here with me? You should be over there making an Acardi sandwich. You could be the lucky middle."

Her heart dropped to the porch. "Macy!" Darn woman was using her outside voice again.

"Sweet baby Jesus, he's a real man." Ignoring her, Macy practically drooled as she continued to stare past her. "Not one of those guys who looks like little boys barely old enough to shave. No sir. Vince is a real man. And…wait…what's that? A tattoo? Girl, why didn't you tell me he had a tattoo?"

Emma knew for a fact her friend was in a loving relationship and would never stray, but the woman did love to window shop. "It doesn't matter."

"Sure it matters." Her friend *tsked*. "I might be taken but you're not. So go on over there and have some wild monkey s—"

Muttering under her breath, she reached out to cover Macy's mouth. "Don't you dare finish that sentence."

Chuckling, her friend sat back out of her reach. "All I'm sayin' is you can't let that man go back to Texas without getting all up in there. Mmm…mmm…he sure is mouthwatering. Six-pack and ridges and muscles…oh my. No wonder you feel something when you kiss him. It's called lust. He's sexy as sin. Hell, I'm happily married and my ovaries are about to burst."

This was all her fault. Why had she confided to Macy how much she enjoyed kissing Vince?

Oh yeah, that's right, it had been during her massage-induced euphoria.

"Thanks for the tea." Macy stood and straightened her skirt. "I've got to go. Those Acardi brothers have me all hot and bothered. I need to track down Dupree and get me some before he leaves for that ball game. I'll see you at Kelley's tonight, but in the meantime, why not think about enjoying Vince while you can? He's only here for a little while, and you're not going out with Stephan yet. Do it for yourself. Do it for all the single women out there. Hell, do it for me, so I can get all the delicious details."

Laughing, she got up and walked her friend to the end of the porch. "I appreciate the suggestion, but you go home and worry about you."

Macy stepped onto the driveway, then turned around to face her. "But that's the problem. Who worries about you? Not you, that's for sure. Tell you what…" A determined gleam entered her eyes. "I'm going to take care of you right now."

Before Emma could respond, her friend pivoted around and marched straight for the open gate in her neighbor's yard. "Macy," she whispered loudly. "Macy! Don't you dare."

It was no use. The troublemaker disappeared next door.

Torn between yanking her friend out of there by the hair, or vanishing into her house, she chose the latter. Face on fire, Emma rushed to the table, grabbed the glasses, then shot into her kitchen. What she didn't know wouldn't hurt her.

Her well-meaning friend—bless her heart—had a habit of complicating the hell out of things. Next time she saw Vince, she'd have to do damage control, but right now, she had a pie to make for Leo.

Her heart rocked.

As soon as she retrieved her pie plate from next door.

. . .

After spending time with Dom to make sure he didn't overdo it in the pool, Vince showered and dressed, hoping to have some uninterrupted time to contemplate Macy's unexpected visit and conversation.

"I just wanted to thank you for putting color in my girl's cheeks, and that sparkle in her eyes."

He hadn't known what to say, so he'd scratched his temple. "Uh, Macy, I didn't see Emma today."

"Didn't need to. She can't stop talking about how your kisses make her knees weak, and that she kind of feels guilty because she wants more."

Warmth spread through his chest again, just like it had when Macy dropped the bombshell. He made her knees weak. And she wanted more.

Two things he was better off not knowing, because... damn, he wanted more, too.

"Yo, Vince," his brother called up the stairs. "What's for supper?"

He smiled. The guy was definitely starting to feel better.

"Beef brisket," he replied. "It's in the oven."

"Explains why it smells so damn good in here."

He had started it before they'd gone outside that afternoon, so it'd be ready for when Leo arrived later. "Still has an hour and a half to go, though."

"Damn. You're killing me," Dom grumbled, moving away from the stairs. "Guess that means I can catch the end of the Mets game before I shower."

Despite his brother's nonchalant attitude, Vince knew accomplishing those things on his own helped Dom tolerate the forced downtime. So even if it meant standing to watch the game because prolonged sitting aggravated his ribs, and that he couldn't bend in the shower, they were still tasks Dom could do without Vince's help.

The sound of his phone ringing sent him back into his room to retrieve his cell from the nightstand. "Hey, Stone. What's up?" he asked, a little surprised to find his friend's name on caller ID. With the guy's wedding around the corner, he had more important things to worry about than Vince.

"Just calling to let you know Leo is on his way, and to check to see how you and your brother are doing. I know when I'm in forced close proximity to mine, there's times we want to wring each other's throats."

He laughed. "Yeah. I remember a few of those times." Straight-shooter and Romeo had two different personalities. "Dom is making slow progress, but it's progress so he's not biting my head off near as much as before."

Stone chuckled. "Good to hear. And speaking of hearing, how's your fake girlfriend?"

He shook his head and sighed. "Leo has a big mouth."

And Emma's was amazing…

Dammit. He clenched his jaw. This was Macy's fault.

"He's just concerned. We all know you're sometimes too nice for your own good."

Ah, hell…

He stiffened as a thought occurred. "Is that why he's coming here today?"

"To him, it is," Stone said. "But to me and the other guys, this trip is to get Leo to leave the ranch. He hasn't been off it since his last incident, other than to visit his grandmother or Cord and Haley."

"We've gone fishing and bowling, and up to Dallas for that rodeo," he pointed out.

"Yeah, he's gone with *you*. But when was the last time he

went anywhere not work related on his own?"

Vince sat down on the edge of the bed and blew out a breath.

"Exactly." A modicum of worry crept into his buddy's tone.

At-Ease was Stone's brainchild. He got them all on board to rally around Leo. Concern for their Ranger brother sent them on the rewarding path they all now traveled.

Including Leo.

"It could just be a coincidence," Stone said. "It's been months since he's had any issues. You know as well as I do that he's a big help at the ranch, and has really stepped up at work, too."

True. The tightness gripping Vince's chest eased with his friend's words.

"The guys and I thought giving him a mission—so to speak—to visit you in Georgia would accomplish two things," Stone said. "One, assuage his concern about your situation, and two, assuage our concern about *his* situation. We all figured you'd be on board."

"Of course."

"Good." Relief lightened his friend's tone. "A night or two should do it. We asked Dom first, and of course, he said it was fine. But we wanted to check with you to make sure your brother could handle another visitor."

He nodded. "Yeah, he'll be all right. I appreciate you checking, though. Dom's a lot like you. Doesn't put himself first and is always eager to help despite his limitations. Although, Christ, don't speak the *L* word around him. He thinks he's fine."

Stone chuckled. "No problem. And I hate to break it to you, pal, but that eagerness-to-help gene runs in your family."

A well-known fact. He laughed. "The Acardi curse."

"Nah, it's a good thing," Stone said.

"So is Leo's visit," he said. "I think it'll do Dom some good, too. Not sure he appreciates me under his feet all the time."

"Can't be all the time if you're going out on dates with the neighbor."

Damn. So much for his friend forgetting about that.

Knowing Stone's interrogation tactics—and results—all too well, Vince rose to his feet and walked out of the room. "You're fishing for something that's not there. Emma and I are just friends. I'm helping her out."

And making her knees weak…

Not even his brother's grumpy demeanor could've stopped the smile from spreading across Vince's face.

Stone grunted. "You seemed to have forgotten the denial I went through when I met Jovy."

"True." He headed downstairs, recalling his buddy's interesting behavior after the first few encounters with his bride-to-be. "Your attraction to the woman was obvious. Everyone seemed to know but you."

"Kinda like the obvious change in your tone of voice when you said Emma's name?"

Frowning, he shook his head. "You're full of shit."

His tone hadn't changed one damn bit. Had it?

A deep chuckle met his ear. "Name-calling is all part of the denial process."

A slew of curses flew through his mind, along with the image of waving his middle finger.

Stone chuckled. "You just flipped me off, didn't you?"

"Yes. Mentally." He chuckled. "Double flamer, pal."

The laughing stopped. "Then you definitely like Emma."

He opened his mouth, but no denials were forthcoming. Damn.

"Don't sweat it, Vince. It goes much smoother when you stop denying."

He nearly tripped off the bottom step. "Wait. You're saying you think it's okay if I like her?"

"Of course. Why?"

Shrugging, he walked into the kitchen, happy to find it empty. "Dom keeps warning me off her, and Leo keeps warning me to be careful."

"That's because they're pessimists. You and I are not," his buddy rightfully pointed out. "Go with your gut, Vince. It's never led you astray."

He blew out a breath. "Kind of hard when another body part wants to call the shots."

Stone laughed. "Damn. I remember those days. I'm just saying give yourself permission to have fun. Because if you don't, and you come back here full of regrets and it places a dark cloud over the wedding, you'll have the wrath of Jeth to contend with."

He cocked his head. "Jeth?"

"Yeah, Jovy and Beth," Stone said. "The two have worked hard to put these plans in place. Trust me, you don't want to mess with their mission."

Vince snickered. "Roger that."

Though sweet, both women were confident in their convictions. Stone was right. Vince did not want to incur their wrath.

"Your mission is to have no regrets with Emma." Stone's tone held a familiar undercurrent of command.

"No regrets," he repeated. Trouble was, no matter what he chose to do about Emma, regret littered the path.

"All right," Stone said. "I'll call you in a few days to get your thoughts on Leo. In the meantime, enjoy Operation Emma."

Before he could reply the line went dead.

Operation Emma…

"Is Leo here already?" Dom shuffled into the kitchen

with a frown. "I thought I heard you talking."

"You did," he said, holding up his cell. "I was on the phone with Stone. He called to make sure Leo's visit wasn't going to be a strain for you."

A grin tugged his brother's lips. "Still mother-henning."

"Always." A trait that had kept Vince and the others alive on more than one occasion.

His brother waved a hand toward the other room. "Game's over. I'm going to go take my shower."

Vince opened his mouth, about to offer help, when Dom sliced him a hard look.

"No. Everything's within reach on the shelf in the shower. I just might take a little longer, but I can manage myself." His disgruntled brother started to turn, when a knock sounded on the door.

Vince took a step toward the back door, but Dom waved him off.

"I'll get it," his brother said, then remained where he was and hollered, "Come in."

A second later, the door opened and a beautiful breath of fresh air breezed in wearing a pretty blue sundress and a smile. "Hi. Sorry to bother you, but I was getting ready to make Leo's pie when I realized my plate was here."

"You're never a bother," Dom said, beating him to it. "Especially when you're going to make pie."

She laughed. "You are so easy, Acardi."

His brother grinned. "I know. I'm a pie whore."

"Among other things," Vince said, garnering another laugh from Emma that spread warmth through his chest.

Gaze twinkling, she nodded. "You've got that right."

Dom's eyes narrowed. "And you've got a glow about you. I take it you had a good spa day?"

She frowned. "How'd you know I went to the spa?"

Dom scowled as he borrowed Vince's words. "Macy told

us…among other things."

Color rose up her neck and into her face, deepening the blue of her eyes. His chest tightened. And swelled.

Yep. She definitely wanted more of his "knee-weakening" kisses.

"Ah, crap." She set her hands over her blazing cheeks. "I can only imagine. Sorry about that."

Vince rushed to her rescue. "No need to apologize."

"Yeah," Dom said. "My brother's an Acardi. Of course you enjoy kissing him. And judging by this crimson look you've got going on, I'm guessing it's true."

Vince stepped in front of his brother and stared him down. "Why don't you go take that shower?"

"I'd like to hear Emma's answer first." Dom cocked his head, daring him to push it.

He dared. "And I'd like to text a certain someone to come and help you in the bathroom."

Aggravation flashed through his brother's eyes. "No need to get hostile. I'm going," Dom said, then stepped to the right to glance around him at Emma. "Good luck with your pie. I look forward to having some later."

His brother flashed Vince a warning glance before leaving the room.

Vince turned to Emma. "Sorry," he said in unison with her. "You don't need to apologize," he added.

"I get the impression Dom doesn't want me to like kissing you."

His brows shot up as something akin to hope rushed through him. "So it's true?"

Her mouth dropped open, and she blinked. "I…I—uh… truthfully, I'm not sure." Sighing, she walked over to the island and sat on a stool. "Maybe the rush was just because both times Stephan was watching."

The possibility of the truth in her words sucked the wind

from his sails. "Could be." Although, he didn't see how Stephan's presence held any influence over the way his body had reacted to hers. Still, it couldn't be ruled out. Unless... "There's only one way to find out."

She straightened and slowly met his gaze. "How?"

"We kiss now. Here." He walked to her, ignoring the red flags his conscious was furiously waving. "In front of no one." That would prove or disprove her theory.

"Okay," she said, a little breathless.

Her agreement trumped the flags. Hell, it snapped the suckers in half.

She slipped off the stool and stood, nervousness clouding her gaze. "Now what?"

Cupping her face, he stepped into her. "Now we kiss."

Chapter Fourteen

In no hurry, Vince slowly lowered his mouth to Emma's and hovered a moment, enjoying the feel of her palms gliding up his chest while they shared a breath. Damn...the woman was intoxicating, and he soaked it all in for a moment. But his need to show her what a real kiss from him was like won out. Closing the gap, he brushed her lips with his, nipping and tasting like she had at the park yesterday. He started at one sweet corner and made a thorough trek to the other as awareness shot through his body.

God, she was soft, and when she sighed and opened up for him, he swept his tongue inside to finally sample her taste.

As sweet and succulent as a juicy peach, she was also hot and hungry, similar to the need ripping through him. But still he took his time, making slow, deep passes, acquainting himself with her essence. This is what he'd wanted to do since that first day when she'd hit him with the door. Even though they'd kissed before, he'd held back, not daring to make such a bold move, or take what she didn't want to give.

But, damn, she was giving now.

A needy, sexy sound rumbled in her throat as she clutched at his shirt and brushed her tongue along his. Fire flickered down his spine and increased his desire for more, but lack of oxygen forced him to break the kiss.

Setting his forehead to hers, he dragged in air while her warm, delicious breath washed over his neck in ragged spurts. Need tightened his groin. He tried to ignore it, but failed. "I think we have our answer," he said, kissing a path to her ear, unable to keep his lips off her. "Our reactions to each other have nothing to do with Stephan's presence and everything to do with chemistry."

Still clutching his shirt, she gasped. "I agree."

"Do you want me to stop?" he asked, brushing his mouth along her jaw.

"No way," she breathed, turning to meet his lips, rocking his world with a deep, hot-as-hell kiss that had him hard and throbbing like a teenager.

The woman made him feel hunger. She made him feel a deep-seated need.

Made him feel...*again*.

Without breaking the kiss, he lifted her up and set her on the island, where she wrapped her legs around him and drew him in. Her heat and desire had him on fire and it increased when her hands sneaked under his shirt and blazed a path up his torso.

God, he needed to touch her. He needed to feel her skin, too.

With one hand cupping the back of her head, he glided the other up her arm and over her bare shoulder, loving the feel of goose bumps covering her soft skin. Yeah, Emma's reactions and responses had everything to do with *him*.

Satisfaction was swift and strong, and it swelled more than his chest.

Basking in that knowledge, he released her mouth to nip

and taste his way down her throat while he lightly brushed his palm over her chest. She moaned, and arched into him, pressing her lush curves into his hand.

Groaning, he captured her lips for a hot, wet, deep kiss that had his eyes crossing and erection denting the zipper in his jeans. He was ready to burst, and when she gasped his name as he grazed his thumb over the nipple poking against her dress, he nearly lost it.

"Vince," she whispered this time, clutching at his back in a move he interpreted to mean more.

He had more. A hell of a lot more.

Kissing a delicious path down her cleavage, he slipped his fingers under the top of her strapless dress and pulled it aside to reveal a mouthwatering, pert peak. "Gorgeous."

Just as his mouth was about to close over the beauty, he heard a thud down the hall, followed by muffled curses, and the sound of a door being wrenched open.

"Vince!" his brother called out.

Shit. In one swift move, he released her and stepped back, taking in his surroundings and the fact they were out in the open in the middle of his brother's kitchen.

"The damn bottle fell, and I can't fucking pick it up," Dom grumbled, but it sounded as if he hadn't left the bathroom.

Thank God.

"I'll be right there," he hollered as he watched Emma fix her dress. "Sorry," he told her quietly, reaching out to help her off the counter. "You had me so worked up I forgot where we were."

Surprise widened her eyes, while a smile tugged at her lips. "I forgot, too. It—"

"Vince? Dammit, come on," Dom snapped, cutting her off. "I'm dripping wet here."

He rolled his eyes at Emma. "Sorry. I'll be right back." Then he turned and rushed to his brother. "Coming, princess.

Hold your tiara."

The idiot either had the worst timing in the world, or perhaps the best. Christ. He'd been so close to ravaging the poor woman right out in the open where his brother could've walked in to witness.

He was an idiot.

"What the hell took you so long?" Dom grumbled the second he saw Vince.

Entering the bathroom, he shrugged and walked past the guy without responding. No way would he say a word. What happened between him and Emma was their business. He secured the bottle of body wash from the shower floor, then handed it to his brother. "Here. Maybe you need to tighten your grip."

Dom chuckled. "Fuck you."

He had someone better in mind.

With a shake of his head, he shut the bathroom door and headed back to Emma. He needed to talk to her about that kiss, but when he entered the kitchen it was empty.

The pie plate was gone.

And so was Emma.

He leaned against the counter as disappointment washed through him. It was probably for the best. Their chemistry was too crazy. Too dangerous. Both of them were better off leaving it unexplored.

Now he just needed to get his body to agree.

• • •

Emma had been on the fast track with Vince earlier. She needed to change course. "Could you jump from a train to a ship?"

Macy frowned as they sat in a booth at Kelley's that evening, confusion clouding her brown eyes. "What are you talking about?"

"Never mind." She shook her head and bit into her slider.

For a Sunday evening, the bar and grille was moderately packed. Which was good. The live band and activity on the dance floor kept her focus from slipping to Vince and their hot kiss. Mostly.

"So are you going to tell me what's got you drinking a huge glass of wine instead of water tonight?" Macy asked.

Emma frowned. "I drink wine."

"Yeah, but not when you drive." Her friend smiled. "Did you have another encounter with Vince?"

Memories of their heated kiss in the kitchen, and the way she'd unexpectedly gone up in flames, flashed through her mind. She went to deny it, but unfortunately, had a mouthful of pinot noir at the time, so she choked instead.

"I'll take that as a yes." Macy grinned, lifting her own glass of wine.

After much coughing and some chest pounding, she managed to clear her airway. "Now I'm not going to tell you."

The smug woman waved a hand at her. "You don't need to. The wine and choking spell it out clear."

"I'm sure it doesn't," she said. "It just went down the wrong way."

"Whatever floats your boat, girlfriend." Macy lifted a shoulder.

Emma burst out laughing and Macy joined her.

"Well, it's nice to see you two having fun," Stephan said, appearing out of nowhere in front of their booth.

Her heart didn't quite rock, but it tipped a little. She hadn't planned a Stephan encounter, and yet, here he was in khakis and a white button-down shirt...smiling at her.

She fixed her posture and smiled back. "Hi, Doct—"

He lifted a brow. "What'd I tell you to call me outside of work?"

"Stephan," Macy replied. "He told us to call him Stephan, Emma. Don't you remember?"

Using her foot, she wacked the woman's shin to relay exactly how much she remembered. "Of course. Would you like to sit down?"

"Perhaps he's not alone." Macy stared up at him as if waiting for an answer.

His smile returned. "I'm here with a few friends, and actually, I came over to ask Emma to dance."

If he told her he was a Time Lord from the future she wouldn't have been more surprised.

"Too bad the band is still on a break," her friend pointed out.

If Emma didn't know better, she'd swear Macy was trying to sabotage her lucky break with Stephan.

A second later, the band retook the stage and started with a rock ballad.

She smiled up at him. "I'd love to."

"Great." He held out his hand and helped her from the booth.

"You two do remember Emma has a boyfriend, right?"

Oh. My. God.

"He's not my boyfriend. It's just a casual thing. There's no relationship." Placing her back to Stephan, she turned to face her friend and mouthed, *What are you doing?* before leading her childhood crush out onto the dance floor. This was *Macy's* freakin' plan. *She* was the one who'd encouraged Emma to have someone help her appear desired, so that Stephan would take notice and make a move.

Well...this was him making a move. Why the heck was Macy trying to sabotage it?

Vince was a casual, not-supposed-to-be-real thing...who happened to make her heart flutter and knees weak. But that was okay because Stephan did those things, too. Sort of.

Holding her hand, he turned to face her and reached out with his free hand to lightly grasp her…purse?

"Sorry." She readjusted the thin designer crossbody out of the way. As much as she'd been thrilled to score a deal on the purse at an outlet, right now, she wished she'd brought her clutch.

A smile spread across his face as he cupped her hip. "No problem."

The light touch of his hand sent a tiny butterfly flickering through her belly. Not exactly the swarm she'd expected, but there was movement. Although, to be truthful, she wasn't 100 percent certain the flickering was due to the man in her arms, or the fantasy of the man she'd created in her mind all those years ago.

Where was this uncertainty coming from?

This was Stephan. She had his attention. The attention Emma had longed for since her teens. Now was not the time for doubts.

Lifting her chin, she smiled at him and wished to goodness she could think of something to say.

It hit her then. Other than high school, they had nothing in common. He came from a higher-class household. She was raised middle class. He went to college and med school. She took a medical transcription course. He'd lived in New York and Boston. She'd always lived in Columbus. He belonged to country clubs. She belonged to the Book of the Month Club.

But Stephan was a nice guy back in high school. And yet, she was strangely uncomfortable and stressing about what to say.

You don't have that problem with Vince, the voice in her head reminded her, sounding vaguely like Macy.

She needed to get her friend out of her head.

The reason she didn't have that problem with Vince was because they weren't really a couple, and didn't have the pressures that come with it, she mentally countered.

"True."

"What's true?" Stephan asked.

Shoot. "Nothing." She shrugged. "Just thinking out loud."

He nodded, but still wore a frown. "Dancing with me won't get you in trouble with Vince, will it?"

"No." That was the perfect lead-in to remind him there wasn't anything serious going on with Vince. That they were just casually going out. But by the time the song ended, none of those words had left her lips.

"That's good," he said, releasing her. "Because he just walked in with two other guys."

Vince was here?

She glanced at the door, and sure enough, there he was in jeans and a blue T-shirt that hugged his lean frame. Emma's heart rocked in her chest.

Now that's what I call movement, the voice in her head said in Macy's tone again.

She ignored it, and when they reached her booth, she turned to Stephan and smiled. "Thanks for the dance."

"My pleasure," he said, then gave them a slight bow. "Enjoy your night, ladies. I'll see you tomorrow."

Macy lifted a brow after he walked away. "Well?"

"That's what *I'd* like to know." She sat down, never taking her eyes off her friend. "It was your idea to go the whole phony-date thing to get Stephan's attention, and the second it starts to work you tell him Vince is my boyfriend?"

"You're right, but as far as I'm concerned, the plan changed when you told me you liked kissing Vince."

Dammit. She had mush for brains. *Why'd she ever tell her that?*

"Still, I'll stay out of it...even though Vince is clearly the right man for you." Her friend held up a hand when Emma opened her mouth to protest. "And enough with the suspense, girlfriend. You're killing me. How'd it go? According to you, you've been waiting for that moment your whole adult life. So, tell me, what happened? Were there fireworks? Harps playing? Heavenly choirs singing?"

She snickered and reached for her wine. "You watch too much TV."

"Ah, come on. You mean to tell me there wasn't even a little flicker?"

Swallowing her wine, she nodded. "Yes, there was a flicker." And it felt good to realize it wasn't a lie.

"And what did you feel when you spotted Vince?" her friend asked with a grin.

Since Emma had felt major fluttering, she kept her mouth shut.

"I thought so." Macy chuckled as she glanced at the guys sitting at the bar. "Mmm...mmm...mmm...hose me down with warm melted butter, who is that extra helping of hunk with them? He's got that delicious bad-boy vibe going on. You know, he kind of looks like that superhero cold soldier dude from the movies."

"Sebastian Stan's character?"

"That's the one."

"Oh, wow." Emma blinked. "You're right." Why hadn't Vince mentioned he was best friends with a sexy Winter Soldier look-alike? "That must be Leo."

Macy turned back to face her. "Leo...he's Vince's friend from Texas you made the pie for, right?"

Before driving to Kelley's, she'd sneaked into Dom's house and set the pie on the counter, grateful to escape without running into anyone.

"Yes." She sipped more wine and tried not to notice how the muscles in Vince's back rippled as he reached for his beer.

"Shouldn't you go say something to him?"

She nodded, watching her wine swish as she twisted her glass. "Yeah. I'm sure Stephan would find it odd if we didn't interact. Even if we are just casual."

"Forget Stephan," Macy said. "Concentrate on the delicious man walking toward us."

Walking…?

Before she could fully brace herself, Vince appeared with a devastating smile that sent more than a flicker of awareness through her belly.

"Hello, beautiful ladies," he said. "Are you having a good time?"

"Yes," Macy answered first. "But you should take Emma out on the dance floor."

Vince's grin grew. "It'd be my pleasure," he said. "But I wouldn't want to intrude on your girls' night out."

Macy waved a hand at him. "No intrusion at all. Go have fun."

Emma raised an eyebrow. It was interesting how Macy was so generous with Emma's permission. Not that Emma would've turned him down. Even though she should. But wouldn't.

He shook his head. "Not without you. I'm Italian from Jersey. I'm more than capable of dancing with two women at the same time."

Winking, he held his hands out to both of them.

Macy laughed and grabbed his hand. "You're on."

Emma took his other one, impressed that the guy was willing to tackle a fast song and beyond touched that he was including her friend so she wasn't left sitting alone. That was sweet. Really sweet. And her heart cracked open a little more for the man.

Vince led them to the dance floor, where he indeed held his own with her and Macy. The guy had more moves than the two of them put together. He was a natural, and so darn cute she couldn't stop smiling. For three songs she danced and laughed at his smooth footwork and his exaggerated ones.

By the time the band announced they were slowing things down, Emma was both grateful for the break, and sad to see it end.

"Thank the Good Lord." Macy fanned herself. "I don't think I could've held up through another one. You can seriously groove, Vince." The panting woman nudged him toward her. "You two go ahead. I need to sit down."

"All right. If you're sure," he said.

Macy nodded. "I'm sure." Then walked away.

Emma was sure, too. She was sure this dance would be the most enjoyable of the night. Which meant she probably— no, *definitely*—should complain about being tired and join her friend at the booth.

Only she didn't. Nope. Instead, she adjusted her purse so it rested on the side of her hip and wouldn't interfere like before. Nor did she stop him from pulling her in close, much closer than she'd danced with Stephan.

Emma's heart leaped and beat erratically, and she suspected it didn't have anything to do with Stephan's presence. In fact, until that moment, she'd forgotten he was there.

Two strong hands lightly squeezed her waist. "You okay?"

Unable to find her voice, she nodded and set her palms on his chest, and that incredible wall of solid muscle. He was magnificent, and she was in trouble. Every part of her body screamed for her to press against him, but she managed to remain strong. Barely.

"That was a nice thing you did," she said when her voice returned. She was trying to keep things light, but it was tough with those talented lips of his so close.

"What do you mean?"

"Asking Macy to dance, too." Looking into his warm gaze, she couldn't help but smile. "She's going to talk about that for years. Did you have ballroom dancing lessons or something?"

His lips twitched. "No. It's an Acardi trait, although it seems to have skipped my brother."

"That explains it." Her steps faltered as a thought occurred. "I've never seen him on the dance floor during a fast song." And truthfully, she'd never equate her tough, muscle-bound neighbor with sophisticated moves, although the man in her arms was full of solid muscles, too.

Vince nodded. "Oh yeah. He has two left feet."

She giggled. "A princess with two left feet. Not sure I can look at him the same again."

"Good."

Wave after warm wave of awareness spread through Emma while her heart raced in anticipation, for what she had no idea.

He glanced over her shoulder, then back at her, an undecipherable look drifting across his face. "Stephan's watching. Do you want me to kiss you?"

Chapter Fifteen

Emma nodded. She wanted the kiss, but wasn't entirely sure it had anything to do with Stephan.

As they continued to sway, Vince slowly captured her lips in a lazy, thorough kiss that stole the strength from her legs and the ability to form a thought from her brain. By the time he lifted his head, she was clutching his shoulders and working to clear the fog from her head.

"I can't seem to get enough of you," he said against her lips.

A thrill like she'd never known raced down Emma's body, leaving her needy and confused. Should she admit the same thing, or run and hide? It was foolish to get involved with him. He was leaving in less than two weeks. Tipping her head back, she drew in a breath. "I…I should get back to Macy."

Disappointment flashed through his eyes, but he nodded. "Of course." He walked her back to her booth. "Thank you for the dances, ladies. I should go check on my brother and friend."

"Okay." She slid into the booth and rubbed at her

suddenly tight chest, feeling that same disappointment, and a bit of remorse.

"Vince?" A stunning blonde approached, a wide smile on her face. Before he could react, she pulled him in for a hug. "It is you!"

His eyes went wide. "Tiffany," he said, trying to draw back. "This is unexpected."

The woman released him much too slowly for Emma's liking. "Are you here alone?"

A strange prickling spread across her shoulder blades. Without thinking, she rose to her feet, stepped next to Vince, and slipped her arm around his waist. "No. He's here with me."

The blonde's brow arched above a disappointed gaze. "And you are?"

Vince wrapped his arm around her shoulder and pulled her in close to his side. "This is Emma. My girlfriend."

Two words.

Two simple words, and yet they held such a heavy impact. In a good way. Which was bad, since they were a lie.

"It was nice to see you again, Tif," he said, then turned to Emma. "I'll be right back."

"Okay." She went along with the ruse, and since it seemed like he was the one who needed a fake girlfriend, she lifted up on tiptoe and kissed him, feeling his smile against her lips.

This was no time for him to be amused. She kissed him again, this time a little deeper, until his smile disappeared and his hands gripped her waist.

Much better.

She broke the kiss and lightly caressed his cheek. "Hurry back." And because she could barely feel her legs, she retook her seat and reached for her wine, ignoring the smirk on Macy's face.

"Will do," he said, then headed toward a snickering Dom

and Leo.

She didn't care. Whatever.

"You're one lucky lady." The woman sighed, adoration in the gaze glued to Vince as he walked to the bar. "He's the whole package. Sweet. Sexy. Loyal. Great in the kitchen."

Emma sipped her wine and nodded. "His meals *are* delicious."

The blonde twisted back to face her. "It wasn't his cooking I was talking about." With envy darkening her eyes, Tiffany sighed and walked away.

"Huh." Macy tapped her chin. "I wonder what she meant."

That persistent prickling across Emma's shoulder blades almost persuaded her to acknowledge she was jealous. But she refused. That was silly. He would have to mean something to her for jealousy to take root. Which was even sillier.

Except it wasn't.

He certainly was "great" in the kitchen. Her body went up in flames just *thinking* about that kiss. Where would it have gone if his brother hadn't called out for help?

Better question. What in the world would've happened if Dom had wandered into the kitchen instead of calling Vince from down the hall?

This was bad. Very, very bad.

Macy grinned. "You're thinking about it now, aren't you?"

"Yes," she muttered.

Her friend sighed. "Me, too."

Their gazes met, and a beat passed before they burst out laughing. Macy was a good friend. So was Vince. He really was, and that was why he meant something to her. But, man, everything was getting all screwed up.

Time to get things back on track.

She exhaled and took another gulp of wine. Then

another. And another. "I should tell Vince to hook up with that blonde."

"No way, girlfriend." Macy shook her head and frowned. "Don't do that."

She downed the last of her drink, hoping it would make things clearer. "Why not?"

"He's your boyfriend."

"No, he's not." The thought made her head spin in delicious little circles. So much for thinking clearer. More wine seemed like the answer, though, so she swiped the glass out of Macy's hand and gulped down the rest of her friend's drink, too.

"Hey." Macy frowned. "That was my wine."

She shook her head and pushed the empty glass across the table. "I needed it more than you."

A smile twitched Macy's lips. "Because Vince is your boyfriend?"

"No, see that's the thing." She nodded, then shook her head, because one of them had to be right. "He's only *pretending* to be interested in me, until I start to date…um…" Shoot. She forgot his name. Her friend from high school. The doctor. Doctor who? It was on the tip of her tongue, but her tongue was too numb to remember.

Or was that her wine-fogged mind?

Why was her mind wine-fogged anyway? She'd only had a glass and a half. Although, a good portion of that was before she'd had anything to eat. And the glasses were pretty huge.

"You mean Stephan? The man who left ten minutes ago?" Macy stared at her, eyes full of knowing with a side of amusement.

"Yes." She slapped the table. "Him. Stephan." She grinned, happy to have a name to go with the face swimming before her eyes. Wait…Stephan left? Funny, she hadn't noticed. But it did explain why the face in front of her had dark hair and eyes the color of warm whiskey. "Does warm whiskey taste good?"

She bet it did.

"Whiskey?" The face frowned. "I thought you wanted wine." He glanced at the glass he set before her.

"It was…I mean. I did," she stammered, willing the room to stop spinning. Sheesh, she was such a lightweight.

"Maybe you shouldn't have any more," he said, joining her in the booth.

The guy with the sexy voice. And sexy mouth. And…

"I know you," she blurted, grabbing that sexy face with her hands. "You're my secret fake boyfriend, Vince."

He laughed. "It's not going to be much of a secret if you don't lower your voice."

"Right." She released him to place a finger to *his* lips. "Shh…"

He kissed her finger, then grasped her hand and set it on her lap. "Yeah, you definitely need to be cut off." He glanced over at her friend. "Isn't that right, Macy?"

The woman had a big-ass grin on her face. Emma blinked, tipped her head, then shook it. Nope. Still smiling.

"Why are you showing so much teeth?" she asked her friend.

"I'm smiling because I've never seen you let loose. This is rare, so I'm enjoying it and you should, too."

"Well, there you have it, Vince." Emma grabbed her new glass of wine and enjoyed a big mouthful per her friend's suggestion.

Why not? Everything was going to crap. She was confused as crap. Might as well get smashed as crap, too. Thanks to her lightweight status, she was more than halfway there. "And no, it's not because of that blonde chick."

He glanced around. "Who? Tif?"

Damn. She must've said that out loud. "Don't mind me. I

still have another three-quarters of a glass of wine to enjoy."

But this time, when she went to reach for it, a large hand whisked it out of reach and set it on a tray of a passing waitress.

"Consider yourself officially cut off." Vince slid from the booth and held out his hand. "Come on. I'll take you home."

Probably a good idea.

After helping her to her feet, he slid an arm around her waist. A nice, muscular, strong arm. And because she liked the feel of him, she stepped close and ran her hands up his yummy torso.

Mmm...hard ridges.

He smiled down at her. "You ready to go home?"

Man, he was cute.

"Sure. You can even drive my car. But Texas is too far. Let's go to my home instead."

His chuckled. "Whatever you want."

"Perfect." She turned to Macy. "We're going home now."

Her friend smiled. "I gathered that."

"How about I walk you out," Vince said to Macy.

Emma patted his chest. It was solid and warm...like the man. "Aw, that's sweet."

"It is. Thanks," Macy said, "but I see some of the girls from book club. I'm going to go join them. You two go on. Have fun."

"Okay." She saluted her friend.

Why?

No clue.

Laughing, she slipped her arm back around Vince's waist and fell into step alongside him. Okay, technically, she was leaning on the guy, and he was doing the walking, but it was all right. She trusted him. He knew what he was doing.

Which was a good thing, because she didn't.

Not by a long shot.

. . .

Although he enjoyed the feel of Emma's sweet curves pressed into his side, Vince would've preferred her to be sober and willing, although, inebriated and willing looked cute on her.

She glanced up at him. "Why are you smiling with all those dimples showing?"

"Because you're adorable." He tightened his hold as he led her toward the bar to tell the guys what was going on and hand Leo his keys.

They were there celebrating the fact Leo's friend had located Dom's buddy Amir, and the two had talked on the phone. When Vince had left them to dance with Emma earlier, his brother and the owner of the bar, Shamus Kelley, a veteran and father of one of the guys in Dom's unit, had been deep in conversation. The poor man had been a little shaken to see Dom back and battered.

It brought back memories from active duty Vince would rather forget.

"Sexy is better, but adorable is good," Emma said, bringing his mind back to the present. "I like adorable."

Happy for the distraction, he dipped his head toward hers. "So do I."

A pretty blush infused her cheeks, and his whole body warmed. He was in trouble. The woman was definitely getting to him without even trying.

"Don't you two look cozy," Dom said as they approached.

Shamus was down at the other end of the bar serving customers, and Leo was reaching for his ginger ale—his drink of choice lately, although he still enjoyed an occasional beer with the guys at the ranch.

As they neared, his buddy turned around on his stool and raised a brow, but said nothing.

Emma nodded. "Vince thinks I'm adorable."

"I bet he does." His brother smirked, but there was definitely a warning in his eyes directed at him.

She smiled at Dom. "And it's okay, because I think he's hot. But don't tell him I said that." Her body pressed closer as she lifted a finger to her mouth. "It'll be our secret."

Another, bigger wave of warmth rushed through Vince. Damn. The woman made him feel good, despite the fact he didn't want her to.

Dom's gaze narrowed under a disapproving brow, while Leo ducked his head and smiled into his ginger ale. At least his buddy saw the humor in the situation.

"You must be Sebastian—I mean Leo," she said, thrusting a hand out to his friend.

Leo shook her hand. "Nice to meet you, Emma. Thanks for the pie. It was delicious."

"I'm going to take Emma home," Vince said.

Her deep sigh rumbled through him. "Yeah. I had too much wine. Who knew a glass and a half was too much? I didn't. Did you?" She continued to stare straight at Dom.

His brother shook his head, apparently still dumbfounded.

"Me, either." She shrugged. "But I think it's making me say things I shouldn't. And I know I shouldn't drive. And I'm talking too much. So I'm going to shut up now."

Dom nodded slowly. "O-kay."

"Because it's the smart thing to do," she continued. "And I'm smart."

A smile tugged at his lips. "Usually."

"Yeah…hey." Frowning, she stepped toward Dom, but clutched Vince's arm. "What do you mean by that?"

Dom lifted a shoulder. "Nothing. Would you rather I drive you home?"

She stepped back and burrowed into Vince's side. "No. You're not supposed to drive yet. Besides, your brother thinks I'm adorable. And I think he's hot."

"So you've said. And you don't think I'm hot?" The idiot conjured a mock-hurt expression.

She snorted. "Of course not. You're Dom."

Holy shit.

It was the first time Vince had ever witnessed his brother being dissed by a woman. It was momentous. Classic.

Too great to hold in.

Vince laughed and tightened his hold on the sweet woman. She truly was a gem, and the fact the barb was unintentional made it all the more humorous.

Leo chuckled and nudged Dom's shoulder. "You're losing your touch, man."

His brother snorted. "Apparently."

"I think Vince should take me home now." She frowned and poked Dom in the chest. "Don't drive drunk!"

Damn, he *really* liked this woman.

Smiling so much his face hurt, Vince fished his keys from his jeans and dropped them in Leo's hand. "I'm sure you remember the way back to Dom's."

"Of course." His buddy nodded, and it was the first time that night a modicum of censor entered his friend's eyes. "Be careful."

That sentence had nothing to do with driving. He acknowledged it with a nod then brushed it aside. The two men were acting like he didn't know what he was doing.

They were wrong.

And it went both ways. "Don't stay too long," he told his brother. "This is your first time out since leaving the hospital. You don't need to overdo it."

A scowl crossed Dom's face. "Yes, Mom."

Emma straightened up. "Your mom's here?" she asked, glancing around. "Where?"

His mother would love her.

Vince chuckled. "She's not here. That's just Dom being

an idiot."

"Oh." She blinked. "He's really good at it."

On that note, he escorted her out of the bar, and was still smiling at her parting shot when he pulled into her driveway seven minutes later.

"I had a great time tonight," she said with a soft sigh. "And it all started when I danced with Stephan."

He'd noticed that the instant he'd entered the bar, but had tried not to think about it. Deciding to play dumb, he raised a brow. "You danced with Stephan?"

"Uhum." She yawned. "Around the time you got there. And my stomach even fluttered."

"Oh." His gut twisted and turned to lead, which was dumb considering that was the goal of all their fake stuff. "What did you feel when you danced with me?" Damn, the question was out before he could stop it.

Turning to face him, she grinned. "With you it was much stronger. Like a tornado with strong gusts, and a whole lot of thundering in my chest. Probably because my heart was pounding so hard." She smiled and got out of the car. "You are one potent guy, Vince Acardi," she stated, then shut the door.

Ah hell…

With her keys in his hand, he sprang from the car and caught up with her in the middle of the driveway. "A tornado, huh?" Smiling, he slipped his arm around her waist again—to steady her—he told himself as he walked with her to her side door.

"Yeah. An F5 because it was intense. Like your kisses." She fumbled in her purse.

Grinning, he jiggled her keys. "Are you looking for these?"

"Yes. I forgot you had them." She rolled her eyes. "My house key is on there."

Locating the key, he opened her door and helped her

inside because she needed help, not because he enjoyed the feel of her brushing against him.

He handed her the keys. "Here, you should put these back."

"Thanks." She dropped them in her purse. "It's a shame, though." She moved away from him to pull the strap over her head and set the purse on the counter.

"What is?"

She waved a hand between them. "The whole tornado F5 kiss thing."

It *was* a shame, and also amazing. But he was suddenly curious to know why she thought so, too. "Why is that a shame?"

"Because you're my 'casual' fake boyfriend," she said, making air quotes, "and we only go on 'casual' fake dates." Then she smiled a brilliant, beautiful smile that lit her whole face from within, and for a split second, he forgot how to breathe. "But...they haven't been fake for me. Confusing, yeah, but not fake, which is probably why it was confusing." She stepped closer and ran her hands up his chest. "And I have a great idea about where you can take me."

Something in her eyes made his blood run hot and completely dried out his throat.

"Where?" he asked, hardly recognizing his low tone.

"To bed," she said, shoving both hands in his hair while lifting up on tiptoe to capture his mouth for a kiss that rocked his world.

Uninhibited from the wine, no doubt, she demanded and gave with a hunger that shocked the hell out of Vince. Over and over she plundered, taking what she wanted, practically climbing up his body.

He knew it was wrong—knew he should pull away—but when her tongue slipped inside his mouth, all reason left his head in a fierce gust of need. An F5 equivalent that leveled his rationale and sent need spiraling through his body.

Chapter Sixteen

With a groan, Vince glided his hands down Emma's back to cup her sweet ass and crushed her close. She moaned and rocked against him. Stars exploded behind his eyes. He didn't think that was possible, but it happened. *Emma* happened. With her gorgeous body and a desire that matched his own.

Her hands were all over him, touching, caressing, driving him out of his mind. He wanted her. Bad. Which was equally bad, for several reasons. First and foremost, she wasn't sober. He'd never take advantage of her. And second, she was his brother's neighbor, and he had no intention of ruining that dynamic with what could only ever be a fling. He had to do the right thing.

So with a control born from years in the military, he broke the kiss and held her back at arm's length. "Emma, we need to stop."

She blinked up at him, confusion and desire clouding her blue eyes. "Why? Don't you want me?"

Swallowing a curse, he released her arms to cup her face in both hands. "Yes, with every last breath in my body."

A smile curved her lips and her palms returned to his chest. "Good. Then let's go to my room."

Damn. Sometimes doing the right thing sucked.

Letting go of her, he closed his eyes and blew out a breath, trying really hard to resist temptation. "I can't," he said, opening them again. "I don't want to hurt you, Emma. So, this is a bad idea. Besides, I'm not sure if it's you or the wine talking."

Her brow creased, then cleared as she glided a hand down his body. "The wine has nothing to do with wanting you."

Christ, she really was making it hard for him...and making him hard. Grabbing her wandering hand, he brought it to his mouth to kiss her knuckles. "But, since I'm not looking for a relationship, and you are looking for one with Stephan, it's better if we don't act on that." He released her hand to slip a finger under her chin and tip her face until their gazes met. "Do you understand?"

"Yes, I think so." She yawned.

Smiling, he let her go and stepped back. "Get some sleep. I'll see you after work tomorrow."

She nodded. "Okay. Maybe then we can have sex."

To say his heart stopped was an understatement, because it stopped, dropped to the floor, then bounced back up into his chest. It took him a full second to find his voice.

"Sure," he finally said, stepping back because he was teetering on the brink and it was obvious not everything he said got through to her. "I'll see myself out. Good night, Emma."

She yawned again. "Good night, Vince. See you tomorrow."

With a nod, he pivoted around and left her house, locking her door behind him. Inhaling the sweet night air, he breathed easier.

Now, she was safe from him making a mistake.

• • •

Returning home from work the next day, Emma tried to sneak into her house without the guys seeing her. The gate was open to Dom's backyard again, and she could hear them talking and laughing. She hadn't seen any of them since getting blitzed the night before, although, she highly doubted it fazed them.

Then there was Vince.

Lordy, how did she face the guy after propositioning him in her kitchen?

"Emma," Dom called. "Come on over."

Shoot.

Short of appearing rude, she couldn't ignore him. Maybe it wouldn't be so bad. Maybe she hadn't really said and done the things she vaguely remembered from last night.

Right, and pigs could fly.

Hell froze over.

And Macy became an introvert.

"Coming." Forcing her feet to change direction, she turned and headed for the open gate.

Once again, it was time to face the music. She was so tired of screwing up lately. Something had to give. Yes, she did crazy things around Vince. And yes, they were out of character, but, if Emma was honest, she kind of liked it. She liked having fun around him and with him.

Shame he was leaving next week. Her chest actually tightened at the thought.

Maybe she should take Macy's advice and enjoy spending time with him while he was here. Lord knew she wanted to. There. She admitted it to herself. Then took it a step further.

She liked Vince and wanted to date him for real.

Expelling a breath, she smiled. The world didn't end. Sky didn't fall. And it definitely felt good to be honest with herself. And while she was at it, she admitted to wanting to sleep with the sexy former Army Ranger, too. Even more weight lifted from her shoulders with that confession.

She'd never been more attracted to a man in her life. It would be foolish, wouldn't it...to let him go home without allowing herself to have fun with him in and out of bed?

Surely knowing ahead of time that he was leaving would keep her heart safe. They could only ever be casual, just like they were already pretending to be. That'd certainly be different than investing herself in a guy she planned a future with, only to have him leave without warning.

Maybe it was time to be in control of the "it's been fun" part.

And once he left, things should be okay for her and Stephan. She'd already started to catch his attention. And she'd still want to date him once Vince left.

Probably.

Damn. She was confused. She had no idea what the right thing was anymore.

Reaching the yard, she screwed up the courage to step inside and found all three men sitting at the table in their bathing suits, their broad chests bared for her viewing pleasure. Heat rushed into her face and her throat dried, but she didn't look away. Heck, she didn't even blink. Though each were perfect lust-worthy specimens, it was the sight of Vince's toned body that threatened her ability to breathe.

He sent her a sexy, lopsided grin. "Hey, Emma, come on over and have a seat."

Warmth spread through her body, leaving a tingling in its wake.

Returning his smile, she urged her shaky legs not to buckle. "Thanks," she said, a little breathless as she sat down. "I should probably apologize and explain about last night. Your brother—"

"Yeah, I know," her neighbor cut her off. "He thinks you're adorable."

Leo smiled from across the table. "And you think he's hot."

Shoot. "I'd hoped I'd imagined all of that stuff."

Vince's deep chuckle rumbled through her as he slid her a glass of iced tea.

"Thanks," she said and immediately took a sip, unable to look at him. Lifting her drink, she set it against her burning face. "Aside from acting like a fool, I had a good time last night." She turned to the man responsible. "I don't remember the last time I had so much fun. Thank you."

"No need to thank me," Vince said. "I had fun, too."

Her heart skipped a beat, giving her the courage to take a walk on the wild side.

"Want to have more?"

That seemed to surprise him because his brows rose, then knit together as uncertainty clouded his eyes. "Uh...where?"

Where, indeed? Where she really wanted him was stretched out naked in her bed, but his hesitancy gave her pause. Did he sense she was starting to like him for real and wasn't a fan of the idea?

"Dinner cruise," she blurted out, not willing to risk it. "Macy said she overheard Stephan mentioning he was going on a Boatwright Cruise tonight at seven."

Rising to his feet, he held his hand out to help her up. "Then we better get ready. I'll be over in twenty minutes."

Disappointment rippled through her. He didn't hesitate once she mentioned Stephan. Seemed she had her answer.

So much for a walk on the wild side.

He glanced at Leo. "Mind keeping an eye on my stubborn brother?"

"No problem."

"Your stubborn brother can keep an eye on himself."

Dom scoffed.

"Are you okay on a boat?" Vince asked her. "Do you get sick?"

"I don't get sick." She shook her head and decided to make the best of it. There were several boats and riverboats that cruised the Chattahoochee, and yet she'd never been on one with a date, even a pretend one. "I used to fish with my grandfather on his boat all the time. Even piloted it when I got older."

"You fish?" Leo asked, brows disappearing under his hair.

Emma nodded. "Yes, although, it's been a while. Too long." She hadn't gone much after her grandfather had passed.

Leo leaned closer to the table. "Do you have a sister?"

She laughed. "Nope. I'm an only child."

"How about a cousin?" Amusement flickered in his dark-blue eyes.

"Sorry." Still smiling, she lifted a shoulder. "He's married with two children."

Dom snickered. "Looks like you're shit out of luck, Leo."

He shook his head. "Figures."

"Cheer up, buddy," Vince said, devilment lighting his eyes. "I'm sure there's a woman out there just waiting to hit you with a door."

"Hey!" She smacked his arm with her free hand, her mood lifting under his teasing. "That wasn't my fault. It was an accident. I don't know why those doors open into the hall like that." She turned to face Leo. "What time do you leave tomorrow?"

Surprise raised his brow. "I'm going to head to the airport around three o'clock."

"Which means I probably won't see you, so have a safe trip." She walked around the table and held out her hand. "It was nice meeting you."

It was her turn to be surprised because he rose to his feet and pulled her in for a hug. "Nice meeting you, too," he said, then lowered his voice for only her to hear, "You'll never find a better guy than Vince."

She suspected it to be true. But he said that as if she and Vince were entering a real relationship, not a fake one. That wasn't in the cards, though she wouldn't mind a temporary one. Still, she nodded so Leo knew she'd heard him.

He drew back and released her. "Thanks for my pie."

"I'm glad you actually got a piece." She grinned, transferring her gaze to her neighbor. "No thanks to you."

Dom shrugged. "Pie whore, remember? I make no excuses."

No, he didn't. And that was one of the things she loved most about Dom.

"Well, if we're going on that cruise, I'd better get ready," she said, walking past Vince.

They didn't have a lot of time to get across town and board. She just hoped she didn't make another fool of herself tonight, because for her, the line between fake and real was definitely blurring.

• • •

The sun was setting, and a warm breeze blew through the open dining deck. Emma sat across from Vince while they finished their meal. He was sweet, and looked hot—*real* hot—dressed in jeans and a white button-down shirt with the sleeves rolled up. Her heart hadn't beat normal since he'd knocked on her door over an hour ago. Thank God she'd opted to wear a backless halter dress to combat the humidity, because her date sent her temperature into the stratosphere.

Tables covered in white tablecloths lined each side of the boat and overlooked the water, with larger tables scattered throughout the middle of the deck. A lit candle sat in the center of each, with a hurricane glass surrounding it to protect the flame from the wind.

She could relate. Unable to keep her traitorous body from dropping her guard, she had nothing to protect her from the heat in Vince's gaze. It had steadily warmed throughout the evening. Had she read too much into his hesitancy earlier? Because the vibe she was getting off him said he was happy they hadn't run into Stephan.

And she liked it. A lot.

As always, he was easy to talk to, and he listened to her with genuine interest in his eyes. They hadn't glazed over. Not once.

He got two points for that.

"You wanted to be a nurse, didn't you?" he asked out of the blue, perception ruling his gaze.

Emma widened her eyes. "How did you know?"

She'd never told anyone. Not even her mother.

A smile tugged his lips as he lifted a shoulder. "You have a caring nature."

"Ah, thanks." She returned his smile as the server freshened their iced tea. "Nursing was definitely something I'd wanted to do. But it's not for someone who can't stand needles."

He chuckled. "No, I guess not. I have a buddy who feels the same. Brick is a bear of a guy, and a big baby when it comes to needles."

"I can relate." She laughed. "I didn't know I had that issue until I cut myself on some glass when I was eighteen. Several stitches later, all my secret aspirations of nursing disappeared for good."

"Do you like what you do now?"

"Yes, I do," she said honestly. "I still get to work with doctors and help patients without dealing with wounds or blood or needles." Just talking about it made her a little queasy. She reached for her drink and changed the subject. "What about you? Do you miss active duty? The adrenaline rush? Helping people to safety?"

"At first, I did," he admitted, sitting back in his chair. "It was tough transitioning into a life without gunshots, constantly looking over your shoulder, or being relied upon to keep people safe. But the hardest part was retiring one man down."

Her heart squeezed. "Drew."

Sorrow darkened his gaze as he nodded.

Reaching across the table, she set her hand over his and squeezed. "I'm so sorry."

Living in Columbus and working on base, Emma had witnessed the toll it took on units when they came back from missions with casualties and deaths. They were scarred. Haunted. Walked around like there was a hole in their collective. It always broke her heart.

Having gotten close to Dom and his unit, Emma knew she'd take it harder should something ever happen to any of them. This past week proved it. Seeing Dom so bruised and banged up was tough.

"Thanks." Vince covered her hand with his free one as the small orchestra on the deck above them began to play. He smiled. "Shall we go up top and see if we can find *Stephan*?"

She nodded and rose to her feet. "I'm beginning to suspect we've been duped."

There hadn't been one sign of the guy since they'd boarded.

Vince chuckled. "Yeah. I think you received some bad intel."

"Don't worry. Killing Macy is top of my list of things to do at work tomorrow."

Or maybe thank her and promise to bake her a pie.

The delicious scrape of calluses from his hand on her bare back as they headed for the top deck made her warm all over. Since entertaining thoughts of giving in to her attraction to Vince, Emma noticed several things. The attraction felt stronger, and he made her feel good about herself. That was a first.

When they reached the dance floor, the band began to play some kind of folk song. Vince glanced around, then turned to face her. "I still don't see him." A devilish gleam entered his eyes and tripped her pulse. "But there's no reason to let a good band go to waste. You game?"

"Sure," she replied, happier than she should be in the knowledge he wanted to dance with her even though he knew he didn't have to.

Taking her hand, he guided her around the floor, with an ease that made her smile. Other's joined in, and soon the whole deck was full of laughing, dancing people of all ages, urging the band for more. Happy to comply, they played several similar songs in a row, and the fun continued. And after the last one, Vince pulled her in for a kiss, which perfectly embodied the dance—robust and pulse pounding, yet lighthearted.

Something Emma would never forget.

But when the songs eventually slowed down, she discovered that was when *unforgettable* happened.

Vince held her close, his hands caressing her bare back, up and down in delicious swirls while they swayed, cheek to cheek under the stars. And as the band continued to play, even after they docked, she closed her eyes and gave herself over to their incredible, pulsing connection.

Something between them shifted.

"Ready to go?" he asked near her ear when the song ended.

"Yes," she replied in a breathless voice, then nodded in

case he didn't hear.

Within minutes they were in his car. All the way home, he held her hand, resting it on his leg as if he didn't want to let her go. The brush of his thumb inside her palm drove her wild and completely dried her throat, making conversation impossible.

After he parked in Dom's driveway, he got out and came around to her side and opened her door. She smiled at him as he helped her to her feet.

"I had such a great time tonight." Sounded lame, but it was the truth.

He smiled. "So did I," he said and shut the door.

Together they walked to her house in silence. A heated silence that held an unspoken promise of an unforgettable night.

Emma's heart dipped to her belly. She'd never done anything like this before. Never hooked up with a guy she knew wasn't staying around. But, years ago, she'd let another great guy leave without taking a chance, then mooned over him for over a decade, wondering how it might've been.

Not this time.

Not with Vince.

Chapter Seventeen

When they reached her house, and he pulled her in for a deliciously sensual kiss that made her whole body tingle, Emma let go of control and gave in to the need pulsating through her veins. For several heart-pounding seconds, the mind-blowing kiss heated and consumed, until the need to breathe eventually took over and forced them to break for air.

His taste, his touch, were intoxicating and heaven help her, she wanted more. This was the tipping point. So she tipped in favor of fierce awareness, aching need, of Vince and the desire he induced.

With a shaky hand, she unlocked and opened her door, anticipation and excitement tripping her pulse as she grasped his hand to pull him inside.

He refused to budge.

"Not a good idea." Regret filled his heated gaze. "You deserve forever."

Still holding his hand, she squeezed. "What if I just want right now?"

His gaze narrowed as he searched her face. "Emma, you need to be sure."

She smiled. "I'm sure. And don't worry. I know you're going back to Texas soon." She tugged him inside, closed the door, then slid her hands up around his neck. "No regrets."

Instead of zapping her strength with one of his delicious kisses, he continued to study her, teetering on the edge. Before she could think twice, Emma leaned forward and brushed him with her curves, hoping to sway him to her side.

A groan rumbled deep in his chest, and the doubt and uncertainty disappeared from his eyes as he used that sexy, rock-hard body of his to press her against the door. "Oh, I can promise you, Emma, regret is the last thing you're going to feel tonight." Then he was kissing her, slow and tantalizingly deep, sweeping his tongue inside her mouth, as if staking a claim.

She moaned and brushed her tongue along his, needing to give as much as she took. And she took, running her hands down his shoulders to the front of his shirt and unfastening the buttons as quickly as possible. She needed to feel him, too. All of him.

Releasing her mouth, he helped her remove his shirt, and she shook in anticipation of finally getting to caress all those muscles and ridges.

She wasted no time getting her hands on him, loving the feel of his taut abs quivering under her touch. "I could eat you up," she said against his collarbone before nipping her way over to his shoulder.

"I was thinking the same thing." His fingers brushed the back of her neck, sending chills down her spine as he untied her dress, then he stood back to watch it fall to the floor. "God, you're even more beautiful than I imagined."

Feeling a little bit naughty standing under his gaze wearing nothing but blue satin bikini-cut panties and her strappy sandals, she also felt incredibly empowered by the heat in his eyes. "If you don't put your mouth on me soon, I might have to hit you."

A sexy, devilish grin dimpled his face as he glided his hands up her ribs to cup her breasts, brushing his thumbs over her sensitive peaks. Before she could protest—or praise—he backed her up against the door again.

"Anything for you," he murmured, dipping down, but instead of kissing her, he sucked a nipple into his mouth.

Gasping at the pure, unexpected pleasure, she thunked her head against the door and closed her eyes.

Praise. Definitely praise.

His mouth was warm, and his tongue flicked her sensitive tip while he gently pulled on the other with his forefinger and thumb. Desire slashed through her belly, straight to her core, and she clutched at his toned biceps, willing him to continue. As if knowing what she wanted, he switched his attention to the other, and she sighed at the sheer pleasure.

"Like that?" he asked, releasing her nipple.

She nodded and mumbled something that must've made sense because he smiled and kissed her nipple.

"Me, too." His lips blazed a path up her chest, throat, and jaw, until he finally covered her mouth with his, kissing her fast and hungry. Threading his fingers in her hair, he knocked the clip loose, and it fell to the floor with a light *clang.*

Heat flooded her belly, making her tremble—making her want more—so she slipped her tongue into his mouth, and a low, sexy sound rumbled in his throat.

Mmm…she liked that sound. A lot.

Removing a hand from her hair, he skimmed a path to the curve of her hip and over the top of her panties, where he slid a finger down the middle, rubbing the material against her sensitive flesh.

Emma broke the kiss and gasped.

"You're so wet," he said against her throat, then without warning, lifted her up and walked over to the island.

She squeaked when the cold counter connected with her heated skin, and a second later, she forgot her discomfort as he regarded her with a dark, smoldering gaze.

"We have unfinished business." He tucked his fingertips inside her panties and tugged the satiny fabric over her hips and down her legs without removing her sandals.

If she hadn't been so turned on, so needy, she probably would've felt self-conscious. "I agree." She trailed her hands up his arms to explore his sinewy shoulders. The man was hard and cut, but not overly pumped like some of the soldiers she saw doing physical training on her way to the office in the mornings.

Vince had a working man's build, which she preferred, and she showed him by running her hands down his torso, brushing her thumbs across his ridges along the way.

He groaned and caught her hands. "Later. I can't think when you touch me."

She was about to tell him she knew what he meant when he released her hands to lift one of her legs and kiss a path from her knee to her quivering thigh.

Need tingled through her body in a delish rush.

"Relax. Open up for me," he urged, his breath warm on her skin, while his fingers skimmed up and down her leg.

Emma didn't know what was more incredible, the scrape of his hands or his chin as both inched closer to where she ached for him the most.

"In fact, lie back and enjoy," he murmured. "I might be a while."

His words, delivered in a low, hungry tone, nearly set her off.

Taking his advice, Emma eased her back onto the counter and clutched the sides as he trailed kisses to her hip and across her stomach, swirling his tongue in her belly button on his way to the other side.

"So soft." He nipped and kissed some more before setting both her legs on his shoulders. "Damn, Emma." His sucked in a breath and gazed down at her. "You're so gorgeous."

Another flash of empowerment rushed through her as his eyes blazed with a need she felt to her core.

Then he brushed a finger over her center, once, twice, then slipped inside. "So wet."

She clutched the counter and moaned, and repeated the processes when he removed his finger in an upward motion.

"Yeah," he said, dipping down to kiss her upper thigh. "I'm definitely going to be a while."

Then he licked her.

Gasping, she lifted off the counter, but he didn't miss a beat, didn't stop, he just slipped his tongue inside and explored every bit of her while gently pressing her back down. Alternating between his finger and his tongue, the talented man had her panting and moaning inside of a minute.

He's great in the kitchen…

Tiffany's words resounded in Emma's head, and Emma wondered briefly just how many women he'd been great with in the kitchen, but then he upped his pace and did something amazing with his tongue. All thoughts disappeared as her world narrowed to what he was doing and how he made her feel—decadent, and sensual, and worshipped.

Closing her eyes, she rocked her hips, matching his pace as heat spiraled through her. Mmm…he was good. So good. And she was so close. Already.

"Vince." She forced her eyes open and stared at him. "If you don't stop I…"

"It's what I want," he uttered, his gaze so dark it appeared almost black. "Lose yourself for me."

Then his mouth was on her again, licking and sucking

and driving her out of her mind. And when he changed the angle of his stroking tongue and held her between his finger and thumb, she indeed lost it, crying out his name as she burst into a million-and-one pieces.

He let her down slowly before removing his mouth to place a kiss to each of her inner thighs, working his way to her left knee and back. "You taste amazing," he said against her skin.

Finding a smidgen of strength, she lifted onto her elbows and met his gaze. "You were the amazing one, Vince." She smiled. "I was the one lying back and enjoying, remember?"

Satisfaction gleamed in his eyes, turning them a rich amber. "Trust me, you weren't the only one who enjoyed that. Thank you for giving yourself to me."

"Thank you for giving me such an amazing orgasm."

"My pleasure." A wicked grin crossed his face. "But I'm far from done with you." Heat still smoldered in his eyes as he lightly brushed a finger over her center.

Emma's heart rocked in her chest, then thundered out of control as he started to take her out of herself again. She knew their attraction was intense, and being with him would be amazing, but the things he was doing, the way her body responded so easily—so quickly to his—blew her mind.

It was something she'd never expected, never knew existed, and as he brought her to climax a second time, she realized he was ruining her for other men, because she might never get enough of him.

• • •

The sound of his name on Emma's lips was the most incredible thing Vince had ever heard. And her taste? Damn, he'd never get enough, not as long as he lived. But this wasn't forever, so he was going to enjoy what she wanted to give him right now.

And right now, he needed to be inside her.

As she trembled on the counter, working to catch her breath, he quickly shucked the rest of his clothes and grabbed a condom from his wallet. The sight of her lush body, glistening and shaking with aftershocks, made him harder than hell. He needed to sink into her heat more than he needed air.

Focusing on the floor, he inhaled, then exhaled slowly in an attempt to regain some control. Their date tonight had been incredible. Their *real* date, because that's what it had turned out to be. Once Emma had let her guard down and let him in, let him see the real her, he discovered everything he'd expected to find. A warm, thoughtful, funny, vibrant woman. She made him smile and laugh, and he enjoyed making her smile and laugh, too.

But his favorite thing was making her pant and call out his name as he satisfied her.

Damn…it made him feel…amazing, on top of the world, like nothing he'd ever felt before.

He needed to do it again, but this time, Vince wanted to be inside her, wanted to satisfy them both.

"Let me," she said, slipping off the counter, her beautiful breasts bouncing in front of him as she grabbed the condom from his hand.

Not daring to breath, he stood still while she slowly rolled it on, taking her good-natured time doing it, too. Testing his control with a few strokes along the way.

"Emma," he ground out through his teeth, then crushed her close and kissed her, hot and wild and frantic.

She moaned and rubbed her breasts back and forth against his chest. Damn, that felt good. *She* felt good. Need throbbed through his groin. The sound and feel of her pleasuring herself with his body was nearly too much. Ah, hell. He wasn't going to last.

In a quick move, he swept her off her feet and carried her

to the couch in her open-concept living room. No way would he make it down the hall to her bedroom. "Is this okay?" he asked, setting her on the cushions.

She moved to the floor instead, and smiled up at him. "Perfect."

Wasting no time, he crawled up her body, kissing and licking his way to her gorgeous breasts, paying extra attention to her tight peaks. She moaned and writhed beneath him. He liked that. A lot. Again and again, he tweaked and sucked, until she clutched his shoulders.

"Vince...I need you in me." She spread her legs in an open invitation. "Now."

Lifting his head from her breast, he stared into her desire-laden eyes. They were so dark, they appeared almost navy. "Anything you want." He positioned himself at her center, and still holding her gaze, pushed all the way in.

Damn...he'd never felt anything so good. So sweet. So... Emma.

He knew being inside this amazing woman would rock his world, but it was beyond anything he could've imagined.

"Vince," she murmured on a hitched breath, her body arching off the carpet. "Faster. Harder."

Not wanting to mar her supple skin with rug burns, he gathered her to him and leaned back until his ass rested on his calves and her inner thighs brushed his hips.

"Oh...wow," she choked out, a decadent smile on her lips. "I can feel so much of you."

Cupping the soft cheeks of her gorgeous ass while she gripped his shoulders, he began to thrust, loving the sexy, low moans he ripped from her throat.

She captured his mouth, kissing him fast and hungry and deep, her body matching his movements. The incredible woman drove him mad, with her peaked nipples scraping against his chest in delicious tandem.

So beautiful and giving and demanding.

Her tongue tangled with his, and he groaned, pumping into her harder and faster. Soon, heat skittered down his spine and tingled through his balls. Release was close, too close; he wanted this to last forever. Wanted to enjoy her decadent body and the feel of her slick heat surrounding him.

But she felt too damn good.

Drawing back, he kissed a path to her shoulder and sunk his teeth near the curve of her neck. She cried out and rode him harder.

Ah, hell. He was done.

Sliding his hand between them, he brushed his thumb over her center and she instantly flew apart, calling his name again and spurring his own fierce release.

After a few brief but amazing seconds, they dropped down to the floor, still tangled together. He held her close as they worked to catch their breath, her body shaking with little aftershocks like she had on the counter. A thrill ran through him knowing he was the cause.

Brushing her damp hair aside, he kissed her forehead. "That was amazing."

"That was…I…wow." She drew in a breath. "We have some killer chemistry."

Something she was not going to find with Stephan, of that he was damn sure.

Vince's gut knotted, but he pushed thoughts of the doctor and her possible future with the man aside, determined to concentrate on the present. Tonight. Right now.

"That we do." As much as he hated to pull out of her, it was time. "Where's your bathroom?"

"First door on the left." She pointed down the hall.

Reluctantly, he left her to go take care of business. Then he returned to the kitchen to grab his phone and text Leo to make sure he wasn't needed next door. When he received the all good sign, he told his buddy he'd see him in the morning before shoving his phone back in his jeans. While there, he dug out the other two condoms from his wallet. They might not have forever, but they did have tonight.

He was far from done with Emma and their killer chemistry.

Chapter Eighteen

The next morning, Emma woke up in bed, sore in places she'd never been sore in before. As the night and all her hot Vince activity rushed through her mind, she smiled and reached for him.

The bed was empty.

He was gone already?

She opened her eyes, fighting off disappointment and hurt, when the smell of bacon registered in her brain.

Her stomach rumbled. The man was the root of both of her hungers.

And her satisfactions.

Chuckling, she glanced at the clock on her nightstand and noted there was still an hour left before she had to go to work. Good. She got out of bed and made a quick stop in the bathroom before heading out to the kitchen in search of her chef extraordinaire.

She found him by her stove, barefoot, shirtless, wearing a pair of jeans he must've hastily pulled on, because when he turned around, she noted they were zipped but not buttoned.

"Good morning, beautiful," he said, then his eyes widened and his mouth dropped open as he took in her naked state. "Damn...you take my breath."

Smiling, she walked to him. "Allow me to give it back." She wrapped her arms around his neck and kissed him just how she'd learned he liked it, slow and deep.

His firm hands cupped her backside, and she rocked into him. A tortured sound rumbled in his throat a second before he took over the kiss, zapping her brain cells left and right.

When they finally broke for air, he smiled down at her. "That's what I call a good morning." Then he blinked and muttered a curse. "Damn. I forgot about the eggs." He let her go to shut off the stove. "They're burnt. Sorry. I've never done that before." He walked to the oven and removed a tray of bacon.

"It's okay." She followed him and lifted a hand to grasp his chin and turn his face her way. "It wasn't eggs I was hungry for."

Heat flashed through his eyes and his lips twitched. "Oh? Care to tell me what entrée you'd like me to prepare?"

She unzipped his jeans, then pushed them down to his ankles. Before he could respond, she dropped to her knees and helped him step out of his pants, thrilled to find him naked and ready underneath. "I think I can prepare it myself."

"Is that right?"

With a few strokes, she watched his erection bob in affirmation. "Yep." Grasping his hips, she leaned in to trace his sexy V with her lips before licking her way down the happy trail. "Most definitely." Encouraged by the feel of his hands on her head, she placed kisses down his length, all the way to his tip, before taking him into her mouth.

His sharp inhale echoed through the kitchen. "Damn, that feels good."

Happy to be on the giving side for a change, she repeated

the process several times before releasing him to rise to her feet. "I have an idea."

Grabbing his hand, she led him across the kitchen toward the bench along the wall and used her hip to shove the table aside. Adrenaline and need shook through her as she pushed him onto the bench before dropping back to her knees.

"Emma," he said, but she reached up to place a finger over his lips.

"Just relax." She grinned and glided both of her hands over his thighs, licking her lips as she stared at his erection jutting out thick and long and proud. "I might be a while."

Then she showed him just how good *she* could be in the kitchen.

• • •

All day, Vince couldn't get rid of the image of a gorgeous, naked Emma kneeling between his legs as she melted every last bone in his body. He couldn't keep the smile from his face, either. A fact his brother noted the instant he'd walked in that morning. Thankfully, Leo had been in the kitchen, too, so it prevented his brother's tirade.

Oh, it was coming.

As sure as Christmas.

He was certain, but he knew his brother. Dom never argued in front of people. If he had a beef with someone, he took them aside and had it out in private. Vince respected that—and his brother's opinion—but he didn't want to hear it right now. Especially since it wasn't going to be favorable.

So he'd nodded to them and headed upstairs to grab a shower before taking his brother to physical therapy. As if knowing he was some sort of buffer, his buddy tagged along.

Leo was a good friend.

And Vince told him that when they sat in the hospital

cafeteria drinking coffee while Dom was in therapy.

Of course, Leo shrugged it off. "Nothing you and the guys wouldn't do for me. We have each other's backs."

"Always." He nodded, noting a slight smirk to his friend's lips.

"I take it all went well on your *date*?"

Leo wasn't fishing for details. It was an unspoken rule between them. No. His buddy was more interested in his mindset. "Yeah, great."

The woman was fun and beautiful, and she listened with interest when he talked about his work. Curiosity had filled her gaze during dinner, then later, when they'd danced, enjoyment had replaced the curiosity, and later still, a fierce hunger had deepened the hue of her baby blues. And ruled his heartbeat.

Leo's brows rose. "That good, huh?"

He blinked and brought his mind back to their conversation. "Let's just say, better than I even expected."

"Bet I know why." Leo regarded him steadily from across the table. "Because you think she's adorable and she thinks you're hot."

He chuckled. "Smart-ass."

No sooner had the words left his lips than his phone buzzed with a text. He removed it from his pocket and sighed. Another shortened therapy session. "The master beckons."

It wasn't until later, much later, after Vince had returned from the store with groceries for dinner—and a box of condoms—that he let his mind drift back to the reason for needing the condoms. He hid a smile as he put away the food.

An image flashed through his mind of a wet, soapy, lush Emma, suds running down her bouncing breasts as he pressed her against the shower wall and thrust inside her.

Yeah, now that he'd had a taste of her, and knew she wanted more, too, he definitely needed the condoms. They were going to enjoy the ten days he had left. He'd make sure of it. Picking up the box, he sprinted upstairs while Dom was in the living room and Leo was packing. Since his brother had an issue with him dating Emma for real, there was no need to leave ammunition lying around to set the guy off.

When Vince returned to the kitchen, he found Dom leaning against the counter, drinking a glass of water. His gaze flicked to Vince, but he didn't say anything. Just scowled.

Whatever. It was Dom's problem. Not his.

Leo entered the kitchen with his duffel bag slung over his shoulder. "Time I headed to the airport." He walked over to Dom and held out his hand. "Thanks for having me."

"No, thank you for helping me track down Amir," his brother said, shaking his friend's hand. "I really appreciate it."

"Glad I could help." Releasing Dom's hand, Leo adjusted the strap. "Take it easy, unless you're back in the sandbox. Then give 'em hell."

Dom nodded. "Roger that."

"I'll walk you to your car." Tired of his brother's dark looks, Vince moved to the door.

Once outside, Leo snickered. "Man, Cord and his intensity have nothing on Dom."

"Don't I know it." He smirked. "He's stewing, and I'm pretty sure I know why."

"Emma?"

"Yes," he replied as they passed his rental and walked to Leo's. "Dom's pissed we went from fake to real. But he'll get over it."

Because it was only temporary.

Reaching his car, Leo opened the door to the back seat and tossed his bag inside before shutting it to face him. "Well, guess I'll see you in a week or so."

Vince nodded. "Dom's had a week of therapy under his

belt and regained some mobility, so I can only assume, by next week, he will have improved that much more. And if he's still not able to drive by Friday, I'll fly in after his therapy, then return here on Sunday."

"Sounds feasible," Leo said. "Although, I don't see your brother being down that long."

"Me, either. He's too stubborn." Vince pulled his buddy in for a back-slapping handshake. "Thanks for picking up my slack at work."

"No problem," Leo said, stepping back. "Just be careful, Vince."

Knowing the guy was referring to Emma and not Dom, he nodded. "Always."

A smile tugged at his friend's lips. "Yeah? What about that time in Cairo?"

"Hey." He sent him a mock scowl. "You can't pin that on me. I thought she told me to dance with her cousin."

His buddy laughed. "Man, they were fighting over you pretty good."

"That was crazy." He shook his head. "And a big misunderstanding. There's nothing to misinterpret with Emma."

"I hope not," Leo said, getting into the car. "Just watch your six. And hers."

"I will," Vince said, "but she's on the same page." That would keep them safe.

Leo waved as he backed out of the driveway, then disappeared down the road.

Over the past two days, Vince had observed the guy in several situations and locations, and not once had his buddy shown signs of inner turmoil, depression, repression, or anger. Leo was coping and coming along well. Vince made a mental note to call Stone to tell him.

But right now, since his buffer was gone, he had to deal

with Mr. Stick-up-his-ass alone.

Back inside, while waiting for his brother to say something, Vince tossed together a big dish of lasagna for dinner. Emma's favorite. Something he'd discovered over pillow talk last night. It was also when he'd asked her to come over for supper after work today.

Not the best idea, he knew. Certainly not the smartest, but he didn't care. They all had to eat anyway.

The whole time he worked, Dom sat at the island, grumbling under his breath while supposedly reading the paper. After the third time in forty minutes, Vince decided it was going to be up to him. Shaking his head, he shoved the tray into the oven and slammed the door.

"All right." He twisted around and stared his brother down. "Out with it. What the hell is bothering you?"

Chapter Nineteen

"You slept with her." Dom slid off the stool, faster than he probably should've since the idiot turned white. "I can't believe you slept with her. After I asked you not to. Dammit, Vince. What the hell were you thinking? Wait, I know, you weren't thinking with the head on your shoulders."

"That's enough," he ground out through clenched teeth. He understood most of his brother's aggression stemmed from worry about his men and was pissed he wasn't with them, but Vince refused to let him insinuate he was using Emma to get his dick wet. "What the hell is so wrong with Emma and I hooking up? Unless you *do* have feelings for her."

"No. I told you, it's not like that," Dom insisted. "She's a friend. A damn good one, and she's been hurt too many times. I was here for the last one. I don't want to see her go through the pain again."

He scrubbed a hand over his face. "Jesus, Dom. I'm not going to hurt her. Yes...this is temporary, but she knows it and I know it. We enjoy being together and we want to have fun. I haven't had fun in a long time. Not since Connie. I know we were young, but I loved her. I would've died for her. But she died first and left me with a big gaping hole in my chest, because a piece of me died with her, too."

Dom exhaled. "I know."

"I buried the rest away, threw myself into training and missions, and lived for keeping my Ranger brothers alive."

Over time, physical need became too much and the groupies too amorous, so he eventually sated that need. But Vince had always been upfront with the women. He never lied. Never felt anything for them, either.

"Now, for the first time in years, I've found a woman I want to see more than once. Those parts aren't so buried when Emma's around." She made him feel things again. And he liked it. "So, while I understand and appreciate your concern for Emma, part of me wishes you'd be a little bit happy for your damn brother."

Silence stretched for several beats and Vince used the time to get his anger under control. A useless emotion. One he rarely entertained. It didn't do anyone any good.

Dom folded his arms across his chest and stared at him. "What makes you think my concern is only for her?"

He blinked as surprise washed through him.

"I was there when you got the news about Connie. I saw what you went through. What it did to you." Full-blown concern darkened Dom's gaze. "I watched you bury that part down so deep, I didn't think you'd ever find it again. But over the past week, I've seen some of it resurrected, and I have to be honest, it's scaring the hell out of me."

It scared him, too.

"I'm fine." He smiled. "Quit worrying."

Dom's arms dropped to his sides. "Fine? Just because you don't intentionally mean to hurt her, or think you'll ever get hurt, doesn't make it fine. There's nothing fine about it.

It's far from fine."

Vince stilled and studied his brother, noting the tight jaw and the way his brother's gaze darted back and forth, signaling agitation more than anger. And then there was the fact his brother mentioned the word "fine" four times.

Who had his brother so worked up?

"So, care to tell me who we're talking about, because that had nothing to do with me and Emma."

Dom stiffened. "I don't want to talk about it," he grumbled.

Had to be a woman. But his brother hadn't been anywhere other than here or at the hospital for therapy and doctor appointments...

Wait.

It suddenly made sense. The shortened appointments, long appointments, rescheduled appointments, yeah, something was definitely going on between Dom and the beautiful doctor who effectively put his brother in his place the day Vince had arrived to pick him up. He grinned, but one glance at his brother's clamped jaw told him not to press it.

Blowing out a breath, Dom turned a shrewd gaze on him. "Let's get back to Emma. I want to know what you think is going to happen to her when you're no longer with her? No longer here? Come on, man. You don't live in Georgia. Your life is in Texas, and it's a good life. It's the right place for you. I've seen it change you, in a good way. Hell, Leo told me you're the glue that keeps that place together. They need you, and you need them. Are you going to give that up?"

Leo said that?

Something akin to pride spread through his chest.

Life outside of Joyful, Texas, had never been on Vince's radar. He was invested and vested in the ranch and the good they were doing there.

He shook his head. "No. Like I told you, this is just temporary, Dom. She knows I'm going back to Texas. As a matter of fact, she literally told me that before we took things further. So it's all right. We're on the same page."

"Then you're setting yourself up to fail. And for you *and* her to get hurt, whether you want to admit it or not. This thing between you and Emma has no future, but your chemistry is strong, and that makes what you're doing dangerous. *That's* why I'm pissed. More at myself than anything. I never should've pushed you to date her."

Vince ran a hand through his hair. "Look, no one knows what the future holds. Believe me, I'm living proof." He was also proof that playing it safe wasn't living. It was time to change that. "I'm not looking for forever, and neither is Emma."

"Are you sure about that?" Dom asked. "Because, as I recall, she was looking for forever with Stephan when you blew into town."

He ignored the fact those words caused his gut to clench as if punched, and answered honestly. "And she'll probably still have that. But right now, she wants this, and I want this, so we're going to live for the moment for a change, and not worry about the future beyond today."

Dom blew out a breath and shook his head. "I hope you know what you're doing."

"So do I."

His brother's lips twitched. "Do I get a piece of that lasagna when it's done?"

A change in the subject. Dom's way of saying he was stepping off his soapbox and done interfering.

Vince rubbed his jaw. "Depends."

"On what?"

A smile threatened to ruin his serious expression. "On whether you get the kitchen cleaned up before Emma gets here."

"Me?" Dom's brows rose with his tone.

"Yeah." He grinned. "I'm going to jump in the shower."

Without waiting, Vince left his brother in the kitchen with all the dirty pots and pans, and some things to digest. He had some digesting to do, too. Like the fact his brother had been more worried about him than Emma. Yeah, he was still processing that one. But, hopefully, he put his brother's fears to rest. There was no way he would hurt Emma and she wasn't going to hurt him.

So why waste time worrying?

. . .

It was Saturday morning, the day of the bake sale, and for the first time in a long time, Emma was excited about the weekend. Thanks to Vince. The more they spent time together, the more it felt as if she'd known him her whole life. It was unreal how he remembered her likes and dislikes. Between food and flowers and songs and movies and…sex?

Yeah. She smiled. The sex was amazing.

Heat rushed through Emma, tingling all her good parts. Vince knew her body better than she did. He was a master and magnificent. And so giving. Even now, just thinking about the man, she ached for him.

She'd see him soon enough. She was heading next door in a few minutes, although not for any "hot stuff." All the baked goods were there, and they needed to get them loaded in the car. Quickly tying her wraparound dress, she smiled. Vince had helped her bake next door, then returned to her house to heat up the sheets. He'd only run back to Dom's for a quick shower and to make sure his brother was up.

Yesterday, Dom had finished his second week of rehab. Even though he was slowly winning the battle over his muscle spasms, he wasn't cleared to drive yet. But he could sit and stand for longer periods of time now, and had insisted Vince didn't need to stay with him at night anymore.

A noticeable attitude adjustment.

Her neighbor executed a one-eighty where she and his brother were concerned. It was as if he took a step back and kind of gave them his blessing to hang out. In fact, he'd been the one to insist they use his kitchen to bake last night. Lucky bugger had a double oven, so she gladly took him up on the offer. Although, she knew the real reason. Dom's sweet tooth. He sampled all their goods. Some twice.

With a lightness to her steps, she headed next door, slipping her purse across her body along the way.

"Morning, Emma," Dom said, carrying a tray of her pineapple squares.

She rushed to take them from him. "Let me help."

He sidestepped her. "No need. I'm more than capable of carrying these. You can, however, open your car door."

Doing as she was told, she frowned. "But you're not supposed to lift anything."

"I'm not. I'm carrying them." He nodded to the covered tray. "And before you complain about that, my restriction for carrying is five pounds or more. This tray does not weight that. I've got these, go ahead inside and grab more."

So she did, and within minutes, the car was almost loaded. Just two more trips and they'd be good to go. She was approaching Vince and the open trunk with two containers of chocolate chip cookies in her arms when her phone rang.

"I got these," he said, grabbing the cookies.

"Thanks." She smiled and fished her phone from her purse. "Hi, Mom. How are you and Aunt Katherine?"

"We're good, hun. How are you? Did Stephan ask you out yet?"

She stiffened. "No, not yet."

"Well hang in there. You still have almost a week left," her mom said.

Her deadline. She'd almost forgotten about it.

She must've been standing there with her mouth open because Vince took one look at her and frowned. Emma forced a smile and shook her head to let him know nothing was wrong.

Although forgetting about Stephan because she was starting to fall for Vince was sort of an issue.

"Not to worry," her mother said. "I'm directing all my thoughts and energy toward wishing you well with Stephan."

Great, although she didn't need them. She had a feeling she would need them because Vince would be out of her life in a week.

Pain stabbed at her heart at the thought of his absence. She rubbed her chest to ease the ache.

"So, what are your plans for today?" her mother asked.

"The bake sale," she replied.

"That's today? Oh. I'd better let you go. I was just touching base again. Good luck with your sale."

After the line went dead, Emma inhaled and shoved the phone back in her purse. She'd worry about picking her plan to date Stephan back up after Vince was gone. Her stomach rolled, so she forced the conversation out of her mind. She only had a few days left with Vince, and there wasn't any room for guilt or negativity.

"Everything okay?" he asked.

"Yes. She was just checking in." She nodded. "Are we good to go?"

He slammed the trunk shut. "That we are."

"Well, you two have fun," Dom said, sounding like he thought it would be anything but.

Vince opened the driver's door, then grabbed her hand and kissed it as he helped her in. "We will."

Warmth washed away the chill her mother's call created. She loved that he had no issue with her driving, and was excited to share one of her favorite days with him. A few minutes passed while she enjoyed the aroma of their cargo, and the feel of Vince's hand on her knee.

"Thanks for helping me last night. You know, with the baking...and stuff." She smiled at him as she drove through town.

After baking, they'd gone to her house and showered off the flour, spending extra time on each other's bodies and making sure they were good and satisfied with the results.

"My pleasure." He returned her smile. "It's my new favorite thing."

She chuckled. "What? Baking?"

"No. You," he said, lightly brushing his little finger over the inside of her knee.

Awareness shot straight to her core. "Ditto."

Since she was pulling into the rec center, she let the conversation drop, hoping it would drop her heart rate back to normal, too. They were there to sell baked goods to raise money for the troops. Her out-of-control desire for the guy needed to take a back seat.

And for most of the morning, she managed to do just that, thanks to the task of setting up, then a constant flow of customers. To her amazement, she discovered Vince was just as proficient at peddling their goods as he had been at making them.

Although, she shouldn't have been surprised. He was a capable man in every sense of the word. A doer, not a slacker.

"Emma, Vince, hi." Chelsea bounded toward them, glancing around. "Is Dom here?"

Emma's heart kind of constricted for the poor girl, knowing that if her neighbor had been there, he would've hid in the bathroom to avoid the eager woman. "No. He's not here. Sorry."

Disappointment washed the smile from the cute brunette's face. "Oh. Well, how's he doing this week?"

"Improving. He can sit and stand a little longer." Vince grabbed a container and loaded it with a few items. "He's at home alone right now. Why don't you take this to him? I'm sure he'd appreciate it."

The woman's face brightened. "Okay. I will," she said, grabbing the container. "What do I owe you?"

"Nothing." Vince grinned. "It's on me."

Chelsea's smile broadened. "Thank you. Thanks a lot." Eagerness, once again, ruled her features as she turned around and rushed toward the exit.

Grinning, Emma slapped his shoulder. "You're bad. Dom's going to kill you."

Vince chuckled. "He can try."

A grin twitched her lips. "Am I bad for wishing I could be there to see his face?"

"No. I'd say you're just right."

So was he. She held his gaze as he held her hand, and the longer they stood there smiling at each other, the more her chest swelled with warmth.

"Hi, Emma, dear."

Blinking, she tugged her hand from Vince's and turned to find her favorite octogenarian stepping up to the front of the table.

"Mrs. Henderson. Hi. Nice to see you." She smiled at her second-grade teacher. "Do you want your usual?"

For ten years the woman had come to the fundraiser and bought the same baked goods.

"Yes, please," her former teacher replied. "You look beautiful today. Even more so than normal. I'm guessing this young man is to blame?"

Heat surged into Emma's face as she introduced the two

and started to put the woman's order together.

"Emma looks beautiful every day," Vince said.

With her heart swelling in her chest, she glanced up at him and smiled. She was really—*really*—beginning to like him.

"You're a very perceptive young man," Mrs. Henderson said.

He grinned, exposing his full dimples. "Thank you, ma'am. I try."

That hooked Mrs. Henderson. Emma could tell by the gleam in the older woman's eyes.

"And you have manners, too. Your mama raised you right. It's nice to see."

"Thank you, ma'am," he repeated.

"Emma's mama did, too," her teacher said. "Emma's an angel. Do you know she comes over to my house every spring and helps me with my garden?"

He shook his head. "No. I didn't know that. But I'm not surprised. Emma has a good heart."

"Yes, she does. And she helps my neighbor Mr. Ross with his Christmas decorations because he can't get up and down the ladder too good anymore."

Emma added two brownies to the six chocolate chip cookies in the container. "Sometimes Dom helps, too."

In fact, they helped several senior citizens in their neighborhood with outdoor decorations.

Mrs. Henderson grinned. "That Dominic is a good guy."

"Vince is his brother," Emma said, patting his shoulder.

The older woman narrowed her shrewd gaze on him. "Yes, I can see a slight resemblance. Are you a military man, too?"

"Former, ma'am. Now I run a ranch that helps transition veterans."

Mrs. Henderson nodded with what looked like approval.

"Admirable. It's so nice to know Emma finally found a man who is worthy of her."

Heat returned to Emma's cheeks. Yes. Vince was certainly a worthy candidate. Worthy enough that she had begun to question her no-military-men policy.

"Are you two coming back for the movie in the park tonight?" Mrs. Henderson continued. "They're showing Emma's favorite Bogart movie out back on their building. Everyone sits on blankets under the stars. It's very romantic." She gave them a dreamy smile.

Vince turned to her. "Would you like to go?"

She nodded. "I'd like that." She'd like a lot of things.

"That's nice." Mrs. Henderson nodded toward Vince. "You hang on to this one, Emma. He's a keeper."

Her heart squeezed uncomfortably. Whether that was true or not, by next week at this time, Vince would be gone.

He wasn't hers to keep.

· · ·

Several hours later, Emma squirmed her sweet ass against Vince's groin, hugging the arms he'd banded around her. Damn. He held his breath and counted to ten. Ranger training should've included this type of torture because he was positive, with this woman, any sane man would break. He was barely hanging on by a thread.

"You make an excellent chair," she told him, shifting again.

Sure was the best kind of torture, though.

The movie played on the back of the rec center building, while speakers dotted the grassy area full of movie-goers sprawled out on blankets. Theirs was spread out under a tree, and he was leaning back against the trunk with his soft, warm woman nestled in front of him.

His woman.

That was a dangerous thought. One he needed to push aside, especially since he liked the sound of it. But was he really worthy of her?

Mrs. Henderson seemed to think so. And she was well respected. Plus, he did admirable, fulfilling work on the ranch. Still, did that make him worthy? Was anyone?

"I could sit here all night," she said on a soft sigh.

God knew he wanted to be. Tightening his hold, he kissed her head. "Me, too. But if you keep squirming like that, we may get arrested for indecent exposure."

She chuckled and turned her face his way. "Then we better save the indecent stuff for my place."

"Deal." He dipped her back and captured her mouth for a deep, tantalizing kiss, savoring her exquisite taste, loving her soft sighs.

After several thorough seconds, he forced himself not to be too selfish, broke the kiss, and let her settle back against him again to watch the movie.

The more time he spent with the woman, the more time he wanted to spend with her. Maybe he could leave Texas and come here. The pros would be he'd have Emma and Dom. And Emma and Dom would still have each other, too. She'd also have her friends and her job.

He didn't like the thought of her giving that up for him. Hell, he didn't want her to give anything up. He wanted her happy.

But would *he* be happy here, Emma and Dom aside?

Could he walk away from At-Ease Ranch and all the veterans he'd gotten to know, cook for, listen to? The crew at Foxtrot he supervised?

His stomach knotted at the thought.

What about Stone, Leo, and the rest of his Ranger unit? Could he leave them? That knot twisted tighter.

And what would he do here for work? Construction? Probably. He could contact the base to find some kind of community service or something to help with veterans. But it wouldn't be a twenty-four-seven thing, and he needed that in his life.

But asking her to move to Texas meant she'd lose the things she loved, too.

Was he worth that?

Tightening his hold on her again, he closed his eyes. He wasn't sure what to do. Didn't know what was right or fair.

He had no damn clue, other than he had started to suspect he wasn't going to be able to just walk away from her.

Christ. Maybe Dom was right.

You're setting yourself up to fail, Vince. And for you and her to get hurt.

He hoped that wasn't true.

All week, red flags had constantly gone off in his head. Just like now, he'd pushed them into a dark corner of his mind and tried to ignore how big that pile of red flags had gotten. But sooner or later, they were going to come back and bite him in the ass.

Emma hugged his arms tighter, tipped her head back to look at him, and smiled.

He couldn't help but smile back. "What?"

"Just enjoying the view."

His hollowed chest swelled at the warmth and affection softening her gaze.

She deserved his undivided attention. He'd worry about red flags and pros and cons later. Holding Emma in his arms was too amazing to ruin with negative thoughts.

Chapter Twenty

Emma was falling for Vince.

Correction. She'd already fallen for him.

Hard.

A military guy, albeit former military, but still. Who was she and what had she done with Emma?

After another night of incredible passion turned into a midmorning romp, she wanted to do something special for him, so when the sexy man headed next door to check on Dom—under the guise of needing to shower and change—she dressed quickly and rushed over there, hoping to catch her neighbor while Vince was upstairs.

Knocking on the door, she mentally crossed her fingers for luck.

Dom opened the door and surprise lifted his brow. "Emma? What are you doing here?"

"Hello to you, too." She chuckled, stepping inside.

Smiling, he shut the door and turned to her. "Haven't you had enough of my brother? He just got back from your place. He's upstairs in the shower."

That brought decadent memories to her mind. With extreme effort, she pushed them aside. "Actually, I wanted to talk to you."

He narrowed his gaze. "To apologize for letting Vince send Chelsea here yesterday?"

She laughed. "Sorry, but I don't control your brother. And that's not why I'm here."

"He's an idiot." Dom snorted. "So what's this about then? Is something wrong?"

"No." She shook her head. "Everything is great. Your brother is always doing stuff for me. So I want to cook him dinner tonight, but it dawned on me that he knows my favorite meal, but I don't know his. I was hoping you did."

"Ah." He headed for a stool. "Besides our mother's chicken cacciatore, the only thing that comes to mind that he probably doesn't have often is pierogi."

A lightbulb went off in her head. "That's right. He did seem disappointed when Leo mentioned...I think it was Beth? When she made it last week."

Dom nodded. "Yeah. Go with that."

Emma happened to have the perfect recipe. A family one. She used to make them with her grandfather, whose mother was from Poland. "Thanks. I will." Excitement skittered through her. "Think you can keep him occupied for a few hours?"

He laughed. "I'll try, but it's hard to keep him away from you these days."

Heat rose to her face. "Sorry. I don't mean to take up all his time."

"Don't be sorry." He shook his head. "In fact, I want to thank you."

"Thank me? For what?"

Dom's gaze turned serious. "For putting the smile back on his face."

Why? What had taken away his smile?

The sound of footsteps on the stairs had Emma swallowing her questions. Now, more than ever, she was glad she decided to do something nice for the guy entering the kitchen.

"Emma." His whole face brightened when he saw her.

Once again, hope stirred in her chest. Maybe he was falling for her, too. "You caught me." She smiled and walked over to him. "I was asking your brother to keep you occupied while I cooked you dinner."

Pleasure lit his gaze. "You're going to cook for me?"

"Yes." She slid her hands up his chest, while his hands settled on her hips. "Don't look so surprised. I can cook. You just usually have something done by the time I get home."

He smiled. "I enjoy it. Please don't feel like you have to return the favor."

Shaking her head, she patted his chest. "I'm not doing it because I have to. I'm doing it because I want to." Then she kissed him. Once…twice…three times, before drawing back. "Come over around four."

He grinned. "I'll be there."

All afternoon, excitement upped Emma's pulse while anticipation tingled through her veins. It felt good to give back to the man who had given her so much happiness the past dozen days.

Opening the door to him when he knocked, she smiled and her heart warmed. He stood there, eager expression on his face, holding her favorite flowers. It never ceased to surprise her, but once again, the thoughtful man had remembered what she said during their brief conversation between bouts of great sex the other night.

"Vince. Thank you. That's so sweet."

"So are you." Stepping inside, he handed the daisies to her and bent to give her a quick kiss before he straightened.

"Pierogi?" He sniffed the air. "You made me pierogi?"

"Yes." She laughed. "It's a family recipe."

He shook his head, disbelief rounding his eyes. "I can't believe you went through all the trouble for me."

"I was happy to." She brushed his cheek with her thumb. "You're worth it."

Lifting his hands to hold her face, he gazed down at her with affection lighting his gorgeous amber eyes. "You are something else, Emma. Thank you."

Warm lips covered hers, and moved unhurriedly in a lazy exploration that had her heart rocking in her chest. At that moment, it felt like their hearts touched.

Weird. Corny. Amazing. It left her feeling appreciated, and needed, and…wanted.

Something, Emma realized, she'd never felt in any of her past relationships. Sure, he was a military man, but he was different, and she was discarding her rule for him. Vince had a way of making her feel special. *He* was special, and she decided, then and there, to do whatever it took to keep the incredible man in her life. He was worth it.

In five days, he flew back to Texas for that wedding. Given the sweet way he looked at her and the emotion she felt in his kiss, he must feel the same way. Even though he'd made it clear it was only temporary when they began, she could only hope he'd want to continue to see her long distance, and wouldn't break things off.

Emma didn't think she could bear it if Vince walked away from her, too.

• • •

Monday afternoon, Vince had an unexpected opportunity to visit Emma at work, thanks to his impatient brother. Dom had called his doctor, requesting his checkup be moved up a few days. He'd tried to tell the idiot it was a waste of time. It was too soon to be cleared to do anything, but his brother had insisted on trying, and got lucky with a cancellation.

So he sent Emma a text and asked her to meet him on her break.

Since he was a few minutes early, he set the smoothie he brought her on a windowsill and watched people outside. Several were in uniform. The soldiers brought back memories of his time on the base for both basic training and when he'd returned for Ranger training a few years later. That was when he'd met Stone and Leo.

A smile twitched his lips. Man, the shit they used to get into.

"Vince?"

He turned toward the familiar voice.

"I thought that was you." Stephan walked to him with his hand out. "How's it going?"

He shook the doctor's hand. "Good. My brother's here for a checkup, so I thought I'd meet Emma on her break."

Stephan cocked his head. "Still seeing each other?"

Something in the man's tone sent his hackles up. "Yes." He may or may not have puffed out his chest.

"I see." The man nodded, gaze serious. "You're sticking around then?"

Vince frowned. "Just until the doctor okays my brother to drive."

Concern darkened Stephan's eyes. "So you intend to leave."

"Yes."

"Does Emma know?"

"Of course." He didn't like what the man insinuated.

"Are you sure?"

"Yes, I'm sure. Look, Stephan, what's this about?"

The guy blew out a breath. "I know I'm overstepping my

bounds, and I apologize, but I've known Emma since high school. She's sweet, and good-natured, and I care about her. I don't want to see her get hurt, and that's what will happen when you leave."

"If you care about her so much, why haven't you asked her out yet?" The question was out before he could stop it.

The doc stiffened. "It's complicated."

"*Un*complicate it."

"The timing has never been right." Stephan shrugged. "Either I was seeing someone, or she was seeing someone." He looked pointedly at Vince. "Among other things."

Vince shook his head. "I've only been in the picture for two weeks. You're trying to tell me you haven't been single long enough since you started working here?"

"No, that's not it." Stephan seemed to study the floor. "I work with her, and I have this rule not to get involved with a coworker. I broke it once, and it came back to bite me. But, I'll be honest, I am having a hard time keeping that rule with Emma."

Too damn bad. He wanted to tell the guy he'd had his chance, but that wasn't Vince's style. Instead, he blurted out, "And if I ask her to come with me?"

Damn. Where the hell had that come from?

The other man reeled back. "Emma's going with you?"

Vince dragged his hand through his hair. Seriously. What was he thinking? He'd already thought this through and the cons were too overwhelming to consider. "I don't know. I haven't asked her."

"Oh." The doc frowned, and silence stretched between them. Finally, Stephan shook his head. "Let me ask you this. Do you think it's wise? Emma's lived in Columbus all her life. Her home is here. Her father's buried here. Grandfather's buried here. Her memories are here. Job is here. Friends are here. That's a lot to ask her to ditch to follow you to Texas to

DONNA MICHAELS   197

live in an unfamiliar place with a bunch of strangers, after having only known you a few weeks."

Yeah, that *would* be crazy. And they were all things he'd already thought about.

"All I ask is that you consider her feelings, too," Stephan said. "I can tell you care about her. I trust you'll do the right thing."

"Hi, Vince." Emma came out, smile on her face as she walked over to slip her arm around his waist. "Hey, Dr. Greenwald," she said to Stephan. "I think Dr. Harper was looking for you."

The guy nodded. "Okay. If I don't see you before you go home to Texas, Vince, have a safe trip back."

Normally, he would've been pissed at that parting shot, but he realized the guy really did care about Emma. If only the guy had figured it out before Emma decided she needed to fake a relationship to get his attention.

The rest of the afternoon, Vince thought about nothing but Emma and pierogi, and by the time he finished the remainder of the incredible meal at her house later that night, he was ready for dessert. After they cleared the table and washed the dishes together, she sprayed him with water.

Her laughter snapped him into action. "Oh, you're going to pay." He grinned, reaching for her.

She squeaked and sidestepped his grasp, then rushed to put the island between them. "Have to catch me first." Excitement sparkled in her eyes and they gleamed a beautiful blue.

She liked to be chased, did she? Vince grinned. Game on.

With adrenaline pumping through his veins, he chased her through the house and caught her in the hall. Using his body to hold her against the wall, he stared into her happy face. "Now what are you going to do?"

Laughing and panting, she held his gaze, and in that instant the playful mood turned heated.

Desire replaced his adrenaline—apparently hers, too—because they lunged for each other, kissing fast and hungry, their hands roving up and down and around, unbuttoning and unzipping, so when they finally drew back for air, their clothes fell to their feet.

As if on the same wavelength, they bent to remove their shoes, stepped out of their clothes, then lunged for each other again. This time when they kissed, he slowed it down, making long, lazy, deep passes, savoring her taste and the feel of her curves melting against him.

Her hands were in his hair, and she made a sexy, needy sound in her throat that sent awareness trickling down his spine. He loved how she pressed into him, like she needed to get close, needed to feel all of him.

He needed to feel all of her, too.

Without breaking the kiss, Vince picked Emma up and carried her to her bed. He wanted to take his time tonight, to kiss and taste every inch of her, imprint it to memory, in case this was their last few days together.

Releasing her mouth, he set her on the bed. "Lie on your stomach," he said, then sucked in a breath at the sight of her mouthwatering ass. His groin fisted tight and his dick ached just looking at her. But he was going to do much more than look. Taking his time, he kissed and licked his way up to her shoulders, paying special attention to the back of her neck.

"Mmm…that feels good," she whispered, thrusting her sweet ass off the bed against his throbbing erection.

Vince saw stars and forgot how to breathe. God, he loved how she responded to him. Needing more, wanting to give her more, he rolled onto his side, bringing her with him. As he continued to brush his lips over her neck, he reached around to cup a gorgeous breast, flicking her peaked nipple with his thumb.

She inhaled sharply and ground her ass against him.

Holy hell, he loved that. So he did it again, and again, pinching her nipple between his finger and thumb the third time.

Her low moan vibrated into him, and when he left her breast to skim his hand over her quivering belly toward the promised land, she tossed her knee over his and opened up for him. Happy to oblige, he reached farther down and slipped his finger into her sweet heat.

"So wet," he muttered against her neck, his body already throbbing to be inside.

Not yet.

In and out, he slowly slid his finger, ripping sexy, erotic sounds from her lips while her hips continued to rock.

The back and forth motion sent her mouthwatering curves thrashing against his erection. He matched her thrusts with his hips and hand, and soon she was panting and gripping his hip.

Vince glanced over her shoulder to watch their connection, mesmerized by her bouncing breasts, loving how her hand trailed from his hip to his hand, as if she were afraid he'd remove his touch before she was done.

No chance in hell.

Changing the angle slightly, he slipped his finger out, and when he slid it back in, he brushed his thumb over her center.

"Vince...yeah..." She gripped his hand tight and bucked as she flew apart.

So damn beautiful.

He watched her for a few seconds, then brought her down slowly, her soft sighs driving him mad. It amazed him how in sync they were with each other.

Releasing her, he kissed her shoulder. He wanted to hold on to her forever.

"Mmm…" She twisted her face toward him and brushed her lips to his. "You always amaze me."

He smiled. "Keep that train of thought. I'll be right back." He kissed her quickly, then slipped off the bed to grab a condom from his jeans in the hall.

It was time to take it to the next level. The thought of losing her, of not having her in his life, cut the breath right out of him. He wanted to share every part of himself with her, show her what he couldn't say. To feel her need for him, let it surround him as he loved her with his body and silently opened his heart.

Chapter Twenty-One

When Emma found enough strength, she lifted onto her elbows and watched Vince stride back into her room, a determined, heated gleam in his eyes that sent desire rippling to her core. How was that possible? He'd just given her a mind-blowing orgasm. She could barely feel her legs, and yet, her body quivered as he grasped her ankles.

"Watching you is incredible," he said, kissing his way up her body. "But I need to taste you." Settling his shoulders between her legs, he held her gaze and blew on her sensitive flesh.

She sucked in a breath and watched his gaze darken before he lowered his mouth on her. Emma closed her eyes and gripped the bedspread, but it didn't help her keep the moan inside. The man was too good. He lapped and licked, brushing his thumbs over her flesh. Her eyes crossed, and her heart thudded in her chest. And whatever he was doing with his tongue was new and so amazing, he had her panting and crying out in under a minute. She flew apart in a stronger, more intense orgasm that stole her breath and remaining brain cells.

"Sweet. So sweet," he said when he drew back and licked his lips.

Her heart hit her ribs. Desire blazed in his eyes as he positioned his erection at her center, grabbed her hips, and slowly slid in. A deep, sexy sound emanated in his chest.

Emma cried out, she hadn't meant to, she'd wanted to just watch his enjoyment, but it'd felt so good. So damn good.

A satisfied smile curved his lips. "Never get tired of that."

"Me, either." She smiled, reaching out to trace a path up his torso, marveling at the way her fingers parted his sexy trail of hair.

He leaned over her, setting his palms on the mattress alongside her shoulders, then dipped down to rub his jaw lightly around her breast.

"Never get tired of that," she repeated his words, meaning every one as his stubble brushed her skin, making her nipples peak. Then he lightly skimmed over them. "Vince." She inhaled, and the wise, giving man, knew exactly what she wanted. What she needed.

One at a time, he captured them in his mouth, until she squirmed with a fierce need for him to move inside her. He had done it again. She didn't know or question why she was ready, she simply rocked against him, making him groan.

He released her nipple to take her mouth in a sensual, drugging, delicious kiss she felt all the way to her toes. Over and over, he took and he gave, making her tremble by the time he drew back. Then he entwined their fingers, set their hands beside her head, and began to thrust.

She watched as Vince's eyes drifted closed and his face tightened with sheer pleasure. It certainly felt good to her. So good, her eyes began to close, too. She wanted to feel him. More of him.

As if on the same wavelength, he lowered onto his

forearms and she let out a sigh.

Yes, that was what she wanted. To feel him everywhere.

As he spread openmouthed kisses up her neck, the hair on his chest tickled her skin, drawing another moan from deep inside. It was so amazing.

He burned a path to her temple, brushing his lips over her eyes and nose, down to her jaw, before finally touching her lips. From one end to the other, he took his time, tasting, dipping, drinking in slow, sweet passes as his hips mimicked the sensual pace.

This kiss was different.

Hotter. More incredible than their frantic, demanding, hungry ones.

It was as if he was baring his heart, offering it to her. Emma had never been so touched and turned on in her life. She wanted to cry and come at the same time.

But since her desire to come was stronger than her urge to cry, she pushed back her tears and gave herself over to Vince. Gave him everything. Kissing him with the same tender intensity, while matching his delicious, lazy, grinding thrusts.

Everything felt stronger, more powerful, meaningful, and the slow, sensual drag and pull of their bodies, as he thrust deep inside her, had her heart melting beneath his.

"*Emma*," he groaned. "Look at me."

Blinking her eyes open, she stared into his eyes, full of heat, and need, and affection so strong it made air clog her throat and desire pulse low in her belly. Something in her eyes must've caused the same reaction in him, because he lifted up onto his forearms and increased the pace.

Release barreled closer, and her eyes began to flutter closed.

"Keep your eyes open," he urged between breaths. "I want to see you come with me."

His words, and the feel of him thrusting deep inside, was all too much.

"Vince," Emma murmured over and over again. She couldn't help it. Didn't want to help it. He needed to know what he did to her. How good he made her feel. She burst in the most intense, beautiful, strongest orgasm of her life.

A second later, he stiffened, then thrust deep, whispering her name in a hoarse breath, and his eyes darkened to nearly black as he followed her over into unfathomable bliss.

Falling half on and half off her, he kissed her shoulder as they worked to catch their breath. When he apparently regained a little strength, he headed to the bathroom. Emma didn't move. Couldn't move. Her bones were mush.

She smiled and sighed at the same time. She liked mush. Loved mush.

"That smile looks good on you," he said, returning to her side, pulling her close as he yanked the covers over them. "Real good."

"You're fault," she mumbled against his chest.

She looked forward to many more nights like this... feeling incredibly satisfied and unbelievably happy.

Drawing her closer still, Vince kissed the top of her head, and Emma fell asleep, wrapped in his warmth and strength, thinking about the possibilities of their future, in whatever form that might be.

Hopefully he'd agree they could have one.

• • •

Showering with Emma... Vince's new favorite way to start his day.

As he watched her finish drying off, he resisted the urge to help. That would lead to more distraction, and she had work in an hour. Instead, he walked over to the shower and draped his towel over the bar to dry.

"Mmm…" Emma wrapped her arms around him and pressed her soft curves into his back. "I can barely feel my legs. Again." Her lips brushed his shoulder blade as she talked. "Which I need to fix, because I have to get ready for work soon."

He twisted around, and his body tightened at the feel of her nipples scraping his skin. He kissed her temple and dragged his mouth down to her ear, while his hands caressed her soft curves.

"Oh no you don't." She pushed out of his arms. "I have to get into work mode, remember? That isn't helping." Laughing, she grabbed a robe from the back of the door and slipped it on. "Coffee. Yeah, that's what I need. I'll go make us some."

"Sounds good." He smiled, following her back into her bedroom. "Do you want help?"

She shook her head. "No. Thanks. I got it."

So did he.

Bad.

Vince drew in a breath. After a night of the best sex he'd ever had, with a woman who made him feel good, strong… whole, he was even more sure he couldn't walk away from her on Friday. But how in the world could he make it work? It wasn't just geography separating them. They had totally separate, totally fulfilling lives. Lives that couldn't coexist without losing a central part of who they were.

Yesterday's conversation with Stephan whispered in the back of his mind.

Could he ask her to give up her life in Georgia to give him a chance?

Exhaling, he sat on the bed. No matter how he looked at it—and he'd looked at it plenty in the last few days—asking her wouldn't be fair. He didn't need Stephan to tell him that.

Which meant if he was going to let her get on with her life here, then he should probably start distancing himself now.

Damn, this sucked.

While he waited for Emma to come back, he grabbed his phone to check the time and noticed he had a missed call and voice message. Must've happened when they were in the shower. He didn't recognize the number. Telemarketer? He pressed the screen and listened to the message.

Stephan. Asking Vince to call.

He stiffened and glanced at the door. No sign of Emma with the coffee. Taking a deep breath, he hit call.

"Hey, Vince," the doc said. "Thanks for getting back to me."

"Is something wrong?"

"Just wanted to know if you've given our conversation any thought."

He would've laughed, but it wasn't funny. "Yeah."

"I need to know what you're doing because there's this gala fundraiser brunch thing coming up this Saturday and I wanted to ask her to go with me, but not if you're still in the picture. I don't want to overstep any boundaries."

As much as he wanted to tell the guy to forget it, he couldn't. Stephan was a good guy. And until Vince showed up, Emma had wanted to be with Stephan. The two had a long history of friendship. Hell, she'd only known him two weeks.

What if he did ask her and she went to Texas, but didn't like it?

He would've screwed up her life.

And if he asked her to continue to see him for a long-distance thing, and she grew tired of his absence and turned to someone close by to fill in the gap...*his* life would be screwed up.

Happened to soldiers all the time.

Vince's gut twisted. He didn't want to set himself up for betrayal. And didn't want to put her in the damn position in the first place. It was the last thing he wanted.

If she was happy before he came, then she'd be fine when he left.

Stephan and staying in Georgia was probably what was right for her. Vince was just a temporary distraction. He was an idiot for even considering a relationship.

"Vince? You still there?" Stephan asked.

He cleared his dry throat. "I'm here, and yeah, you should call her in about five minutes and ask her to the gala," he rushed to say before he changed his mind.

"You sure?"

"I want her to be happy," he said, his chest crushed tight.

He hung up right as she walked back into the room with two steaming mugs.

She handed him one and frowned at the phone. "Is everything okay?"

No.

"Just checking on Dom," he lied, hating what was about to happen. Hating what he was about to do because he knew she had feelings for him. It'd been evident in her kisses and touch, and somewhere in his dazed mind, he'd thought it would all be fine.

But he had to make things right for Emma, and he'd do anything for her.

Even leave her.

So Vince drank his coffee and pretended things were fine while he waited for her damn phone to ring. A minute later, it began to buzz on her nightstand.

"Probably my mom. She's the only one who calls this early," she said, setting her mug down to pick up her phone, then stiffened. "It's Stephan."

Vince waited to see what she'd do. He gave himself one

last chance. If she said she didn't care that Stephan was calling, he'd explain things to her. Find some way to work this out. But she just stood there, the ringing phone in her hand, uncertainty clouding her gaze.

His insides fisted tight. He had his answer. She still wasn't sure who she wanted, and that made his decision a whole lot easier.

Though no less painful.

"Looks like you got what you wanted," he said, nodding toward her phone. When she didn't deny it, Vince began to get dressed. "You should answer."

She drew in a shaky breath. "You're okay with that?"

Hell no. But he couldn't be selfish. He had to be real. He turned to face her. "I'm leaving in three days, Emma. I have to go back to my life in Texas. I *want* to go back to At-Ease."

Her phone *dinged* with a message.

The last thing Vince felt like doing was smiling, but he did, and nodded to her phone again. "I bet that's him asking you out. Call him back."

She stood there, phone still in her hand, staring at him with a mixture of disbelief, disappointment, and pain. That last one nearly killed him. Vince almost caved. But she hadn't chosen him, and caving wouldn't be fair to either of them. He had to go. Needed to go. Needed to let her get on with her life.

A life he'd only interrupted.

Now that it came down to his final minutes with her, though, he realized there was so much he wanted to say. So much he should've told her.

He didn't want to let her go. Didn't want her to be with anyone else.

She'd broken down his barriers and found her way into his heart. But all of it would seem like a lie since he was about to walk away. And he had to. It was the unselfish thing to do.

Grabbing his boots off the floor, he relied on his training and conditioned himself to do the hardest thing he'd ever done in his life.

Leave the woman he was falling in love with.

"Goodbye, Emma. It's been my pleasure...my *honor*...to know you," he said, then let himself out.

Chapter Twenty-Two

Vince just walked out on her.

He left her. Just like…

Emma sucked in a breath. Not again. Not him. Not Vince.

She couldn't believe what just happened. It didn't… It couldn't have. She blinked and pinched herself, hoping to wake from this horrible nightmare.

But it was real. She was awake. And he had left.

At least he hadn't said, "It's been fun."

God, she couldn't have handled that.

As it was, she wasn't handling things so well anyway. She swiped at her wet face and fought to keep the pain at bay.

She'd always known he wasn't staying. That was never in question. But she'd thought, she'd hoped, especially after the way he'd made love to her the night before, that he'd want to continue to see her.

Apparently, it hadn't—no, *she* hadn't—meant enough for him to stick.

That hurt. God…that hurt. So bad.

Seriously, what was it about her that made it so easy for

men to leave her behind? At that point, she couldn't believe her streak would limit itself to military men—Vince wasn't even active duty and had long-since returned to civilian life.

Which left her. And whatever it was about her that drove men away.

Her phone rang, again.

Hope flickered through her tight chest, until she looked at the cell and saw it was Stephan again.

Drawing in a shaky breath, she answered her phone while she still had the ability to function. "Hi, Stephan."

"Hi, Emma," he said. "Sorry to call so early, but I couldn't really do this at work."

She sank onto the edge of the bed only half hearing him. Her chest felt on the verge of caving in.

"I know Vince is leaving at the end of the week, and I wanted to know if you'd go to the gala brunch with me this Saturday."

Opening her mouth, she tried to speak but nothing came out, so she cleared her throat and tried again. "Y-yes. I'd like that."

"You would? That's great," he said. "Maybe we can go outside for lunch and discuss it a little more today?"

"I'd like that," she repeated, numbness starting to fog her mind.

After telling him she might be a little late that morning, she hung up and set the phone on her nightstand.

There. She'd done it. Emma had gotten what she'd wanted for so long. And she even had three days to spare on her deadline.

She should be thrilled. Overjoyed. After fifteen years, she was finally going out with Stephan Greenwald. Her dream man.

Only he wasn't her dream man anymore, was he?

No. Her dream man just walked out.

Left her.

Didn't stick.

Unable to hold in the pain any longer, Emma crawled back in bed, curled up into a ball, and cried her heart out.

• • •

That afternoon, Vince stood by the sink, staring unseeingly out the window. All day he'd walked around with a crippling pressure on his chest. It hurt to think. Hurt to talk. Hurt to even breathe.

"Sit down." Dom's voice drifted through his mind.

When he turned around, his brother pulled two stools from the island and pointed at one.

Vince shook his head and leaned back against the counter. "Too keyed up to sit."

"What's going on?"

Nothing good. He shrugged. "Stephan finally called Emma this morning."

His brother stiffened. "Damn. I'm sorry, man."

"Don't be." He shook his head. "She didn't answer. But I told her she should."

Dom's brows crashed together. "Why the fuck would you do that?"

"Because she belongs here. You were right. I should've listened to you. Not sure what I was thinking. Wait…yeah, I do. I was only thinking about myself. Being selfish." He inhaled, then exhaled slowly. "Well, not anymore. I told her goodbye, and that she should call Stephan back."

"And she actually called him back?"

He shrugged. "Don't know. I left."

"Ah, Jesus, Vince." Dom threw his hands up. "That's exactly what I was afraid of. You left her. Just like her last boyfriend. And the last few ones before that."

"No. It wasn't like that," he insisted, clenching his fists. "I didn't leave her. She knew I wasn't staying. And she didn't ask me to, either. Didn't tell me she didn't care about Stephan. Didn't tell me she cared about me." He sucked in a breath and unclenched his fists. "So I did the right thing by bowing out. This way, she can hopefully work things out with Stephan. I want her to be happy. He was the one she wanted in the first place."

God, that hurt to admit.

Pain intensified and spread from his chest to his gut right before Dom's phone rang.

Maybe it was Emma. Vince glanced at the microwave clock. Too early. She'd still be at work, and he couldn't see her calling his brother while there.

But he was certain she was going to look to Dom for answers.

Surely she'd realize Vince never lied to her, not once. And he'd told her from the start he was leaving. Never made any promises. Never promised her a future...even though, in the end, he'd wanted one with her.

Some of the tightness in his chest eased a little.

"That's great, man." The excitement in his brother's tone caught Vince's attention. "When? Roger that. I'll see you then." Dom hung up and smiled at him. "The guys will have boots on the ground here at fifteen hundred tomorrow."

Vince straightened from the sink, the good news momentarily pushing back his pain. "All of them?"

"Yes." Dom grinned. "According to Jax, other than a few scrapes and bruises, they're all good. Mission accomplished."

Vince grabbed two beers from the fridge, opened them, then handed one to Dom. "To their speedy return." They clanked bottles and drank to his brother's men.

It was great to have something positive to occupy his mind. He was happy for his brother. Hell, already there was a change in Dom's posture. Just knowing his brothers-in-arms were safe and on their way back no doubt went a long way to healing him on the inside. Vince was glad for his brother.

He was also glad for another reason.

And once again, it was selfish.

The return of Dom's buddies meant Vince could go back to Texas two days early. It would be a big help for Beth and Jovy for sure. And for himself. He wouldn't have to see Emma, or possibly Emma with Stephan, if the guy started to come over to her house.

"You going to book a flight home?" his astute brother asked, setting his bottle on the counter.

Vince nodded. "For tomorrow night if I can get one." He wanted to be here when the guys got back to make sure there weren't any last-minute hiccups in transport. "But I'm not leaving until the guys are here. Think Jaxon will stay?"

Dom grinned. "Hell, yeah. They'll probably all stay, if I know them."

He nodded. "You're right." The mission would also have been tough on the guys, having to function while worried about Dom. They'd no doubt camp at the house until his brother kicked them out. "I'm going to go book that flight."

After finishing his beer, he headed upstairs. And after booking a flight to Dallas the following evening, Vince sent Leo a text telling him the arrival time. Yeah, that was chickenshit, but he wasn't in the mood to talk just yet. There'd be time enough for that on the hour drive from the airport to the ranch.

Yesterday, he kind of hoped maybe Leo would be picking up more than him from the airport. Not that he'd done anything to make sure that happened.

Hell, maybe he hadn't been as selfish as he thought. Because if he had, there's no way he'd have let Emma go.

Vince set his phone aside and began to pack.

• • •

The next afternoon, Emma pulled into her driveway as Vince began to back out of Dom's crowded one. When he saw her, he stopped.

Emma's heart thudded hard for the first time in two days. She got out of her car, willing him to do the same. They needed to talk. She shouldn't have let it go on this long. For a moment, it looked like he was reaching for the handle, but then he lifted his hand and waved.

She stood there like an idiot, watching his car back out of the driveway and disappear down the road. After a minute passed, maybe more, she snapped out of it. The last thing she needed was to still be standing there when he got back from the store, or wherever he'd gone.

With a shake of her head, she turned around and was walking to her house when a sudden ruckus from Dom's backyard caught her attention. Glancing that way, she gasped at the sight of four burley men rushing out to greet her.

Dom's unit. The guys were back. All of them. Safe and sound. This time her chest tightened for a good reason, and she realized that was the reason Dom's driveway was crowded.

"Emma," they chorused, taking turns hugging her.

She hugged them back, a little harder than normal, because…darn it, she really needed the hugs. Fighting back tears, she sniffed, then shrieked as Jax, the embodiment of tall, dark, and dangerous, picked her up and carried her into Dom's yard.

Happy that her friends were home and safe, she stayed and talked with them a few minutes, trying not to panic too much as time went on. She didn't want to be there when Vince got back. It was just too hard.

She glanced at a silent Dom who regarded her with a

knowing look in his eyes. God, that made her want to cry.

"It's a shame you didn't get home a little sooner," one of them said. "You could've met Dom's brother before he left."

"Idiot, he was here for almost three weeks." Jax shook his head. "Emma's obviously met him already."

Wait...her mind stuttered to a halt. Vince left? As in back to Texas? She couldn't bring herself to ask, so she let her gaze drift back to Dom. He must've read the question in her eyes because he nodded.

Her chest squeezed so tight, she could barely breathe.

Vince left without saying anything to her? With only a wave?

That just about cracked the dam. She needed to leave. Now.

Rising to her feet, Emma hoped it was a smile she brought to her face. "I'll see you later. I want to go home and change."

They said stuff in response, but she didn't really hear them. Didn't hear anything except the sound of her heart shattering.

She entered her house in a pain-filled daze.

A wave? Had she meant that little to Vince?

The sound of someone knocking on her door somehow filtered through her haze. She was tempted not to answer. God, she didn't want to answer it. But if it was any one of those guys next door, they would eventually just walk in, stating concern trumped manners.

Finding her voice, she called, "Come in."

Dom entered and quietly shut the door behind him. There weren't any signs of judgment, or anger, or I-told-you-so in his gaze. Just warmth and concern.

She needed both. Bad.

So when he silently opened his arms, Emma didn't hesitate to step close, hug him tight, and pray she wasn't hurting him as she gave in to her tears.

• • •

Thursday morning, Vince glanced around his kitchen and nodded. It was good to be back. No one had bombarded him with questions. His friends had welcomed his return last night, especially Beth and Jovy. The women happily handed cooking back to him. Surprisingly, his kitchen hadn't been too messed up. It'd only taken him ten minutes to get things back in order.

Now he could start breakfast, and afterward, begin to cook and freeze entrées for the wedding. He glanced at the list pinned to the corkboard next to the industrial fridge. Should keep him busy until well past midnight.

Good. He didn't want time to think. To feel.

The side door opened and Haley walked in, followed by Cord. The couple lived an hour away, and hadn't been at the ranch when he'd gotten home.

"Hey, Vince." She came over and hugged him tight.

Cord waited until his girlfriend moved to the side before holding out his hand. "Good to have you back."

He shook it. "Nice to be home." He just wished he hadn't come back alone.

A shaft of pain slipped past his control and ricocheted through his chest, just as the rest of his friends entered through the swinging door that led to the dining room.

Apprehension spread across his shoulders and down his spine like branches on a tree.

"Cord, Haley, right on time." Stone nodded before turning his attention to him. "Vince, we're all glad to have you back, man. But we're calling an intervention. On you."

Chapter Twenty-Three

Vince's heart slammed into his ribs a second before he stepped toward the side door, intending to escape outside.

Cord stood in front of it with his arms folded across his chest. When the hell had the guy moved there? He glanced at the swinging door that led to the dining room. Brick smiled from his post in front of it.

Yeah, he wasn't getting past him, either.

"Fine," he said, leaning against the counter. "But you're wasting your time on me."

"You are not a waste of time, Vince," Beth said.

Leo stood across from him with his back against the island. "We can see you're in pain. You're quiet. Closed up. You and Emma were dating for real when I left. What happened?"

He stared at his buddies and knew from the staunch set of their shoulders and determined gleam in their eyes, the only way to get back to cooking was to start talking.

He shrugged. "Stephan happened."

Leo leaned forward. "He finally asked her out?"

"Yes." Dom had confirmed it when Vince called last night to let him know he'd arrived at the ranch. "But before that, Stephan opened my eyes to the fact I was being selfish."

The room erupted in protests.

"Bullshit."

"No way."

"Not you."

He shook his head. "I was only thinking of myself when I got involved with her. We both knew I was going to leave upfront, but I should never have crossed that damn line with her in the first place." He shoved a hand through his hair. "That's all on me."

"No," Jovy said. "It's not. You weren't the only one involved. The only one consenting."

Fierce emotion shined in his buddy's eyes as he gazed at his bride-to-be. Oh, right. She'd moved to Joyful to be with Stone.

The man in question shook himself out of his adoration long enough to eye Vince. "Did you at least try talking to Emma about continuing with some sort of relationship?"

He blew out a breath. "No."

Leo frowned. "What? Why not? I got the impression you liked being with her."

"I did. I do." He straightened from the counter and shook his head. "But if I did ask her to continue with a long-distance thing, it doesn't change the fact I'm not leaving here. She'd have to come here, and there's no way I'm putting that on her shoulders."

Beth sighed. "No, Vince. You are." She walked over and placed her hand on his arm. "You had no right to take her choice away. Chances are, Emma would've been happy to eventually come here because this is where you are. Where you belong."

He shook his head at the woman who had *also* done

exactly that for her fiancé, Brick. He was sensing a trend. And yet… "It's not right to ask her to give up everything for me."

Jovy lifted a shoulder and slid her arm around Stone. "Still, it's her choice."

Guilt and pain mixed to sink like lead in his gut. "And if she came, and realized down the road it was a mistake? Or worse, blamed me for taking her away from everything she knew and loved?"

No way could he live with that.

"Maybe *you* are her everything," Haley said quietly. "Or could be, given half the chance. But you didn't give her that chance, did you?"

"And what if she didn't blame you?" Cord asked. "I think you need to ask yourself something, Vince, and be honest. Are you sure you're not just running scared? I did it without realizing." His buddy draped his arm around Haley and drew her near. "Luckily, I had good friends to help me see things clearly, and a good woman to forgive me."

Vince blinked. "Are you saying I deliberately walked away from Emma because I'm falling for her?"

Cord raised a brow. "Did you?"

Leo folded his arms across his chest. "And are you?"

Christ, he could barely breathe again.

"Loving someone makes you vulnerable," Cord continued. "And open for pain if they leave. Or die." He looked at Haley, a sad smile on his lips.

Vince stared down at the floor and contemplated what they were saying. He'd loved Connie and losing her had ripped everything out of him. He swore he'd never let anyone get that close again. Except someone did.

Emma.

Old hurts and new ones instantly collided, wrapping around Vince's chest like a thick, steel chain.

"Bowing out was probably the most selfish thing you

could've done," Stone said. "It kept your heart safe. Guarded. So it couldn't get too invested and possibly go through the pain of loss again. Because loss happens to everyone. You know that better than most."

Feeling like he'd been sucker punched in the gut, Vince sank back against the counter again, slowly shaking his head. The thought of losing Emma like he had Connie knocked him on his ass.

God, is that what he'd done? Got scared because Emma got too close?

Had he hidden behind the noble deed to step aside so she could be happy all to safeguard his heart? To eliminate the risk of ever having to go through the pain and grief of losing someone he loved again?

Ah, hell...he left her before she could leave him.

Tipping back his head, he stared at the ceiling while his mind tried to process everything his friends had just pointed out. He'd done so many things wrong. Kept his feelings to himself. Never gave her a choice. Deserted her. Bottom line, he didn't like what it all said about his character.

He was a coward.

Christ. He never should've left Georgia without talking things out with Emma.

Realizing the room had gone quiet and all eyes were on him, he straightened and blew out a breath. "Not sure there's ever been a bigger screwup than me."

"Nah." Stone shook his head. "Brick screwed up massively with Beth and she forgave his sorry ass."

Vince glanced at the sorry ass who now stood by the island with his arm around Beth.

"I'd argue, but you're right." Brick grinned, hugging his fiancée close.

Haley set her head on Cord's shoulder. "There are two people in a relationship, Vince. Both parties usually share blame. Trust me."

"What are you going to do?" Leo asked.

"What I should've done." He straightened his shoulders. "Talk to her."

Brick grinned. "Right now?"

He shook his head. "I'd rather do it in person." Emma deserved a face-to-face explanation for his desertion. He met Leo's gaze. "Can you take *my* sorry ass back to the airport on Sunday?"

His buddy grinned. "No problem."

"Sunday?" Jovy frowned. "Vince, don't think you need to wait because of the wedding. You can go tomorrow."

He smiled at the bride-to-be. "Thanks. I appreciate that. But I'd never miss witnessing you marry Stone. Besides, Emma's supposed to go to that gala with Stephan on Saturday, and I think she needs to go. She needs to see for herself he isn't right for her. Twenty years from now, I don't want her wondering what might-have-been if she had gone on that damn date."

Haley squeezed his arm. "You're a good man, Vince."

Beth smiled. "The best."

Brick frowned down at her. "Last night, you told me *I* was the best."

Beth elbowed the sorry ass in the ribs.

Then Jovy moved in to replace Haley. "Just remember, although women don't need men thinking for us, we screw up, too. I can guarantee you, Emma has regrets."

Not that Vince wished that on Emma, but it did give him a bit of hope. Maybe she'd at least hear him out on Sunday.

• • •

Saturday morning, Emma stood staring at herself in the mirror. The cobalt-blue dress she'd bought for the gala brunch two months ago, with all the excitement of a girl going to her first prom, didn't even spark a flicker of joy today.

Neither did going to the brunch. In fact, she'd thought about backing out a few times since Stephan had asked on Monday. The two enthusiastic phone calls she'd received from her mom that week were all that had kept her quiet.

Besides, she owed it to herself to go, otherwise, she'd always wonder if she'd missed out by not following through with the long-awaited date. Straightening her dress, she thought about her conversation with Macy before leaving work.

After putting away her headset, she'd glanced at the woman. "What's wrong?"

"You tell me," Macy said. "It's finally here. Your big date with Stephan. How do you feel?"

She'd felt nothing. Since Vince left, she'd operated on autopilot. Emma tried to resurrect a smidgen of joy, but failed, so she shrugged.

"And if Vince was taking you?"

Pain had ricocheted through her chest. "Since that's not feasible, there's no need to answer."

"Girlfriend, it's the twenty-first century." Macy waved a hand in the air. "It's okay for a girl to call a guy and apologize."

"Apologize?" She'd frowned so hard her brows had hurt. "What for? I didn't do anything wrong? He left me, remember?"

"Uh-huh." Her friend had stared without blinking. "After you told him how you felt, right? He knew you were falling for him. He knew you wanted to date him and not Stephan."

She'd cleared her throat and looked away. "Uh, no. Not exactly." She hadn't told Vince any of that.

"So then, is it *feasible* Vince could've left because he thought you still had the hots for Stephan? Did the chivalrous thing by stepping out of the way, putting his feelings aside so you could be happy?"

Shaking herself back into the present, Emma sank onto her bed. Had Macy been right? Is that why Vince had left without a word?

Dom had been nothing but supportive the past few days. Never said anything about Vince, so if his brother had confided anything to him, he kept it to himself.

A knock sounded at her door. That was him now. She could tell by the knock, and the fact it was too early to be Stephan. Her date wasn't due for another half hour.

Walking through the house, she managed to paste a smile on her face by the time she opened the door. "Hey, Dom. What's up?" She stood aside to let him in.

"Still going through with the date, I see." He motioned to her dress.

She shrugged. "Why shouldn't I?"

It wasn't like Vince had gotten a hold of her to apologize for leaving.

Dom stared at her a long moment. "There's something I think you need to know about Vince."

Just hearing his name cut like a knife. Her heart stopped. "Is he okay? Is he hurt?"

"He's fine, in large part because of you. But there was a time when he wasn't."

"I…I don't follow."

Dom blew out a breath. "He's probably going to kill me because I'm sure he'll eventually tell you about her himself, but I want you to know how important you are to him."

Her? *Her* who?

"Back in high school, Vince had a girlfriend named Connie," he said. "They met freshman year and were together until she died right before graduation."

Died?

"Oh my God." Emotions burned her throat at the thought

of Vince going through something like that…and so young.

"Yeah. After getting his diploma, he joined the Army, and hasn't dated a woman more than twice ever since. Until you."

Emma couldn't even begin to imagine that kind of pain. She knew how bad she hurt at the loss of not having him next door.

She was still stunned when the ringing of her phone echoed through the kitchen. As happened every time it rang that week, her heart leaped, hoping it was Vince.

Emma glanced at the caller ID and sighed. "My mom."

"I'll let you talk in private." Dom stepped close. "You look beautiful today." He kissed her cheek, then left.

Autopilot kicking in once again, she answered the phone. "Hi, Mom," she said, moving to the bathroom so she could check her hair and makeup.

"Hi, sweetheart. Getting ready for the big date? Make sure you take a picture and send it to me."

She smiled, obliged, then sent it. "Just did, you should get it soon."

"I'm so happy for you," her mother said. "You're finally going out with Stephan. Oh, hang on, your picture just dinged."

Funny how none of the excitement was there anymore.

"The dress is gorgeous on you," her mom said, sounding odd. "And you're smiling, but you look sad. Really sad. Why didn't you tell me?"

Emma moved into her bedroom and slipped on her strappy silver heels. "Tell you what?"

"That you'd fallen for Vince."

She closed her eyes to ride out the pain. How had her mother known? She'd only told her about the fake dates.

Must've been one of her many motherly superpowers.

Her chin trembled without her permission. "He made me

happy, Mom. Being with him was kind of…amazing."

"Oh, sweetheart, I'm so sorry. What happened?"

She shook her head as if her mother could see. "I screwed things up. I never told him how I really felt, and he left. I'm not sure it would've made a difference, though. He probably wouldn't have asked me to go anyway."

"But you don't know that."

The doorbell rang.

"I've got to go, Mom. Stephan's here." He was the only one who ever used her front door, and while she used to think it was polite, it now struck her as oddly formal.

"Okay, call me later. It's not too late. I'm sure we can figure something out."

"Okay." She'd only agreed to make her mom feel better. Wiping under her eyes in case her emotions had smeared her makeup, Emma hung up and headed for the door.

Stephan's eyes widened as soon as she let him in. "You look amazing."

"Thanks." Grabbing her purse off the nearby credenza, she forced a smile. "Ready."

Between Dom's visit and her mother's call, Emma was operating on overload. Emotions and thoughts cluttered her mind. It felt like someone rammed their fist into her chest, grasped her heart, and squeezed tight. The closer Stephan drove to the gala brunch, the tighter the squeeze.

Why? What was her body trying to tell her?

Only one thing came to mind.

She didn't want to go.

Emma glanced at Stephan. He was still handsome. Still a great guy. But her heart no longer ached for him.

It ached for Vince. Much harder and stronger than it had ever ached for Stephan.

Her pulse hiccupped. "We need to go back."

He frowned. "Did you forget something?"

"Yes." She nodded. "My suitcase."

Stephan met her gaze, and dawning flickered through his eyes. "Texas."

She nodded again. "I'm sorry. I really am. Trust me, up until three weeks ago, I would've given my eyeteeth to be in this seat."

Silence, then a sad chuckle. "I waited too long. You fell for Vince."

"Yes." She gripped her purse tight on her lap as he turned the car around in a vacant lot. "I don't even know if he'll want to see me. He never said anything about a relationship. But I need answers. I need to see him."

Stephan glanced at her again, this time with guilt clouding his gaze. "He wanted to ask you to go with him."

"What?" Emma's heart dipped to her knees. "H-how do you know?"

He returned his attention back to the road. "He told me. Said he was thinking about asking you, but then we talked about you being uprooted and leaving everyone you know and love."

"I love *him*," she blurted.

Holy revelations…it was true.

She loved Vince.

Emma's heart rocked back into place. Clicked. Became whole. Everything was suddenly so clear. How in the world had she not realized it sooner?

Even though it'd only been a few weeks, they'd shared so much in that short period of time. No wonder his absence hurt so bad. Worse than anything she'd ever felt before.

With shaky hands, she pulled out her phone and booked the first flight out. She was in luck. The last local commuter to Atlanta left in ninety minutes, then she'd catch another to Dallas. It was done. She'd taken a step. Took a chance. It felt good. Great, even. And as Stephan pulled into her driveway, she drew in her first real breath in days.

"Can you wait and take me to the airport?"

"Of course." He nodded, guilt still evident in his eyes. "It's the least I can do. I'm sorry, Emma. It's my fault. Don't be mad at Vince. He's a good guy."

Her heart twisted. And although part of her wanted to wring his handsome neck for meddling, she reached out to touch his arm instead. "You both are." She just wished they hadn't tried to make decisions for her. "I'll be quick."

Packing so fast she wasn't even sure what was in the small suitcase, Emma was back outside in record time. Stephan immediately got out of the car to take the luggage from her.

"Thanks. I'll be right back," she said again, then rushed into Dom's without knocking.

She found him watching a ballgame in the living room with the guys, but when he spotted her silently motioning for him to join her in the kitchen, he came out.

"Hey, what's up?"

"Hi." She thrust her phone at him. "I need you to put Vince's address in here, please."

She could've texted him for it in the car, but wanted to tell him in person.

Approval gleamed in his eyes. "Need a ride to the airport?"

"No. Stephan's taking me."

"Stephan?" His head snapped back. "You're one of a kind." Admiration lit his face as he handed her phone back. "Say hi to my brother for me. Does he know you're coming?"

She shook her head. "No. He has the wedding to worry about today. I don't want to distract him."

"Emma." Dom grinned. "You showing up at the ranch is going to distract him something fierce."

Hope flickered through her heart.

With luck, she'd arrive after the nuptials and they'd be

able to talk in private. She needed to tell him how she felt. Something she should've done last week.

God, she couldn't believe how stupid she'd been. Stupid from day one.

But at least she'd figured it out and could still tell him in person. And pray he was happy about it.

Otherwise…

She straightened her shoulders. *Otherwise* wasn't an issue. If need be, she'd deal with it. By then, at least she would've given it a shot. Not wait around, over a decade, wondering what might have happened. Regretting she hadn't tried.

Not this time. Not with Vince.

He was too important to her. He was worth taking a chance. Worth getting on a plane and flying several hours. Worth renting a car and driving over an hour through an unfamiliar state.

He was worth the effort.

Chapter Twenty-Four

The morning of the wedding was hectic. Vince was glad. Once again, it kept his mind occupied. He heated what he could ahead of time, prepped for later, helped set up, and met up with Stone and the guys in time for pre-wedding photos.

Afterward, Brick ushered them all into the office and locked the door. "We only have about eight minutes." The guy rushed over to the filing cabinet, removed a bottle of scotch and six glasses, and set them on the desk.

Stone's eyes bulged. "Better hope Jovy doesn't find that in the filing cabinet."

"Don't worry, I'll remove it by Monday," Brick said, spilling a little scotch in each glass. He handed them out, then turned back around and raised his glass to the sixth one sitting untouched on the desk. "To Drew."

A ritual. The first toast was always in honor of their fallen friend. The rest of them automatically raised their glasses and echoed Brick before drinking. Once finished, they set their glasses back on the desk and Brick repeated the process.

"To my brother, Stone," he said this time. "The first of

our Ranger Rifle Squad to tie the knot."

"To Stone," they echoed, holding their drinks high, then tossing them back.

Vince was grateful Brick had the sense to only spill a little in the glasses, or the whole ceremony could take an interesting turn. One, he suspected, the women would not appreciate.

"Brick? Where are you?" Beth's voice echoed down the hall.

The men made a mad scramble to shove the booze and glasses back into the filing cabinet, and unlocked the door just as Beth twisted the knob.

"Oh, there you are." She blinked. "There you *all* are." Narrowing her gaze, she sniffed the air, then shook her head. "Here." Ever the prepared event planner, she pulled a bunch of mints from her purse and handed them out. "Eat this quick before Jovy finds out you're in here toasting."

"Thanks," Vince said, and they all did as directed.

Beth nodded. "Now get your handsome tuxedoed butts out back to the gazebo. The ceremony starts in fifteen minutes. You gentlemen need to start seating guests."

Nodding and saluting, they obeyed and headed out back. They were tasked with ushering people to the rows of chairs divided down the middle by a white runner that ran to the gazebo that Stone's grandfather had made his grandmother. The whole space was decked out in white fabric and lights and flowers, and several misting fans flanked the whole area, keeping the air tolerable. The reverend stood at the front of it all, waiting for them.

Vince took his place between Leo and Cord. Brick, the best man, stood next to the groom. Anticipation ruled Stone's features as he stared at the house, waiting for his bride to arrive.

The music started, and two of Jovy's childhood friends,

along with Beth and Haley, began to walk single file down the aisle, looking pretty in fancy light-blue dresses, with their hair up and smiles on their faces.

Intense pain tore through Vince's chest. He missed Emma. Missed how she looked at him the way Beth and Haley were smiling at his buddies, with their entire heart in their eyes.

Why hadn't he realized she'd felt so strongly for him? Christ. His leaving must've hurt her bad. He rubbed at the ache in his chest. Tomorrow, he'd do whatever it took to patch things up with her.

As the last bridesmaid took her place across from the men, the second most important female of the day began her walk down the aisle.

Lula Belle.

The lovestruck cow wore a flower necklace Beth had fashioned to match the bridesmaids' bouquets. Since the neighbor's cow was in love with Stone and would've crashed the wedding anyway, Jovy decided to include her by making her the token flower girl.

Catching site of Stone standing at the altar, Lula Belle upped her pace and jogged to him, mooing all the way. Laughter broke out. Stone was still scratching the cow's neck when the music changed and Jovy stepped out of the house.

Stone straightened, and Vince was pretty sure everyone felt his buddy suck in a breath at the sight of his bride. Beautiful in a long white gown, the bride smiled adoringly at her groom, until she got to the end of the runner and her grandfather couldn't set her hand in Stone's...because there was a cow in the way that wouldn't budge.

After several amusing seconds, Stone persuaded Lula Belle to move to his other side and the ceremony continued.

As the two professed their love and commitment to each other, Vince felt the familiar pang of envy. And hope.

Those two had a similar relationship to him and Emma. If they could work it out, then surely he and Emma would.

"I, Jovy Larson, take you, Stone Mitchum, to be my lawfully wedded husband," Jovy said, gazing into Stone's eyes. "And Lula Belle to be my awfully, dreaded cow."

Lula Belle mooed.

The guests chuckled.

Before long, rings were exchanged, and after slipping a ring on Stone's finger, Jovy dug in the pocket of his tux and pulled out a carrot that she placed in the palm of her hand and held in front of the cow.

Lula Belle sniffed it, looked at Jovy, then turned around.

"Oh, sweetheart." Jovy shook her head. "You do not want to show me that end of you while I'm holding a carrot."

Snickers went through the guests.

Stone snatched the carrot from his bride and shoved it back in his pocket.

When it got to the part where the bride and groom kissed, everyone clapped. Then the reverend had them turn to face the crowd.

"I now pronounce you husband and wife."

The guests cheered.

Lula Belle mooed.

"And cow," the reverend added with a grin.

Then, with a huge smile on Stone's face, he walked down the aisle, new bride on one arm, and cow under his other hand. Chuckling, Vince escorted a smiling Beth to the back. That was definitely not your typical wedding ceremony, but it'd been the perfect one for his friends.

Two hours later, after everyone had eaten, and the bride and groom were mingling, Vince checked to make sure there was still enough food in the trays and Sterno cans in the heaters should anyone want seconds or thirds.

"All packed for tomorrow?" Leo asked him.

Vince smirked. "Haven't really unpacked." He hadn't had the time...or the heart.

"Or called her yet?" Jovy drew near with her arm around her new husband, but minus the cow, who was banned to the outside of the tent. "You do know women love phone calls, right?"

"Especially from men who apologize," Beth said, joining them with her arm around Brick.

Haley and Cord rounded out the gang. "And tell you they love you," she said.

Many times over the past two days, Vince had stared at his phone, finger hovering over Emma's number, but he always shoved it back in his pocket. "The things I want to say should be said in person," he reminded them.

Jovy quirked a brow. "Remember the 'women love phone calls' part?"

"Yeah." Beth nodded. "Especially if it shortens our grief."

"And I'm betting with you leaving like you did, Emma's hurting," Haley said.

His gut twisted. He didn't want Emma hurting. That was the last thing he ever wanted. Prolonging their talk so he could do it in person was also prolonging her pain.

Dammit. He was such an idiot.

Determined to put an end to it right now, Vince pulled out his phone and hit Emma's number. Better to do things over the phone—to explain himself—than to have her hurting any longer.

If she was indeed hurting.

It started ringing...and echoed behind him.

His heart slammed to the ground. That sounded close. As if she was... He stiffened and slowly turned around. "Emma?"

Chapter Twenty-Five

God, it was good to see him.

Emma's heart throbbed in her throat, where it had leaped the instant she'd spotted Vince standing off to the side, talking with the bride and groom and several others.

Awareness rippled through her body. The man she loved—the man she'd traveled half the day to see—stood a few feet away, in a tux that fit his lean form to perfection. He made it look good…and her heart flutter out of control.

The best thing about him—besides the fact he just tried to call her—was the hope and affection lighting his eyes.

The same emotions rushed through her.

"Hi, Vince," she finally said, stepping closer. Nothing else made it out, even though she had so much to say. So much to tell him. So much to ask him.

"I can't believe you're here." A smile tugged at his lips as he shoved the phone into his pocket.

"You have a magic phone, Vince." Another guy wearing a tux, a tall guy, smirked. "You should've called her sooner."

Vince nodded. "Damn straight." Then he introduced her

to everyone.

She smiled when she saw a familiar face. "Hi, Leo."

"Hey." He smirked. "What took you so long?"

Feeling a little more at ease thanks to their warm welcome, she turned to the bride. "I'm so sorry for crashing your wedding."

Jovy smiled and waved a hand. "Are you kidding? This is the best present. I'm thrilled that you're here. Carry on."

Beth stepped forward. "Okay, everyone. Let's give them some privacy." The pretty woman made a shooing motion with her hands. The group backed up about ten feet, but continued to watch.

Emma didn't care. The only thing that mattered was telling Vince what she'd traveled there to tell him. Turning to face him fully, she took a deep breath, and it seemed to dislodge the words stuck in her throat.

"I came here to tell you I'm sorry, Vince. I should've t—"

He stepped close and placed a finger over her lips. "You don't have anything to apologize about. I was the one in the wrong. You don't have to say anything else."

"But I need to tell you things," she said against his finger.

Smiling, he removed it to cup her chin. "Emma, the fact you came here tells me all I need to know."

Tears filled her eyes. The man was so damn sweet. She swallowed and shook her head. "But you deserve the words, Vince." She tilted her face into his hand and kissed his palm. "All of them. I'm sorry I never told you how I felt. I started caring about you—and not Stephan—before our first real date. I should've told you then, but I didn't realize how deep my feelings ran until you left."

"I have feelings for you, too," he said. "I thought I was doing the right thing, stepping back so you could have a chance with Stephan. I'm so sorry."

Her heart was eating up every single syllable.

"I thought I was being selfless," the wonderful man continued. "Until my friends made me realize why I'd really left. I was scared." He released her and exhaled. Pain and guilt darkened his gaze. "When I was young, I lost someone I loved."

She nodded, her heart squeezing tight. "Connie."

His eyes widened.

"Dom told me this morning," she said. "Don't be mad at him, though. He was just trying to help me understand why you left. He suspected it was because of her."

And it'd made all the difference in the world.

He blew out another breath and nodded. "After Connie died, I closed myself off. Buried everything deep." He lightly brushed her cheek with his thumb. "But you made me feel things, *really* feel them, for the first time in over a decade." His happy gaze turned haunted. "I don't know, I guess self-preservation kicked in, and I subconsciously tried to save myself from that pain again. But, Emma, being here—without you—it was the same kind of pain. Unbearable. That's why I was flying back to Columbus tomorrow."

Her pulse leaped. "You were?"

"Yes," Leo chimed in. "I was driving him to the airport in the morning."

"I was miserable," Vince said. "I needed to see you, to talk to you and work things out." Fierce affection warmed his gaze, and her heart swelled so much she thought it might burst. He cupped her face, as if he couldn't stop touching her. "I'm so glad you're here, Emma."

"Me, too." She smiled, covering his hand with her own. "I should've told you how I felt. Should've told you I was falling in love with you."

Joy erased the remaining darkness from his expression. "You love me, too?"

"Yes." Wait...too? Her heart rocked. "What do you

mean, 'too'? You love me?"

His gaze softened. "I do. I love you. I just realized it too late. Maybe if we would've talked about all of this, we could've figured out a solution to be together, instead of hurting ourselves and each other."

She nodded.

"We'll figure things out." He smiled, dropping his hand to her shoulder. "Commute. FaceTime. Whatever it takes."

Emma smiled. "I'd like that. Very much. Because I want you in my life, Vince. I want a real relationship with you. A real everything with you."

"Good answer," Brick said behind him.

"Shh…you big galoof, I can't hear," Beth whispered.

Vince's gaze softened, and his hands trailed up her arms. "I want all those thing with you, too. I want to be in your life. I'm not going away. You're stuck with me."

Finally.

She'd finally found someone who stuck. Someone who left Georgia behind, but not her.

With the last of her fears and hang-ups vanquished, she held nothing back, letting him see she was happiest in his arms. Setting her palm on his chest, she smiled up at him. "You said the *S* word. I love it when you talk dirty."

He grinned. "'Stuck' isn't a dirty word, or scary. Especially if it's with you. It's part of that glass three-quarters full," he murmured before brushing his lips over hers for a slow, achingly sweet kiss full of promises and hope and love.

And Emma felt the love—so much so her legs shook, and she had to clutch at his tux to keep upright. When the kiss ended, she drew in a breath and glanced over his shoulder at a flash of movement that caught her eye.

"Um…" She blinked to make sure she wasn't seeing things. "Why is there a cow eating the bride off the wedding cake?"

A gasp filled the air as Jovy twisted around. "Mother-heifer!" The bride picked up the skirts of her gown and rushed toward the cow, her husband and Beth in tow. "Drop it! Dammit, Lula Belle! If you don't drop it, I swear I'm divorcing you right now."

Divorcing?

Still holding her in his arms, Vince turned his attention back to her, a big grin on his face. "The cow's in love with Stone. She wants Jovy out of the way so she can have him for herself."

Emma smiled. She had the feeling she was going to fit right in. "That's adorable."

"Jovy doesn't think so."

They laughed.

After a few seconds, Vince sobered. "I can't believe you came. Did you have a good flight?"

"Yes, but I had to hurry to catch the commuter," she said, playing with his bow tie. "I'm a bit thickheaded. I didn't have my epiphany until I was in Stephan's car on the way to the gala brunch this morning. All I could think about was I didn't want to go."

"You didn't?"

"No." She shook her head. "I wanted to be with you. So, I had him turn the car around and drive me home so I could pack. Then I asked him to take me to the airport."

He stilled. "Stephan drove you to the airport to see me?"

A smile tugged at her lips. "He felt bad for making you leave." She nodded at the question in his eyes. "He told me he'd talked to you. So it seemed only right that he fix it by driving me to the airport."

"Oh, I like her." Haley snuggled against Cord and gave her a thumbs-up.

Vince's gaze turned serious. "Emma, I think you should know I don't have my own house. I live in the main house with Jovy and Stone and Leo."

"That's okay." She smiled. "It doesn't matter to me where you live. Just that you want to continue to see me."

"Another good answer," Brick said, adding in an overly loud voice that reminded her of Macy. "Good thing Vince is part owner of a construction company who happens to be really good at building houses, like the one they're building for me and Beth right now."

"Yeah," Cord said, just as conspicuously. "He also happens to be part owner of this ranch, which has plenty of acres for another house."

"Okay, okay." He grinned at the men. "I'll keep that in mind. But right now, Emma and I are in no hurry. We have all the time in the world. We're going to do this the right way."

She patted his chest and regained is attention. "Exactly, and do you know why?"

"Why?"

Her lips twitched. "Because you think I'm adorable, and I think you're hot."

"God, I love you." He kissed her again, this time long and deliciously deep. She didn't care that his friends stood just a few feet away, but she was glad for the air-conditioning in the tent because her body temperature spiked.

Mrs. Henderson had told her Vince was a keeper, worthy of being hers, and the wise woman had been right. Emma had found a man who wanted her with him, who loved her, and she felt the same way. He was so much more than her dream man. He was her everything.

When Vince broke the kiss, he set his forehead to hers, his heart beating strong and sure under her palm. "Promise me you'll hold that thought until later."

There were a lot of things she was ready to promise him.

Sliding her hands up around his neck, she smiled into his dimpled face. "Anything for you."

Epilogue

The day after Christmas, Vince stared up at the ceiling, Emma's hot, naked, satiated body draped over him while they worked to catch their breath from an incredibly good morning. It was his favorite way to wake up—buried deep inside the woman he loved while she sighed his name.

Rise and shine, indeed.

Several amazing months had passed since they decided to have a real relationship. He and Emma had jumped in with both feet, FaceTiming every night, and once a month, he'd fly to Georgia to spend several days with her, and she'd fly to Texas to stay with him a few days at a time, too. But each visit, they found it harder to part, until last month when they decided they didn't want three states between anymore. She'd jumped right in at the ranch on her visits, so on Thanksgiving, he asked if she'd consider moving to Texas.

He'd been thrilled when she said yes.

As of last week, after her lease had run out, she was fully moved in, thanks to Dom and his buddies helping them pack up her house in three days.

A shaft of guilt ricocheted through Vince's chest. He felt bad for taking her away from his brother. The only person Dom trusted and relied on to watch over his place during deployments.

"Mmm…" She kissed his neck and sighed, sending goose bumps down the right side of his body.

Yeah, Dom could find another friend.

Besides, with the house empty, maybe the new renter would be someone just as trustworthy as Emma.

She reached for her phone that *dinged* with a text on the nightstand. "Oh my God." She laughed, the vibration shaking through her sweet curves straight into him.

"What's up?"

"Macy. She sent a picture of the outfit she bought for Dupree to wear when they come next weekend. A bolero, shiny snakeskin cowboy boots, and…is that a ten-gallon hat?"

Vince glanced at the screen and smiled. "Yes, ma'am, it is. I take it she still thinks At-Ease is a working dude ranch?"

"Yes. Despite the fact I repeatedly told her it wasn't." Her sigh washed over him. "She said, and I quote, 'We can't wait for the full dude ranch experience.' Boy, is she going to be disappointed."

"Nah." He took the phone out of her hands and set it back on the nightstand. "This is a ranch, and there are a lot of dudes on it. I can pretty much guarantee her visit is going to be an experience."

"Yeah, but for who? Her and Dupree? Or everyone here at the ranch?" She laughed.

He trailed a hand down her spine and over the sweet curve of her ass. Damn, she was soft. "Guess we'll find out."

"Hey." She snickered, pushing his hands away. "You're going to make me late for work."

"It's okay," he said against her temple. "I have a good

relationship with your boss."

When Emma had tried to give notice at work, they asked her if she'd be interested in transcribing remotely from home. She was her own boss and didn't have a set start and stop time, just a deadline to get the work handed in. Being able to keep working with everyone at the practice, albeit remotely, seemed to make leaving her coworkers and Macy a little easier.

On the days she wasn't transcribing, Emma helped Vince out in the kitchen because he'd officially handed over the baking reins to the amazing woman.

His amazing woman.

Setting her palms on the bed near his head, she lifted up to smile at him. "Do you now? How good are we talking?"

"Good enough to do this." In a swift move, he rolled them to the edge of the bed and rose to his feet with his arms full of soft, warm woman. "I figured if I gave you a hand in the shower, you might…finish…quicker. Then you could keep your boss's schedule."

"Good thinking," she said, kissing his neck. "I appreciate your helping…hand."

"My pleasure."

It was his pleasure, and his joy to have Emma in his life.

Setting her down in the shower, he stared into her warm gaze. "Happy?"

"Very." She trailed a hand up his body. "I'd never wish your brother ill will, but God, I'm so glad you came to help him out back in August."

"Me, too." Running his finger across her temple, he brushed a strand of hair behind her ear. "Never in a million years could I have imagined I could be this happy," he told her honestly. "Thank you for taking a chance on me."

"Thank you for not leaving me behind."

That broke his heart.

"Never, Emma. I'll never leave you behind." Reaching down, he grabbed her hand and set her palm on his chest. "You're in here. You're a part of me. It'd be like leaving my heart behind. No can do. I need it to survive. Need you to live."

She smiled a watery smile. "I love you so much."

Emma lifted up on tiptoe to capture his lips. And in her kiss, he tasted the salt of her tears, and in her tears, he tasted the promise of forever.

Acknowledgments

As always, a huge thank you to my editor, Heather Howland, for all your time, patience, and suggestions, and yes, more patience, for helping me get Vince and Emma to their HEA! They were a lot of fun to write!

Working with everyone at Entangled, the Lovestruck team, is always fun, so thank you for all you do!

To my husband for his military knowledge and for being a "writer's widower" at times. Love you! To my parents who live with us, for making sure my coffee mug never ran out and supplying me with chocolate during some late nights. And to my cats for keeping me company in the writing cave. Love you all!

A thank you to my street team. Your support and suggestions were a big help!

And, finally, to you, the readers, thank you for picking up my books, and for taking the time to email me with kind words, and your wonderful reviews.

About the Author

Donna Michaels is an award-winning, *New York Times* and *USA Today* bestselling author of Romaginative fiction. Her hot, humorous, and heartwarming stories include cowboys, men in uniform, and some sexy primal alphas who are equally matched by their heroines. With a husband recently retired from the military, a household of six, and several rescued cats, she never runs out of material to write, and has rightfully earned the nickname Lucy...and sometimes Ethel. From short to epic, her books entertain readers across a variety of subgenres, and one was even hand-drawn into a Japanese translation. Now, if only she could read it.

To learn more about Donna Michaels and her books, or to join her mailing list, visit www.DonnaMichealsAuthor.com.

Find love in unexpected places with these satisfying Lovestruck reads...

Romancing the Ranger
a *Cotton Creek* novel by Jennie Marts

When Reese Hudson accidentally sets fire to a park structure, she's sentenced to rebuild it herself under the supervision of the sexy park ranger who helped her put out the blaze. But Wade Baker wants nothing to do with a rich city girl like Reese, no matter how tempting he finds her tenacious spirit or her lush curves. Women like her don't fit into his world. But if they could work together half as well outside the bedroom as in it, there might be a chance for them after all...

Neighbors with Benefits
an *Anderson Brothers* novel by Marissa Clarke

CEO Michael Anderson might be something of a "control freak." Still, he's not quite sure why his therapist thinks dogsitting will fix anything, especially since he and the canine share a kind of mutual loathing. To make matters worse, Mia Argaropolis, the artist house-sitting next door, disrupts his peace—and his dates—with the worst possible music at the worst possible times. But when Michael comes to Mia's aid unexpectedly, they find themselves engaged. Now this neighborly feud is about to take a whole new turn...

TROUBLE NEXT DOOR
a novel by Stefanie London

McKenna Prescott is the queen of picking the wrong men. When her latest boyfriend dumps her, she decides to devote her time to "exploring herself" (read: drinking wine and ordering sex toys online) and starting her freelance makeup business. That is, until an embarrassing delivery mix-up puts her sexy, gruff neighbor in her path...

THE PLAYER NEXT DOOR
a novel by Kathy Lyons

NBA star Mike Giamaria believes that love and basketball don't mix. *Ever.* While he recovers from an injury, Mike moves into a new home next to Tori Williams, his cute, quirky neighbor. When she falls from her roof and into his arms, Mike wonders if he just caught a whole heap of trouble. It's not long before he and Tori are indulging in a hot summer fling. But Mike won't mix girls and basketball...unless Tori can convince Mike that love doesn't belong on the sidelines.

Made in the USA
Middletown, DE
02 July 2022